The Lane That Leads to Christmas

The Lane That Leads to Christmas

✳ ✳ ✳

by Melanie Lageschulte

The Lane That Leads to Christmas
© 2023
by Melanie Lageschulte
Fremont Creek Press

Kindle: 978-1-952066-34-4
Paperback: 978-1-952066-35-1
Hardcover: 978-1-952066-36-8
Large print paperback: 978-1-952066-38-2

Cover photo: Cheryl Images/Shutterstock
Author photo: © Bob Nandell

Also by Melanie Lageschulte

MAILBOX MYSTERIES SERIES
The Route That Takes You Home
The Road to Golden Days
The Lane That Leads to Christmas

GROWING SEASON SERIES
Growing Season
Harvest Season
The Peaceful Season
Waiting Season
Songbird Season
The Bright Season
Turning Season
The Blessed Season
Daffodil Season
Firefly Season

SHORT FICTION
A Tin Train Christmas

✳ 1 ✳

The snow wasn't going to amount to much. In fact, it melted as soon as it touched the ground. But the few flakes now floating around certainly helped Kate catch a bit of holiday spirit.

She turned off at the next field drive to double check all the letters and parcels were in order for the upcoming section of her mail route. But before she pulled back out on the gravel road, she switched the radio to a station playing seasonal songs.

Kate was northeast of town today, filling in for Jack. This section of the county was mostly gently sloped fields, but up ahead was a sizable ravine where a creek slipped under a steel-spanned bridge. The road twisted and turned as it left the waterway behind, and Kate could see how this section of gravel would make for tricky travel in ice and snow.

Kate Duncan had been back in Eagle River for six months, but this would be her first winter driving the Hartland County back roads as a mail carrier. Bertha, the mail car Kate purchased from a recent retiree when she joined the Eagle River office, was supposed to be nimble in even the worst kinds of weather. But Kate, who'd always walked her mail routes in Chicago, wasn't sure she'd be the same behind this wheel.

"One more challenge to face, I guess. I'll just have to take it one day at a time." She slowed for yet-another twist in the gravel, and shook her head over how this winding road was a fitting metaphor for her life this past year.

Happily married (at first), Kate now found herself single again. She'd traded big-city mail routes for drives under open skies and occasional hikes through a town of just over a thousand residents. The chic bungalow in an upcoming Chicago neighborhood was long gone; she now owned a farmhouse as dated as it was charming.

One indoor, Himalayan-mix cat (Charlie) was now part of a menagerie of five furry friends, including three (stubborn-yet-slowly warming) barn cats and a (sometimes-obedient) German Shepherd mix who'd flunked out of doggie-companion school.

"Things have certainly changed." Although Bertha's wiper blades made quick work of what landed on the windshield, Kate leaned forward to try to see around the next bend. "This holiday season is going to be very different, for sure."

The mailbox's odd angle was the first thing to catch Kate's eye. The container was old and a little rusted, like so many along these rural roads, but still in serviceable condition. Or at least, it must have been until recently. Its wooden post was now awkwardly askew, and Kate guessed a vehicle had taken the curve too fast, possibly with an inebriated driver behind the wheel.

The closer she got to the mailbox, the worse the situation looked. Someone had tried to secure the container's warped door with a length of twine. But it wasn't enough, and it was clear to Kate that any mail dropped inside would be exposed to the elements. Not only that, but the knocked-back box meant the carriers couldn't pull up close enough to service it and would have to get out of the car.

This mailbox was too far gone; something had to be done. Kate carefully inched to the shoulder of the road, mindful of the steep ditch that was soon only a tire's width away, and reached for the clipboard that waited on the passenger's seat.

"Oh, regulations." She pawed through the stack for the form she needed. "The Taylors aren't going to like this."

The proper document included an illustration of a mailbox, and Kate's drawing abilities were put to the test as she noted the specific problems that had to be addressed. Until they were, the carriers couldn't drop mail at this location.

Her easiest option was to leave the form in the mailbox, but she wasn't going to do that. The irony of such a gesture wasn't lost on Kate, first of all. And Roberta Schupp, Eagle River's postmaster, believed in personalized service and wanted her carriers accessible to the people they served.

The right move was to drive up to the house and break the bad news in person. Besides, there was some important mail that needed to be delivered today: a letter that looked to be from a collection agency, and another from the county assessor's office.

Kate had been through this before, in Chicago, and the conversation was always a difficult one. Her knock at the farmhouse's kitchen door was likely to be met with anger and frustration, maybe even tears. People wanted their mail, and it was their right to have it delivered. But the federal government was a stickler for regulations, and everyone had to follow those to the letter.

At this struggling farm, that meant a new mailbox. And a new post, which should be set in concrete given its precarious location along this winding road. If another reckless driver didn't take out what was left of the current box, a county snow plow just might finish it off over the winter.

The farm lane wasn't long. And given what Kate could see from her car, the place didn't look too promising. The house had been white once, but its paint had faded and peeled until it was mostly gray. An older car rested by a slanted garage.

While the now-brown lawn had been mowed to a reasonable height before the end of the growing season, towering weeds huddled around the outbuildings and caught the wayward snowflakes in their outstretched tentacles.

Kate studied the dark skies and the worn-down house, and hesitated for a moment. She was alone; and, while these letters were addressed to "Wyatt and Candace Taylor," Kate had no way to know what sort of person might answer her knock at the door.

She fished the pepper spray out of her purse, and deposited it in the pocket of her parka. Then she texted Roberta, and explained exactly where she was and what she needed to do.

Thanks for letting me know, Roberta texted back. *I want to hear within fifteen minutes that you are OK. I'll start calling you if I don't.*

But Kate felt a little better once she was in the farm yard. She noticed the now-dormant flower beds on the west side of the house had been carefully cleared in the fall, and several plump, sassy chickens strutted about near the back porch. A medium-sized black dog hurried out from behind the barn, its tail wagging a friendly greeting.

Kate had been away from Eagle River for over a decade. Had it been so long that she was quick to misjudge those around her based on the appearance of their house, or what kind of vehicle they owned?

"Just because they might be poor, that doesn't mean they're dangerous," she chided herself as she gathered the federal form and the mail. "Really, I've seen worse around here since I moved back."

The dog nosed Kate's hand for a pet when she got out of the car, then accompanied her to the back porch. Kate knocked, and waited. Just when she thought no one was home, she heard steps on the other side of the door. A tired-looking woman about her age opened it.

"I see you've met Champ." The woman tried for a smile, but her expression was still wary. Given Kate's emblazoned parka and the magnetic sign on Bertha's side, it was obvious Kate was a mail carrier. But without a package in her arms, it wasn't clear why she'd come up to the house.

Kate searched for a good opener; animals were usually a safe topic. "Champ is a great name! He's such a sweet dog. Or is it a girl?"

"Oh, he's a boy all right." That brought a grin, and a quick pet for Champ. "He likes to dig in my flower beds, but I'm willing to overlook it."

"I'm Kate." She kept her free hand to herself, as this woman didn't seem inclined to shake it. "Looks like your mailbox needs a little help. I'm guessing you're Candace?"

The woman gave a short nod and self-consciously brushed one hand through her light-brown hair.

"I'm so sorry about this," Kate said gently, "but we can't leave anything in the box until it's repaired. You can arrange to pick up your items in town."

"I tied it closed." Candace looked like she was about to cry. "Why isn't that good enough?"

Kate explained the regulations. Candace gave a nod of defeat, then studied Kate more closely. "You look familiar, maybe. Are you from around here?"

"Yes, I went to high school in Eagle River. Kate Duncan. I moved back from Chicago earlier this year."

Candace gave her a surprised look that said, *why would anyone do that?* "Oh, yeah! I think I was a year behind you. Thompson was my maiden name."

All the pieces fell into place. "Now I remember!" Kate grinned. "Haven't seen you in a long time."

She stopped herself before she blurted out: *How are you?* Because based on Candace's weary expression, Kate sensed all was not well with her former schoolmate.

Candace had been very outgoing in high school, always

the life of the party. But as Kate glanced around the other woman's narrow shoulders and took in the worn kitchen, with its grumbling refrigerator and scuffed linoleum, she felt a mix of sympathy and guilt. She had been blessed with so many opportunities in life; Candace likely couldn't say the same.

"It's really good to be back here, at home," Kate said instead. "Especially with the holidays coming up."

That elicited only a small smile. "They come around faster every year, seems like." Candace shook her head. "I don't know how we'll manage."

Somewhere inside the house, a baby started to cry.

"Jenny, honey, see what Martin needs," Candace called over her shoulder. "Give him the rest of the bottle, maybe." She turned back to Kate. "Sorry. Now, what do I need to do?"

Candace had plenty on her plate, that was obvious. A scolding from the federal government was the last thing she needed.

"Just give this a look, when you get a moment." Kate wrapped the post-office form around the ominous-looking letters before she handed the bundle to Candace, as a young girl with curious eyes had just wandered into the kitchen and opened the refrigerator. "It explains everything. And, please," she added with a smile, "call the post office if you have any questions. We'd be happy to help."

Candace didn't even glance at the packet. She seemed far-more interested in making sure Jenny had left the kitchen before she turned back toward Kate. Why was that?

Kate needed to return to her rounds, but it was important to get as much information as she could for Roberta. If Candace had any idea who might have destroyed her mailbox, that could help move the situation along.

Vandalism was a possibility. And even if the destruction had been accidental, the sheriff's department and the Taylors' insurance company might help them recoup some of the replacement costs from the guilty party. And given the downtrodden look of this farm, the Taylors needed all the help they could get.

"Is there something you want to tell me?" Kate tried to move the conversation in that direction. "If this isn't your fault, and I'm sure it isn't," she added quickly, "we can certainly try to get to the bottom of what happened."

Candace didn't say a word, and Kate hurried on. "I know that might not be feasible. I mean, without a security camera, you'd never be able to prove who did it, anyway."

"Oh, I know who it was!" Candace narrowed her eyes. "He's at work, or I'd have you chew him out for me. We've had quite the fight about this already. Because my husband can't hold his booze, especially when he's had too much of it. It's his damn fault about the mailbox."

"I see." A stunned Kate wasn't sure what else to say.

"I keep telling him, he needs to stop. It used to be one night a week. Now it's two, or three. He goes off into town, down to that nasty bar I can't stand, and comes home late." Candace crossed her arms. "I almost wish he had another woman somewhere, rather than this. Anyway, last night he didn't show up until nearly three. He was still passed out on the couch this morning. I saw the mailbox, first thing, when I went out to do chores."

A busted mailbox seemed to be the least of Candace's problems, and Kate decided she needed to talk to her away from young eyes and ears. A glance at the kitchen clock showed her the fifteen-minute deadline with Roberta was quickly approaching.

"You know, I think there might be another page to that form," she said brightly. "How about we step out on the porch and I'll check, just to be sure?"

Candace was quick to oblige, and lifted a chore coat from one of the hooks just inside the kitchen door. Kate decided she'd been right to press the issue, as it seemed like Candace was willing to talk. Maybe *needed* to talk.

"I'm so sorry about all this," Candace said once the door was closed. "We'll find a way to make it right. Don't know where we'll get the money, but ..."

"Let's just get the paperwork squared away," Kate said warmly. "Be right back."

Kate already had the complete form, but it gave her a reason to duck into Bertha long enough to text Roberta. *OK so far. Will let you know when I leave.*

"Well, that is all of it. Just the one page," Kate told Candace when she returned to the porch, then thought of something that gave her pause. "When does Wyatt get home?"

"His shift at the factory runs until six. And I have to get ready for work. I'm a nurse at the hospital in Charles City, and I need to drop the kids off at my parents' place." Candace must have noticed how Kate's shoulders relaxed, because she smiled. "Don't worry, he's sweet as pie when he's not drinking. I guess that's where the three kids come from, huh?"

That might be, but Kate couldn't let this conversation drop. Not yet.

Eyes and ears, Roberta always said, and it was true. The post office was one of the few organizations that had close contact with residents on a regular basis, and Kate's boss took its secondary role as a social lifeline very seriously.

"I have to ask you something." Kate weighed her words carefully. "Do you feel safe here, at home?"

Candace stared at her for a moment, then nodded. Kate wasn't sure that was the truth. And she had to know, before she left, that Candace didn't need help with more than her mailbox. People around here tended to keep their problems to themselves. But it wouldn't be right to look the other way.

"We're OK. The kids, too. And I mean that," Candace said with conviction. "He doesn't hit us, any of us. Yells, yeah, and he's a big baby when he's hungover." Then the tears came. "I mean it, I do. I'd take the kids and leave if he ever tried anything like that."

"Can I ask why you're crying, then?"

"Because it's been a long time since anyone's bothered to ask me that, if ever." She glanced behind her to make sure the door was closed, and wiped her eyes with her coat sleeve. "It's just so hard, we barely get by." Then she let out a rueful laugh. "Heck, you've seen our mail. The wolf always seems to be at the door."

Kate wasn't sure if it would fly with Roberta, but she quickly made an executive decision.

"Well, for a few days, you're going to see a mail carrier at your door. Jack's back tomorrow, so it'll be him. We'll bring your mail up to the house. I can't promise how long we can get away with that," she added quickly, as Jack was likely to protest this plan, "but that'll give you a chance to sort things out, at least."

Kate knew a few days wasn't enough time to fix everything that was wrong at this farm, but it was the best she could do. Postmaster Schupp often applied the fed's rules only as she saw fit, so Kate was willing to push her luck.

She looked around. "If you're not home, where should we put your stuff?"

Candace suggested the carriers leave the mail between the storm door and the kitchen door, and profusely thanked Kate for her understanding.

"I've tried to get him help, and he won't take it." Candace threw her arms up in frustration. "My parents say it's hopeless, but we have kids. What am I supposed to do?"

Kate didn't have an answer for that. All she could do was try to be a friend.

"We know lots of people, down at the post office. People who might be able to help." She reached into her pocket for a scrap of paper and a pen.

"I don't know if this is regulation or not, but I'm giving

you my number." She handed the note to Candace just as Champ came back around the house, a few stray snowflakes glittering on his thick, black coat. "You need anything, you call me, OK?"

Candace hesitated for a moment, then nodded. "I'm glad you came by." Then she gave a wry smile. "Welcome back to Eagle River, by the way."

"Thanks."

Kate didn't know what else to say. Coming home had been her escape route when life in Chicago got too hard, and she'd never regretted her return. But for Candace, Eagle River had apparently offered only a difficult road that might be a dead end.

After Candace went back inside, Kate took another look around the forlorn farm yard, and sighed. She suspected the holidays might be a hard time here this year.

"You're a good boy," she told Champ as she gave him another pet, then slipped him a few doggie treats from the pouch she kept in her parka pocket.

All is well, she texted to Roberta once she was back in the car. But that wasn't quite true.

I'm fine, at least, she added. *But the Taylors need more than a mailbox.*

The snow had stopped by the time Kate finished at the post office, but the dark skies looked as if they planned to hold on through the evening. Sunset came early this late in November, and Kate hurried home in hopes of accomplishing a few things around her farm yard before night fell.

The sight of her brick, four-square farmhouse was normally a comfort to Kate at the end of a long work day. But even the faint glow from inside the living room's windows wasn't enough to lift her spirits this time around. Three curious kitties were lined up by the garage, however, and the way they hurried toward her, tails held high in greeting, brought a smile to Kate's face.

"Well, hello!" She balanced her purse and tote on one shoulder so she could reach down and scratch Scout's back. He was the largest of the outdoor cats, with a long black coat punctuated with white feet and a white vest. "You're turning into a wooly mammoth these days, what with the change in the weather."

The other two hung back a bit, but didn't shy away when Kate approached. "Jerry, your orange coat is almost as thick! And Maggie, I know you hate the brush, but I think we need to try again."

Kate was relieved the cats loved their insulated hangout inside the machine shed. All three had made great progress since she adopted them two months ago, but Kate held no hope she'd ever be able to chase any of them down, pick them up, and carry them into their shelter.

Letting the cats think they were in charge was probably the easiest way to win them over, Kate had decided. Especially after the fur-raising trip Jerry and Scout were forced to make last week.

Milton Benniger had made sure Maggie was spayed at one of Prosper Veterinary Services' reduced-fee clinics, but the retired farmer had never taken his two boys in for their surgeries. With the help of some raw hamburger and tuna, Kate had managed to wrestle Scout and Jerry into carriers for their trip to the neighboring town.

Scout was normally calm and confident, but he'd morphed into a snarling, howling fiend before they made it down the driveway. Emboldened by his brother's meltdown, Jerry had done the same. Kate was sure she'd added a few grays to her strawberry-blonde hair during their morning road trip, but at least the boys were too groggy on the way home to give her more than a few howls of disapproval.

Jerry and Scout had spent the next several days giving

Kate a wide berth and several side-eyes of distrust. But tonight, Scout followed Kate toward the house. Even if he lagged a few steps behind.

"Am I forgiven yet?" She smiled at him as she pulled her house keys from her purse. "You know I had to do it. And I'm counting on you to help Jerry come around."

Barks of happiness echoed out of the enclosed porch before Hazel popped through her second doggie door to reach the back stoop.

"There's my girl!" Kate rubbed the dog's ears. "Have you been good today? I guess I'd better get inside and see."

Hazel was most interested in meeting up with Maggie on the sidewalk. The gray cat with the dainty white paws was the shyest of the trio, but she and Hazel had quickly bonded. Side by side, they set off across the yard to sniff out what little vegetation remained in the cleared-off garden.

Charlie met Kate on the other side of the kitchen door. "Here's my special boy!" Kate set her things on the counter. "Now, don't tell Scout," she said in a mock whisper as she knelt on the linoleum floor, "but you're still my favorite. I don't think Jerry or Maggie care, either way."

Charlie meowed his greetings and swirled around the legs of Kate's canvas work pants as his fluffy, brown tail swayed in time. "I have to say, I'm impressed by how quickly you turned into a country cat. We have our peace and quiet out here, don't we? You're in charge of the house, and Scout handles the yard and the rest of it. No drama."

As much as Kate wanted to linger in the warmth of her dated-yet-cozy kitchen, there was work to be done. The wind had calmed until it was a mere ripple of breeze, and she couldn't put off one new chore much longer.

The county picked up rural residents' recycling, yard waste and garbage, but the trucks only came around once every two weeks. When winter took hold, snow, ice and tricky roads were bound to slow the crews down.

"It's just like us, at the post office," Kate muttered as she went upstairs to change into warm layers of old clothes. "So I'd better get acquainted with that ancient iron beast behind the chicken house."

Decades before Hartland County offered such services to its rural residents, farm families handled those needs in the easiest, most-economical way they had at their disposal: fire. Of course, they'd salvaged and reused whatever they could, long before recycling became popular. And farm critters had always been eager to gobble up most of the scraps and peelings from the kitchen.

Kate had a compost pile percolating next to the garden, and would hang on to her recyclables until the trucks could make their rounds. But the dirty, smelly stuff that was no longer of use? That's where the incinerator came into play.

It was now only a few days until Thanksgiving, and the snowflakes that had fallen for most of the afternoon were a sign of what was to come. Kate gathered her courage as well as a small sack of garbage, drew a bucket of water from the sink, then pocketed a long-barreled candle lighter from the kitchen's catch-all drawer.

"No way am I going to strike a match, then reach in there," she told Charlie, who flicked his tail in disgust over the sack's odor. "This is safer, I think."

Hazel had other activities in mind. As soon as she spotted a bundled-up Kate coming down the back porch steps, the dog snatched up a small, wind-fallen branch and ran toward the house, eager for a game of toss-and-fetch.

Kate had work to do, but there was always time for what really mattered.

"OK, let me have it." Kate held up the twig, and her dog wriggled with excitement. "Are you ready?"

The stick went flying, and Hazel sprinted after it. Scout watched his doggie friend for a moment, then gave Kate a bemused look that said, *she's so predictable, isn't she?*

"And look at you, King of the Farm." Kate gave him a gentle pet. "Now that we have the leaves under control, and the flower beds and garden are cleared off, what are you going to do with all your free time?"

Scout's answer was to flop down and roll over on the cold ground. "A belly rub? Are you sure? I mean, last week we were barely friends at all."

But the moment Kate's glove touched the thick patch of white fur on Scout's stomach, the cat changed his mind and sprinted away.

"Too good to be true, I suppose." Kate picked up her stuff and started across the yard. "Let's get this over with."

The fields around her little acreage were now clear of crops, a beige carpet that rolled away in every direction. Birds still flitted among the bare-limbed trees but only the tough fliers were left, the ones ready to ride out winter rather than wing their way south. The squirrels were busy, too, snatching up the last of the fallen nuts scattered around the yard.

Once Hazel noticed Scout and Kate were on a mission, she couldn't bear to be left behind. Jerry and Maggie appeared around the corner of the empty chicken house, as if they'd been expecting their friends, and joined the parade down a dirt-packed path to the iron incinerator.

It was brown with rust, and the last of the ashes from a way-back fire remained in its belly. Kate wondered how often the elderly woman who'd last lived at this farm trundled out here to burn her trash, not willing to break a habit that had surely started in her childhood.

"If an old lady can handle this, so can I. But I need all of you to stand back." Kate gave Hazel a level stare, and the dog obediently dropped to her haunches.

"Excellent. Now, if only the rest would be that easy."

The dampers were checked, the refuse piled inside. A tiny flame appeared at the end of the lighter, and Kate was relieved to step back from the growing fire.

The water bucket waited next to the chicken house, and Hazel soon decided that was for her. Busy getting a drink, the dog didn't even look up as the first whiff of smoke drifted through the cool air.

The cats, however, were transfixed by what they saw and smelled. Eyes wide and noses twitching, the trio crouched in a loose huddle at Kate's feet. She was relieved they had reverence for the fire, knew better than to get too close.

As they studied the growing flames, Kate wondered if her kitties recalled other fires from other times. Milton had surely burned the trash at his place. Kate pondered how he wasn't here for this change of seasons, the gathering of the leaves as well as the harvest, and tears sprang into her eyes.

But it wasn't just Milton who weighed on Kate's mind that dreary afternoon. She thought again of Candace, and the resignation and desperation on her former schoolmate's face. The look that had momentarily switched to awe and interest when Kate mentioned Chicago, but was just as quickly snuffed out.

Kate knew she'd done the right thing by coming home. But what if she'd never left in the first place?

She hadn't thought about her high-school boyfriend for some time, but Luke was on her mind that afternoon. Sure, he'd liked to party a bit more than Kate; but wasn't that what being a teenager was about, breaking the rules?

Many of their friends assumed the two of them would find work around Eagle River after high school, and get married. Kate yearned for more, however, and quietly applied to several colleges around the Midwest.

She'd expected a reaction of surprise, maybe even a few tears, the night she told Luke she'd been accepted by the University of Wisconsin, but the depth of his anger had been unnerving as well as heartbreaking.

Kate had cut him loose the next day, and never looked back.

The bright flames inside the incinerator shifted and grew as the scent of smoke spread across the quiet farm yard. But fire was as dangerous as it was fascinating, and Kate knew it would be several more minutes before she was willing to close the dampers and leave the incinerator to do its work.

"You never know where life will take you." Hazel was watching her closely, and Kate reached down to rub her dog's velvety ears. "I mean, look at you." She then smiled at the three cats. "If I hadn't come home like I did, came back to Eagle River, things would be so very different for all of us."

A spark flew out of the incinerator's opening and landed in the packed-down dirt below. The little piece of paper burned bright for just a moment. Kate reached for Hazel's collar, and held her breath. But then, like thoughts unsaid, the tiny flame went out.

✳ 2 ✳

The next morning dawned cold but bright, and every outdoor surface was etched with a delicate layer of frost that sparkled in the sun's first rays. As Kate drove through this winter wonderland on her way to work, she noticed something that brought a big smile to her face: Her closest neighbor, Gwen Ashford, now had a beautiful artificial wreath anchored to her mailbox's post.

"I love that!" Kate slowed for a closer look. "She must have put it out last evening, after I was at home. It'll stand up to the weather, for sure. And it's not impeding delivery, so there won't be a problem."

Gwen's mailbox was in the clear, but Candace's certainly wasn't. Kate felt she'd done the right thing to extend a few days' grace to Candace, and Roberta had agreed wholeheartedly when Kate returned to the shop yesterday afternoon.

But as Kate waited for a truck to pass by on the county blacktop, then turned west to drive the mile into Eagle River, she wondered just how annoyed Jack would be with the ladies' plan.

"I'll let Roberta handle him," she decided. "After all, it's her shop. But it is the holiday season. Maybe he'll decide a little goodwill is required this time of the year."

Eagle River's eastern boundary was marked by a row of houses with generous back yards that adjoined farm fields. It was only a few blocks to the little town's lone stoplight, where a north-south state highway also served as Main Street.

Her hometown was quiet at this early hour, but a bit of commotion just down Main caught Kate's eye. "Oh, they're putting the lights up! I'd almost forgotten about those!"

A trio of Eagle River municipal employees had already unloaded a portion of the city's holiday decorations and leaned them against a nearby lamp post. The oversized round cutouts, painted a festive gold and trimmed with clear lights, circled dark-green tree shapes peppered with multi-colored bulbs.

As Kate prepared to take a right at the stoplight and cross the river, a ladder truck pulled out of the fire department's shed. With its emergency lights off, the engine cruised down to where the first batch of holiday decorations was being unloaded. Only the fire department had ladders tall enough to reach the mounting brackets on Main Street's vintage-looking lamp posts.

Eagle River's post office was a red-brick building, like so many others within the business district. Even so, its boxy, single-story style lacked the charm and character exhibited by the taller, historic properties along most of Main Street. The spacious back room wasn't much to look at, with its bare-concrete floor, fluorescent light fixtures and federally mandated safety posters plastered over faded-cream walls, but it had felt like home from the day Kate joined the team.

Of course, Grandpa Wayne Burberry had worked out of this post office for decades before becoming Prosper's postmaster at the end of his public-service career. Kate had made countless visits to this shop as a girl, and she sometimes still got a bit of a thrill when she opened the back door and came through its tiny vestibule.

But this morning, the shop's mood was gloomy compared

to the bright outdoors. Kate sensed the tension before she made it three steps inside the door.

"I can't believe this!" Jack O'Brien leaned across one of the metal-topped counters to stare Roberta in the eye. "You mean to tell me that I'll have to hike the Taylors' mail up to their house for ... what? Days, even weeks?"

Roberta pushed her black-framed reading glasses up over her brown hair, a gesture that Kate knew meant business.

"You don't have to hike anywhere, you know." A raised eyebrow brought her point home. "That's what your truck is for. Just cruise up the lane, leave their stuff, and cruise back down."

"And what about the dog?" Jack changed tactics. "He barks up a storm when I stop. *At the mailbox,*" he added, "where I'm supposed to be. What's he going to do if I come up to the house?"

"Champ's a sweet boy," Kate interjected as she dropped her purse and lunch tote on the end of the counter. "He won't give you any trouble." Too late, she realized she'd positioned herself as a sort-of referee between her boss and one of the senior carriers.

"Oh, I see." Jack turned his sharp gaze toward Kate. "I guess you're the expert, Duncan. And not just on the Taylors' dog, but my route in general. You took it upon yourself to make a ruling yesterday. One that, must I remind you, doesn't exactly follow our playbook."

Jack was right. What Kate promised Candace yesterday didn't follow the rules. Maybe she shouldn't have done it, she should have let Roberta decide. But Kate had known Roberta would feel the same. And as much as Kate didn't want to admit it to Jack, she felt sorry for Candace. Their shared history, however distant, had made what Kate observed at the Taylors' farm even harder to accept.

And maybe there was a bit of guilt thrown in for good measure. Guilt about Kate's good fortune in life. If she'd done things differently when she was younger, Kate might have ended up in a similar situation. But she wouldn't try to explain that to Jack. He'd just point out that she'd let her emotions get the better of her, which wasn't professional. And the handbook said ...

"I would have done the same thing, no doubt." Allison Carmichael wandered over with an apple muffin in one hand and her coffee mug in the other. She was one of the younger carriers, but she was always eager to speak up when Jack climbed too high on his soapbox.

"I don't know the Taylors well, but they don't have much money." Allison pointed at Jack with her half-eaten muffin for emphasis. "Like too many around here without a public-employee gig. We're better off than most, you know."

That brought a nod of acknowledgement from Jack. A small one, but Allison took it as a point in her favor. "If I were in Candace's shoes, I don't know what I'd do. It's one thing to not have a lot of cash, but Wyatt ..."

Kate stopped Allison with a cautious look. Word of Candace's domestic troubles would likely soften Jack's stance, but Kate didn't think her former schoolmate wanted her personal business spread around town. Of course, in a place as small as Eagle River, Wyatt's battle with the bottle might be old news.

"I had to make a decision. Look, I only promised we'd do it for a few days or so. I didn't say indefinitely, or even a few weeks, or whatever." She softened her tone. "Besides, it's the holidays. Surely we can take a few extra minutes to make things easier for someone."

It wasn't a question. Jack sighed with irritation, but Kate had quickly learned that while he always spoke his mind, he was likely to change course if he thought he was outvoted. And given the united front of the two women bracketing his work table, as well as the one glaring at him from the postmaster's desk, Jack was clearly in the minority.

"Fine. I'll play Santa for a few days." He picked up his coffee thermos and turned toward the break room. Then he paused. "But Duncan, I'll remind you who has seniority at this shop, and who's the newbie. You might be a legacy hire, but you've got a long way to go to fill Wayne's shoes."

Kate almost made a sharp retort about how badly *Jack* had wanted to fill Grandpa's shoes when he retired from the top spot in Prosper, but decided to let that slide. Jack had lobbied hard to be recommended for the Prosper postmaster gig, but in the end Grandpa had endorsed Glenn Hanson, a longtime Prosper carrier, to lead that office.

Kate knew Jack was still a little bitter about that, several years later. But she could roll with it. Besides, Jack's mood often changed as quickly as Iowa's weather.

So much drama so early in the morning meant Kate was starving, even though she'd had a bowl of cereal at home. "Where are those hiding?" She pointed at Allison's muffin. "They look amazing."

"Break room." Allison tipped her head in that direction, then took another bite. "Marge brought them in. Might as well get an early start on our holiday treats. After all, we'll get a real workout lugging packages in the coming weeks."

"Need to keep up our strength," Randy VanBuren said as he breezed by with a stack of parcels in his arms. Even though he was in his early sixties, Randy still hiked a town route five days a week. "The public is depending on us."

Kate was more-than-willing to do her civic duty, and quickly caved to Marge Koenig's insistence she take two muffins. One for now, and one for the road.

Steering clear of Jack, Kate arranged her snack and first coffee fix of the day next to Bev Stewart and reviewed Aaron Thatcher's itinerary. As the newest team member, Kate floated from route to route to cover for the other carriers on their days off. And sometimes, she took Roberta's place behind the front counter.

Although Kate and Bev's life experiences were very different, the two had quickly become friends. Bev and her husband had both grown up near Eagle River. They had farmed north of Prosper for decades, and had grown children living nearby. After retiring from teaching, Bev joined the Eagle River post office as a part-time carrier.

"I would have done the very-same thing," Bev whispered to Kate as they organized their deliveries. "I know Candace's parents; things are tough for her. You were right to cut her a little slack."

"It's just too bad, that's all. And not just about the mailbox. The holidays came up while we were chatting. I'm sure the kids have high hopes for Santa; I just don't know if he's going to be able to deliver."

Bev shook her head in sympathy. "Clyde and I had very little when our kids were young. But at least we had each other's backs." Then she gave a rueful laugh. "As for our deliveries here, we've been swamped for a few weeks already. No one waits for Black Friday, anymore."

"No kidding." Kate eyed the stack of boxes at her feet. "Not when the holiday sales start the second Halloween is over, if not before."

Roberta called a quick huddle before the carriers loaded their vehicles. The holiday rush was officially on, with tomorrow being Thanksgiving, and there were a few things they all needed to keep in mind.

No vacation days were allowed this time of year unless absolutely necessary. Overtime was expected and that budget had been finalized, but those extra hours had to be approved in advance. Starting Friday, the counter would expand its hours for the public.

"All in all, it's shaping up to be our busiest season of the year, like always." Roberta smiled at her charges. "So I hope you all have ways to unwind when you're not here; you're going to need them. As usual, we'll find an evening to gather to celebrate the holidays. Time and place TBA, but I promise to wrap up by nine so we can all get a good night's rest."

"Pace yourselves," Randy offered from his side of the huddle. "This is a marathon, not a sprint. We'll get through it just fine if we slow down and do things right the first time."

Jack looked like he was about to chime in, but Roberta refused to catch his eye. "It's about time to get going. Anything else we need to cover?"

A few other carriers offered questions and suggestions, then Bev raised a hand.

"I have something to share. It's not our responsibility, but I think we all should be aware."

Word had begun to spread about a string of burglaries in rural areas of the county. Bev's husband had brought home tales from the latest livestock sale at Eagle River's auction barn, and a few neighbors had heard the same.

"My dad said something about that." Jared Larsen frowned. "Not his place, of course. But there's been talk. So it's credible, then."

"Apparently so. I ran into Sheriff Preston yesterday at the grocery store, so I asked him about it."

That might have seemed like an overly forward move by someone like Bev, but none of the carriers showed surprise at such a turn of events. After all, Jeff Preston had been Bev's high school sweetheart.

Jack was all ears. "What did Jeff say?"

There had been over a half-dozen reports filed in the past few weeks, Bev told the group. Most of the break-ins had been relatively minor, such as taking advantage of a rusted-out padlock on a machine-shed door, or rummaging through an outbuilding that wasn't secure.

The kind of forced entry that caused building damage wasn't reported until just a few days ago. Sheriff Preston was increasingly concerned those behind the burglaries were growing bolder or, possibly, more desperate.

"It's been small things so far," Bev said. "Some tools, extension cords, garden stuff, I guess. Not that it doesn't matter," she added quickly. "Because it does. Especially to the folks who have to replace their things."

Allison frowned. "What's the black market on rakes and shovels these days? I can't believe these people are getting much cash for the things they swipe, even if they find someone to buy them."

"Probably some stupid kids." Randy crossed his arms. "They're bored, out to make trouble just for the thrill of it."

"Some tools are worth serious money, though," Jared pointed out. "It depends on what they are."

Bev noted the burglaries were happening at night, long after the carriers finished their rounds. "But as you all are painfully aware, it gets dark awfully early these days."

Sheriff Preston requested the carriers keep their eyes open for anything that seemed out of place, and admonished them to be especially careful if their extended holiday shifts kept them out and about after sundown.

Roberta sighed. "It's sad we need to have this conversation at all, but the sheriff is right: safety comes first. And if you come across anything of note, please let me know."

Even Marge's tasty muffins weren't enough to keep the carriers' spirits up once their impromptu meeting was over.

"Happy holidays," Jack muttered to Randy as they suited up for their routes. "It's bad enough that we're loaded down with deliveries, but now we have to watch out for criminals, too?"

✻ 3 ✻

Kate held up Hazel's favorite leash, and the dog responded with a wriggle of joy.

"Do you want to come with me? Thank goodness, because I need a co-pilot today."

Hazel always brought a ray of sunshine into the post office, and her engaging ways would be welcomed on this gloomy Saturday morning. Even Jack, who was still sore about Kate's ruling regarding the Taylors' mail, had a soft spot for Hazel.

Kate had considered offering her dog the ride-along slot yesterday, but it had been just as well that Hazel was too tuckered out from spending Thanksgiving running around Kate's parents' farm with Waylon, Curtis and Charlotte's black Lab. Friday's package haul had been larger than even Roberta had expected, and she'd switched the lineup at the last minute to have Kate deliver in Eagle River rather than the country.

Today, Kate had a route west of town. If the past few days were any indication of what was to come, her best hope for a lunch break was to turn off in a field drive and snarf her sandwich as quickly as possible.

The hour was still early, but Charlie had already bedded down on his padded throne by the fireplace. He'd enjoyed his breakfast and spied on the bird feeder for a few minutes; what else was there to do?

"Glad to see somebody gets the long holiday weekend off," Kate said to him as she checked the front door was locked. "I trust you to be good, since your babysitter's coming with me. We might be a bit late today."

Charlie merely blinked a response, as if to say: *Who, me? Get into trouble?*

"We'll have more turkey and trimmings when I get home." The mention of "turkey" caused Charlie to lift his pink nose in interest, and Hazel barked her enthusiasm from the kitchen. "Don't worry, we'll be feasting for a few more days yet."

A little snow had fallen the night before, just enough to dust the fields and road margins with a bit of white powder. Eagle River's sidewalks and rooftops were also frosted with snow, which added a fairytale quality to the streets filled with older homes and quaint shops. More snow was expected to move in by evening, and the carriers would have to hurry to finish their heavy holiday rounds by dark.

Hazel, however, only saw the potential this new day offered. She started watching for the post office as soon as Bertha crossed the river bridge. And when they pulled into the back lot, Hazel barked and wriggled so much that Kate took a few fluffy-tail swipes to the face.

"You're our emotional-therapy assistant today," she told Hazel as she traded the car restraint for the regular leash. "Hopefully some of your enthusiasm will rub off on the rest of us."

Just as Kate had hoped, Hazel's arrival brought smiles to the weary faces of her co-workers. It was the same along their rural route. Many residents were at home on this holiday Saturday, and the sight of Hazel co-piloting from Bertha's backseat elicited extra smiles and waves as they made their stops.

Kate kept the holiday tunes in heavy rotation, and tried to look ahead to all the excitement the next month would bring.

For the first time in a long time, she'd be home for every extended-family holiday gathering. Tomorrow afternoon, she would visit a nearby Christmas tree farm with friends Karen and Melinda for some hot chocolate, fresh air, and the chance to meet a few members of a local reindeer herd.

And then, just a week before Christmas, hundreds of visitors would descend on Eagle River for its nostalgic holiday festival.

"It's going to be so much fun!" she told Hazel late that afternoon as they traveled the gravel roads just a few miles from Curtis and Charlotte's farm.

"Well, for me, anyway. I think you and Charlie will be content to hang out at home."

Kate had been a mail carrier for almost a decade, but this year had brought her first chance to drop deliveries in the box at the end of her parents' lane. There were three holiday cards for them today, and Kate recognized the return address on every single one. That stop gave her a heartwarming thrill, to be sure, but her energy was dragging again only a few minutes later.

"We're almost done," she said as much to herself as to Hazel, who'd nearly fallen asleep in the back seat. A few fresh snowflakes landed on Bertha's hood, and Kate was glad they'd be off the roads before dark. "About ten more places, and we can wrap up for the day."

It wasn't long before they started down a gentle slope to one of Kate's favorite places in this remote part of the township. Panther Junction Christian Church stood tall and proud at the next crossroads, where its gray clapboards, intricate stained-glass windows, and corner bell tower were in stark contrast to the snow-dusted fields.

The congregation was formed by the area's early German settlers, and the church itself was constructed in 1868. At that time, local lore said, it was the only public building between Eagle River and Swanton, which was twenty miles to the southwest. This beautiful little church predated the entire town of Prosper by nearly thirty years, a fact that had always fascinated Kate while she was growing up.

After the church celebrated its centennial, the congregation's leaders lobbied to have the structure named a historically significant site.

That certification had come in handy several times over the years, as it allowed for occasional grant money to keep the church in good condition and its doors open for services every Sunday.

Panther Junction itself, however, had little to offer beyond its colorful name. There was just a gravel crossroads, with the church on the northwest corner and the cemetery beyond that. A still-active railroad line that ran between Eagle River and Prosper crossed the gravel just south of the corner.

Long ago, there'd been a grange hall on the southeast quadrant, next to the tracks, and a tiny post office had operated out of its front room for several years. A country school had been located close to this corner as well, but Kate couldn't recall exactly where it had stood.

"Panther Junction Christian Church, coming up on our right," she sang out to Hazel in her best tour-guide voice. "I don't think you're going to encounter any wildcats today, but it sure is a beautiful building, isn't it?"

Like the other stops on this rural route, the church's mailbox was on a post close to the road. An extended width of gravel served as a makeshift parking lot on the east side of the church, and Kate pulled Bertha in close to the box and cut the engine.

The Panther Junction church didn't receive much mail, as most of it was directed to the pastor's residence. But today, there was a small package to deliver along with a few letters. Panther Junction had a new pastor that lived in Eagle River, if Kate remembered right; maybe he had yet to be schooled on the congregation's delivery preferences.

It was highly unlikely anyone would tamper with the church's mail, and Panther Junction's remote location meant the only people who regularly drove through the crossroads were neighboring farmers. Even so, several days could pass between congregation leaders' visits to the little church.

Kate was glad tomorrow was a Sunday, as the box wouldn't have to wait long for someone to retrieve it. In fact, since Advent started tomorrow, someone might stop by yet this evening.

As she readied her delivery stack and reached for Hazel's lead, Kate wondered what was in the box. She was glad it was unlikely to contain food, which would have made it a tempting target for a rambling raccoon after sundown.

"It doesn't seem right to leave the package on the front steps," she told Hazel as they stopped at the mailbox. The main entrance looked as if it had been swept or shoveled in the past day or so, but it was still exposed to the elements. "We'll take this around to the back entrance. That little porch roof will keep it from getting wet."

Kate was glad to see the sidewalk that went around the church was also free of old snow and ice. A gust of colder air hit Hazel and Kate when they reached the north side of the building, and the snow was falling steadily now. The bare limbs of the towering oak and walnut trees shivered in the rising wind.

"I'll be glad to get us home." Kate urged Hazel toward the shelter of the back porch. "It'll get dark early tonight."

Hazel suddenly stopped and began to bark. Kate looked around them, perplexed. "Is there a squirrel? I'd think they are too smart to be out on a day like this. Either way, they live on holy ground. Show some respect."

Another bark, and a tug on the leash. Hazel didn't want to stay on the sidewalk; she wanted to veer off into the brown lawn, which was now heavily frosted with snow. Kate may have adopted Hazel only six weeks ago, but she already knew when to pay special attention to her dog's behavior.

"What? What do you see?"

Hazel pulled Kate into the grass. As she studied the ground between the sidewalk and the line of evergreens that marked the north boundary of the property, Kate noticed a snaking line of indentations that appeared to travel from the concrete path down toward the road.

Were those footprints? Whatever they were, Hazel was sniffing them intently, hopping from one to another as her tail worked overtime.

Kate blinked rapidly, tried to peer through the haze of snowflakes to focus on the uneven, white-frosted ground. Maybe, maybe not.

While a few bands of light snow had moved through the area in the past few days, there had been noticeable melting and thawing during the daytime. The snowpack lacked the depth required to create clear outlines of anyone's shoes or boots, much less the delicate prints made by animals. And Kate was sure the shelter of the church's tree line was a popular destination for the local wildlife.

"Let's go." She tugged on the leash, and was relieved when Hazel gave up her investigation. There probably wasn't anything there, Kate reasoned as they returned to the cleared path, but something didn't feel right.

Why would anyone trudge through the slushy snow when the sidewalk was easily accessible?

The wind was just as relentless on the west side of the church, and Kate averted her eyes from the desolate cemetery as she urged Hazel onto the covered back porch.

"Lots of people have been here in the past few days, I'm sure." Kate tried to soothe Hazel's nerves as well as her own. "I bet they've been busy getting this place decked out for Christmas."

Kate made sure the parcel was snuggled up to the side of the church, right next to the porch's door. She was ready to retrace her steps, but Hazel put her paws up on the steel storm door and whined.

"No, we're not going in." Kate shook her head. "We need to get back on schedule."

And then, she noticed a dark gap inside the storm door's tall window. The insulated main door wasn't locked tight. In fact, it was standing open. About six inches, enough that Kate could feel warmth when she placed her hand on the storm door. The furnace was on in the church, of course. Heat had to be leaking out around this entrance; was that what Hazel had noticed?

"Good girl!" Kate pulled the dog back, but gave her a pet of encouragement. "It's hard enough to find the cash to maintain this place, I'm sure. These folks can't afford to heat half of the church yard, too."

When Kate reached in to pull the insulated door closed, Hazel pushed around her and slipped inside.

"No, no, we can't stay." But Kate followed the dog into the vestibule and eagerly welcomed its warmth, just for a minute. She'd left her heavier gloves at home today, as she hadn't expected it to be this cold.

This wasn't Chicago, and there were months of bitter, sometimes sub-zero, temperatures to come. Kate had better step up her work-gear game.

But right now, there were more pressing matters. Hazel was in her element, exploring a new place filled with dozens of strange smells, and she wasn't about to leave.

Other than the hum of the furnace, the church was almost unbearably silent. Was anyone else here? A handful of steps opened into a truncated hallway, which offered access to the sanctuary on one side and a closed door, probably to the pastor's office, on the other.

"Hello?"

The only answer was a high-pitched whine from Hazel. Kate let the dog lead her the last few feet to the sanctuary's side entrance, and tried again.

"Hello, post office! I have a delivery."

Nothing.

Something was wrong. Kate wasn't sure what, exactly. She recalled the sheriff's warning about the rash of burglaries around the county, and turned back to give the side door's frame a good look.

The jamb was intact. The wood was a bit weathered, of course, but there were no signs of forced entry. No splinters, no scratches. "A crowbar would have busted that right in two," Kate told Hazel, who didn't look up from her sniffing investigation. "Well, that's a relief."

In a congregation this small, several members either had a key or knew where a spare was hidden on the property. Someone had probably forgotten to lock up, didn't make sure the door was closed tight behind them when they left.

It was the sort of easy mistake an older person, especially a woman with a feeble grip, might make if they were in a hurry.

And given what Kate and Hazel found in the sanctuary, it must have taken an army of creative, dedicated ladies several hours to transform this historical church for the holidays.

The artificial tree in the corner by the organ had to be almost twelve feet tall, Kate guessed, and it glowed with hundreds of multi-colored lights. Satin ball ornaments wrapped with glitter trim, and hand-crocheted crosses in shades of cream and gold, dangled from its countless branches.

Burgundy velvet bows and faux-evergreen garlands decorated the front of the pastor's pulpit and the sides of the pews. More of those festive touches graced the front of the antique altar, whose red and pink poinsettias were matched by more plants displayed on the organ and piano.

Beyond its Christmas finery, the sanctuary was stately and impressive in an old-fashioned way. A rich, warm stain covered the narrow-plank oak floors, woodwork and antique pews. The window and door trim featured carved designs in every corner, and the curved spindles nestled in the railings on both sides of the altar steps had likely been hand-turned by a local craftsman.

While the ceiling fixtures and sconces looked relatively new, they radiated with a vintage vibe and cast a warm glow over the cream-painted plaster walls and curved ceiling. And even in the day's dimming light, the church's renowned stained-glass windows shimmered with a kaleidoscope of colors.

Despite the genteel beauty all around her, Kate still felt uneasy. Hazel was busy sniffing the burgundy carpet at the front of the sanctuary, and Kate wondered exactly what her dog was discovering.

They were alone; or at least, they should be. But what if someone was still here? Someone who needed help?

There were no other vehicles parked nearby, and the closest farm was over a quarter-mile away. Even so, it was possible someone helping decorate the church had been dropped off and promised to call for a ride when they finished.

Soaring ceilings meant tall ladders were needed. And this old church was full of steps, the steep and narrow kind grandfathered into modern building codes. The sanctuary was definitely empty. But what about the main entrance hall? And the basement?

The thought of someone's mother or grandmother crumpled on the floor, unable to call for assistance, pushed Kate and Hazel to start up the main aisle.

"OK, you get your way." Kate let out a little slack on Hazel's lead. "We'll look around for just a few minutes. We can't leave until we're absolutely sure no one needs help."

More decorations filled the entry, where faux garlands were draped over the paned windows and a side table nearly overflowed with more poinsettias. Eager to investigate the lower level, Hazel took the basement steps in a hurry.

"Easy, easy!" Kate gasped as she tried to keep her balance. "This is exactly why we're checking everything out!"

The kitchen was dark and quiet, except for the hum of the refrigerator. With Hazel in the lead, they checked the handful of Sunday school classrooms and the restrooms, a walk-in storage closet, and even the dusty, secretive space where the mechanicals were housed.

With a sigh of relief from Kate and a snort from Hazel (maybe one of disappointment), they turned around.

Hazel seemed to lose interest until they were back to the front of the sanctuary, where her tail began to work overtime along with her nose as she tried to pull Kate up the altar steps.

"What?" No one was here, that was certain. So why was Hazel so obsessed with this part of the church? "I can't figure you out. And I can't imagine why someone would want to make trouble here, anyway. We need to leave."

Kate would make sure the side door was locked when they left. Even so, maybe she should let someone know? It didn't seem quite right to just drive off. She didn't know the name of the new pastor, couldn't give him a call.

But Bev was a member of this congregation, and she picked up on the second ring.

"I don't see anything out of place." Kate let Hazel sniff around a little more while she chatted with her friend. "The side door's not damaged. We went into the lobby, down into the basement. No one's here. Hazel wanted in so badly, I was worried someone needed help. But thankfully, that's not the case."

"So nothing's missing." Bev sounded relieved.

"Well, I guess not." But Kate couldn't be sure. After all,

while this church was just a few miles from her parents' farm, they attended services in Prosper.

"Hazel, no! Leave it!"

The Christmas tree's glow was reflected in an oversized button hiding under the railing closest to the pastor's pulpit. Hazel saw it first, of course, and was about to snatch it up in her jaws. But Kate was quick, and dropped the button into her parka pocket. The last thing she needed today was to have to call a veterinarian because Hazel swallowed something she shouldn't.

"Well, we don't have any rare artifacts that I know of." Bev's usual good humor came through in her voice. "No Ark of the Covenant, no priceless paintings. You know, the most-valuable items at our little church are those stained-glass windows." She thought for a second. "And the hand-carved nativity on the altar."

Kate pivoted to check the front of the church. "The nativity?"

"Oh, yes! It's one of a kind. The women's auxiliary dusts it carefully every year before they pack it away." Bev laughed. "You should hear the debate *that* causes. What kind of polish to use, no polish at all ... you know how it is, everyone wants to be in charge. Kate?"

"Yeah," Kate said absentmindedly as Hazel's leash slipped out of her hand. "Did you say the nativity is up on the altar?"

"Oh, yes." Bev was certain. "There's no other place to put it where it can really shine. One year, I think someone brought a folding table from home and tried to put it in the lobby. But everyone had an opinion on that, too, and ..."

Kate didn't hear what Bev said next. She was too busy staring at the altar, whose center section was bare. No poinsettias, no candles. Just an empty stretch Kate had assumed was meant to be a visual respite from the glorious riot of color and texture that filled the sanctuary.

"It's not there."

"What do you mean?" Then Bev sighed. "Gladys is in charge of it this year. She was going to set it up yesterday. I can't believe she's waiting until tomorrow morning! I mean, our service starts at nine. It's in a heavy wooden crate, there's something like a dozen pieces and a backdrop, too. It's not a rush job, for sure."

"Everything else is done, it has to be." Kate's heart began to pound as Hazel sniffed around the front of the altar. "This place looks lovely, but I can't imagine where anyone would tuck even one more sprig of greenery."

"You said the side door was wide open?" Bev now sounded worried.

"Yep. And Hazel wanted to ..."

"Oh, dear."

Kate stared at the altar again. "I think the nativity is gone."

✳ 4 ✳

After a few moments of shocked silence, Bev promised to call Pastor Oliver Thorne and pass along Kate and Hazel's discovery.

"I'm sure this is all some sort of misunderstanding," she told Kate before she hung up. But there was a note of doubt in Bev's voice. "He'll take care of it."

Kate checked that the church's main entrance was indeed locked, then hustled Hazel out the side door and ensured the building was secure. While she had her hand on the doorknob, it occurred to Kate that her fingerprints were now all over inside the church. But many other people's marks were, too.

"And that's going to make things difficult," she told Hazel as Bertha's engine purred back to life. Then Kate shook her head. "We don't know yet that the nativity has been stolen. Or that it's even missing. Maybe one of the church ladies took it home, for some reason. Or it's still in storage."

Hazel gave a bark from the back seat, and Kate had to laugh as they took a left at the crossroads. "If only you could fill out a report for Sheriff Preston, describe everything you sensed and smelled in there, I'm sure it would be a big help."

Kate's stomach sank as Bertha braved the falling snow on the way to their next stop. Hazel couldn't account for what she'd experienced inside the Panther Junction church, but Kate might be asked to do that very thing.

"It all happened so fast, it seems like a blur." But the dashboard clock said Kate and Hazel had been inside the church for twenty minutes, at least. She'd found no one, but that was the easy part. She and Hazel had been looking for someone in medical distress, not evaluating the location for the possibility of theft.

Kate pulled down the next mailbox's door, stuffed the family's envelopes and catalogs inside, and quickly slapped it shut against the elements.

She tried to remember the last time she'd been at the Panther Junction church, and came up with a neighbor's daughter's wedding that occurred while Kate was still in high school. But that wasn't during the holidays, so the nativity had been in storage.

"I don't remember anything unusual from today, other than that door being open." She shook her head. "And I don't think I've ever seen this nativity, either. Looks like I'm not going to be much help if it really has been stolen."

Bev soon called back. Pastor Thorne was on his way out to the church to evaluate the situation. She had passed along Kate's number, and urged the pastor to ring Kate up for any details she had to share.

"That's an excellent idea." Kate slowed for the next crossroads, then pushed on. "I'm happy to help. Hazel acted so strangely, but I don't know what it all means."

With her work apparently done for the day, Hazel was now asleep in the back seat.

"When he calls, I might as well circle back and meet with him for a few minutes. I'm already behind as it is. Can you please call Roberta and let her know? Thanks!"

Finally, the last delivery of the day. Half an hour had passed since Kate last talked to Bev, and Pastor Thorne had yet to call. Surely he was at the church by now. Kate wondered if he'd neglected to take down her number in his rush to head out of town. Either way, going back to the church would help solidify what she, and Hazel, had experienced earlier that afternoon.

"This won't take long." She turned at the next intersection and headed back to Panther Junction. "Because if I do have to file a report or anything, I need to get it right."

A newer-model pickup was parked close to the church's main entrance, and Kate sighed with relief. "Good, he's here."

Hazel perked up when Bertha's engine turned off. "You stay in the car, at least for now. It'll stay warm; I won't be long."

All Kate knew about Pastor Thorne was that it had taken a great deal of effort to hire him.

Pastor Reginald Fiske, who'd served the Panther Junction church for over twenty years, had given an extended retirement notice because he knew it would take the congregation a long time to find his successor.

Rural and small-town churches were rarely flush with cash, and there were no other paid employees to help steer the ship. While members volunteered for everything from paying the bills to mowing the lawn, so many duties fell on the pastor's shoulders for relatively low pay. The posts were often taken by church leaders edging toward retirement, or recruits fresh out of the seminary.

Pastor Thorne certainly fit into the latter category, Kate decided when she walked into the church's lobby.

He was young; Kate guessed him to be in his late twenties. His short, dark-blond hair was carefully combed, and his navy sweater and pressed khakis didn't look like the attire of someone who'd been sorting laundry or wrestling with Christmas lights when he was called away on such an unusual errand.

Oliver was hard at work on the coat rack along the far wall of the entryway, adjusting the wayward coat hangers so they all faced the same direction. It seemed like an unnecessary activity, given the late hour and the fact that the church's stunning holiday decorations would quickly divert visitors' attention from something so trivial when tomorrow morning rolled around.

Or maybe that was the point, Kate thought as she lingered just inside the pair of front doors. The pastor's slight frame seemed filled with tension, and perhaps tidying up offered him a little peace of mind. Kate wasn't even sure he knew she was there. "Hello?"

Pastor Thorne's shoulders twitched, just a bit, and he turned toward Kate with a look of wary surprise that was quickly replaced by a big smile. "Oh, hello. May I help you?"

"I'm Kate Duncan." She stepped forward and pulled off her gloves. "Eagle River mail carrier, obviously." She gestured at her parka. "Hazel, my dog, she's out in the car. I can't stay long."

Pastor Thorne's face brightened substantially at the mention of Hazel, but it dimmed just as quickly as he halfheartedly shook Kate's hand.

"Bev Stewart passed on my number. She said ..."

Oliver merely studied Kate with a level gaze. When he made no reference to trying to call her, she hurried on. "I was here earlier, and I want to help if I can."

"Bev told me, yes," he finally said, then went back to sorting hangers. "Thanks for giving her a call."

"I'll just walk around a bit." Kate didn't know what else to say, since Oliver made no mention of the fact that he could have, even should have, reached out to her given what transpired just an hour ago. Then she remembered how his face lit up over Hazel.

"I could bring my dog back in, maybe that would help? She was with me before, of course. She was the one that noticed the side door was open, and it seemed like she was trying to track something, or someone, here in the church."

Oliver's hands froze. "She did?" His voice was flooded with caution, and he paused for a moment before he turned around. "Where did the two of you look, exactly?"

"Oh, everywhere."

His expression darkened considerably, and Kate suddenly felt very uncomfortable.

"But it was quick." Why was he glaring at her like that? "That's why I wanted to come back, to make sure I remembered everything correctly. I mean, the sheriff may ask me some questions, and I want to be as accurate as I can."

Pastor Thorne turned away and lifted a poinsettia from the side table, then put it back. His cheeks were now as red as the festive plant in front of him. "There's no need for that. I'm sure nothing's wrong here at the church."

"But I think that ..."

Oliver spun on his heel in a hurry. "I highly doubt our nativity was stolen." The irritation in his voice made Kate flinch. "This is a very old church, Miss Duncan. It's over a hundred-and-fifty years old, and filled with storage cabinets and cubby holes that you may have missed on your self-guided tour this afternoon. I'm sure one of the ladies simply misplaced the set."

Kate recalled Bev's observations, but stayed silent. It was obvious Pastor Thorne wasn't in the mood to be corrected. Especially by a nosy mail carrier who wasn't even a member of this congregation.

"I see." She let her flat tone and doubtful expression say the rest, and the pastor set his jaw.

"There's nothing to worry about here." He crossed his arms. "As for the side door, I can assure you that several people have access to a key. Many of them have been here in the past day or so, and they've done a wonderful job of decorating our little church for the holidays." Pastor Thorne gave her an evaluating look. "Do you attend services, Miss Duncan?"

It was a challenge, but one Kate could meet. "I certainly do. At the Lutheran church in Prosper." Maybe she'd only been back from Chicago for less than a year, but she wasn't the outsider here.

"And my family has lived in this rural neighborhood for generations. I grew up just down the road from this church, and know some of the current members of the congregation."

"Being a local, then, you can certainly understand why there's nothing to get upset about." Pastor Thorne started toward the entrance, and an astonished Kate realized she was about to be ushered out of the building. "This is all just a misunderstanding, and I'll take care of it."

Through the doors' beveled-glass panes, Kate could make out Hazel patiently waiting in Bertha's back seat. Pastor Thorne opened the right-side door for Kate, even though her hands were empty.

"Have a good night, Miss Duncan," he said crisply. "I think it's time to head home before this snow picks up."

Both Kate and her offer of assistance had clearly been dismissed. Stunned and too uncomfortable to push her cause further, she merely nodded and hurried out to the car.

As she drove away, Kate noticed that Pastor Thorne, despite his concerns about the weather, still stood inside the lobby's main window. Was he merely watching the snow, or making sure she was gone?

"That was really strange." Kate gripped the steering wheel and gave Bertha a little gas, suddenly eager to see the welcoming lights of Eagle River on the horizon.

"If he's not worried about the nativity, then what *is* he worried about? Because something is certainly bothering Pastor Thorne."

✳ ✳ ✳

By the time she finally arrived home, Kate's mood was as dim as the darkness that had settled over the countryside.

Even the sight of Scout scooting out of the machine shed's kitty door to greet her and Hazel wasn't enough to raise Kate's spirits.

"It's getting cold out here, you should go back inside," she told Scout as she rubbed her gloved hands over his thick coat. His demanding meows reminded Kate that, regardless of what had happened at Panther Junction Christian Church, she needed to deliver his supper as quickly as possible.

Hazel's priority was to make mad dashes around the yard, sniff the snow-dusted ground to determine if anything had changed while she was away. Kate saw Jerry backlit in one of the lighted shed's windows, and knew Maggie was also checking her internal clock.

"Let me get my things inside, and I'll be back," Kate promised Scout. "There are still some turkey snacks in the fridge, I'll heat them up for a special treat."

The farmhouse was warm and welcoming, but felt rather empty and quiet after all the afternoon's excitement. Normally Kate waited until the dishes were done to light some logs in the fireplace, but not tonight. The glowing flames and their *pop* and *crackle* brought some cheer into her home, and were a welcome contrast to the snow still falling outside.

Kate didn't realize how exhausted she was until all her pets were fed and she settled in at the dining-room table with a plate of her own Thanksgiving leftovers. She yawned and picked up her fork while Charlie snoozed by the fire and Hazel watched Kate from her post in Kate's reading chair.

"Work somehow gets more interesting when you're along for the ride." Kate pointed her fork at Hazel. "But you did a good job today, a very good job."

This made Hazel's ears perk and twist, and she gave a happy little whimper.

"I *might* have noticed on my own that the inside door wasn't closed. But you never know." Then Kate frowned. "I just hope someone can find that nativity, and before Christmas."

She peered through the open doorway to study the calendar on the kitchen wall. "Let's see ... that's four weeks? No, a little less than four weeks."

Kate considered the situation as she rounded up more gravy to mix with her mashed potatoes. Bev didn't hold out much hope that the priceless display had simply been misplaced. And as Kate reviewed the afternoon's events, she had to agree.

"You wouldn't even have to break in to steal it," she muttered. "Too many people have a key." Her fork paused over her sliced turkey and cranberry sauce. "But who's enough of a low-life to swipe a nativity? I mean, come on! Stealing is bad enough; stealing from a house of worship is even worse."

The theft itself was troubling, of course. But this incident would also undermine the little congregation's sense of safety and trust. Even if the set could be found, those emotional scars would take a long time to heal.

"A nativity is sacred; or at least, it should be." Kate's ramblings stirred Charlie from his nap, and he now stared at her in wonder. What was all this about?

"Just steal Baby Jesus' bed," Kate said sarcastically as she speared a few green beans. "Kidnap Him, too, while you're at it. And all the animals, even the barn! What's wrong with people these days? I guess everyone's just looking out for themselves, they don't care about anyone else. So much for a 'Merry Christmas.'"

As she finished her meal, Kate didn't know when she'd last felt this discouraged and deflated. She tried to boost her spirits by wondering about the early settler who'd carved the nativity.

He'd likely been a farmer. Maybe he'd sat next to his own blazing hearth on countless cold, blustery nights with a carving tool in one hand and a scrap of wood in the other. How many hours, how many months had it taken him to craft such a stunning display? Had he sketched the characters first with a stub of pencil, or just let his fingers bring to life what he saw in his mind?

Kate imagined an older man, his beard threaded with gray and his hands calloused from a life of hard work, carefully working a carving to get its shape just right.

He would have proudly shown the pieces to his wife and children, maybe even a neighbor or two, and shared how wonderful it would be when he completed the collection and it could be on display at the church for everyone to enjoy.

And for decades, that's exactly what had happened. The nativity made its appearance at the start of every Advent season, Bev had told Kate, then kept its place of honor on the altar until Epiphany.

While several generations had admired the figurines and pondered their message of renewal and hope, one member of the women's circle was apparently responsible for the nativity each year.

Was this a volunteer position, or something you had to be nominated to hold? Whatever it was, poor Gladys was likely to get an earful at services tomorrow morning, if not before.

Paster Thorne said he'd take care of the situation; in fact, he'd literally ushered Kate right out of his church. She needed to step aside, at least for now. She was certainly bothered by Oliver Thorne's odd behavior, but Sheriff Preston and his small-but-smart staff had a good reputation around Hartland County. They'd sort things out.

Kate took her plate to the kitchen and carefully scraped its residue into the trash can. She rinsed all her tableware and stacked everything in the sink, but couldn't find the energy to properly scrub them just now. It was a bad habit, and one she needed to break. Because no matter how much she wished for one, Santa wasn't likely to bring her a dishwasher this year.

Hazel still had the reading chair, so Kate and Charlie settled on the couch. She was too tired to do more than stream a few television episodes, and her mind kept wandering to the missing nativity.

Where was it now? Were its antique pieces carefully stowed in their custom crate, or had that already been tossed aside? The thought of those revered carvings jumbled in a cardboard box, then stuffed in the trunk of a car or in the back of a closet, made Kate shudder.

"No respect for the past. None!" She worked Charlie's favorite comb around his substantial ruff of neck fur, and he purred with contentment. "I can't believe the nerve of these people, whoever they are. It's too bad they need money; but can't they find another way to get it? Why swipe a priceless, sacred artifact from a historic church when there's more boring stuff to steal?"

Charlie didn't have an answer for that one, and neither did Kate. As her mind tried to land on a sensible scenario, she studied the outdated wallpaper in the dining room, and the worn drapes and carpet that were everywhere she looked, and sighed.

A few strings of lights and a Christmas tree wouldn't transform this old farmhouse, but they would at least perk things up a bit. She really should put out her holiday decorations this weekend, because the season was sure to get away from her in a hurry. Kate recalled the holiday splendor now on display at the Panther Junction church, and wished she could hire a team of bustling grandmas to do her decorating.

"It looks like we're on our own this year." Kate was too weary to start that task tonight, but maybe she could sort her decorations and review what was available. Perhaps inspiration would strike. "There are a bunch of *boxes* upstairs," she told Charlie. "Want to come?"

Charlie's blue eyes lit up with interest. After all, there

were few things cats loved more than boxes that begged to be explored.

"Hazel, you in?"

The dog wagged her tail, but didn't rise from her cozy spot. *I had a busy day tracking thieves,* her expression said.

Kate was glad for the oversized cardigan tossed over her tee shirt and sweatpants as she and Charlie made the turn on the stairwell's landing. Now that winter was on their doorstep, it was always five to ten degrees colder on the second floor. Kate had sealed plastic sheeting over all the old windows a few weeks ago, as she'd have to win the lottery to afford to get them all replaced.

The snow had finally stopped, but the wind was stronger now. It swished against the windows' panes and whispered around the farmhouse's corners. Kate was very glad for Charlie's company as he followed her into the smallest bedroom, whose only unique feature was its generous window seat.

Because along with her decorations, bittersweet memories awaited her on the other side of that closet door. And tonight, when she was so discouraged about the holiday season and the state of the world in general, she didn't really want to do this alone.

Ben and Kate had divided their possessions before he moved out of their house in Chicago. She'd then pared down the leftovers before she came home to Eagle River, and settled in an apartment over the furniture store on Main Street.

That space had been as old as it was charming, and the lack of closets meant some items had to be stored at her parents' farm. Kate had culled that stash earlier in the fall, and donated what she hadn't wanted to bring to her new home.

"I don't even remember what I have." She shook her head sadly at Charlie, who'd taken up his usual perch on the window seat. "Well, I guess we're about to find out."

The *creak* of the paneled oak door's hinges was too much for Charlie to resist. Before Kate could slide the first totes and boxes out onto the faded carpet, he'd climbed over them on his quest to visit the walk-in closet's back corners. Every plastic container and cardboard box had to be sniffed and studied before Charlie was content to settle at Kate's side.

She reached for something lightweight wrapped in a garbage bag, and had to smile for a second. "Oh, I know what this is!" She undid the knot in the plastic sack's ties and pulled out a minimalist, if large, holiday wreath.

"We had this on our front door, remember? But then, you never went outside. I suppose you never saw it." Charlie sniffed the faux greenery, then turned his attention to the plastic bag.

Kate blinked back tears as she realized Ben was the only other person who would find any meaning in this wreath.

And he wasn't here. Never would be. She was on her own, now.

The memories came rushing back: Kate had found this wreath at a big-box crafting store, and justified its purchase by the massive, pre-holiday discount offered for one weekend only. She and Ben had spent too-many minutes debating exactly where to display the decoration, and finally decided on the front door. Then they'd jogged out onto their front lawn, which was dusted with a bit of snow, to admire the wreath and its welcoming vibe.

"You did it!" Ben had said before he kissed Kate so hard she hoped none of their neighbors were watching. "It's perfect. It's all we need this Christmas. That, and each other."

Why had she kept this wreath? Because she'd held out hope that, someday, she'd have a different front door to display it on, another home filled with joy where she would welcome friends and family during another holiday season.

Well, it was that time of year again. But Kate didn't expect anyone to knock on her front door anytime soon.

All of her family's holiday activities were held at her parents' farm, or other relatives' houses. It was tradition. And while Kate had made a few friends since she'd moved back, her social circle didn't feel big enough to justify a party. Besides, she wasn't feeling very festive these days.

Even Charlie had lost interest in the wreath, and had moved on to the contents of the cardboard box that was next in line. Kate stuffed the wreath back in its plastic bag and put it behind her. Maybe it was time to let it go.

The next carton held a jumble of the usual stuff: strings of lights, boxes of newer ornaments and a plastic pouch filled with a few of Kate's childhood decorations, a random length of faux greenery, and a cardboard sheet missing more than a few of its red-velvet bows. Was this all she had to work with?

Kate had started over in so many areas of her life, but she didn't know if she had the motivation to start over with this, too.

"We'll probably use most of it, at least this year," she told Charlie, who was fascinated by a clear package of iridescent plastic snowflakes whose silver cords were tantalizingly out of his reach.

"All that matters is that we get the tree up, put some things on it. We don't need to be fancy. Maybe next year I'll feel ready to do more." She frowned. "Where is the tree?"

She went back into the closet and, by the shadowy light of the single-bulb fixture over her head, studied the rest of the boxes and totes. "The tree's in here somewhere. It was a pain, sure, but we somehow always squished all the branches back into that box."

She moved a few cartons aside to get to the back of the closet, and her heart sank with every step.

"It's not here." Charlie had followed her, and now studied Kate with a questioning gaze. "Where did I put it?"

She checked the other extra bedroom, then studied the contents of the front entryway's closet. Nothing. By the time she searched the basement's shelves and corners, tears of frustration and regret had started to spill over. Discouraged and sad, Kate trudged back up to the spare bedroom and started to stuff everything back into the closet.

"I can't believe it! Where did I put that thing?"

And then, she remembered. There had been a nasty fight over the tree.

Kate and Ben were adults and fairly mature, but both were so hurt and angry about the end of their marriage that it had taken very little to bring discord into their soon-to-be sold home.

Ben had wanted that fake tree, for some reason Kate couldn't fathom. It was only a six-footer, not too big around, and didn't take up much space in their bungalow's living room.

But there was nothing special about it. Fifty bucks and a trip to any superstore, and Ben could have bought his own. Kate had yelled at him, she remembered now. Something about how she'd been the one to find it on sale, years ago, and it was rightfully hers.

Of course, their fight wasn't really about the tree. In that heated moment, Kate had been determined to hang on to something Ben thought he had to have. He hadn't wanted her anymore, or the life they'd built together. But the Christmas tree? She wasn't about to let him take that, too.

"And then, I must have given it away." Crying harder now, Kate dropped to the floor. Charlie climbed into her lap. "Was it when we left Chicago, or when I cleared out the stuff at my parents'? Oh, I can't even remember."

So much was gone. So many things Kate couldn't replace.

"Maybe we'll just forget it," she whispered to Charlie as she stroked his soft fur. "Who says we must have a tree? We could hang that little garland in the archway downstairs and call it good." And then, she thought of another, practical excuse.

"You've always been such a good boy with the tree. But we don't know if Hazel will leave it alone. It's just as well. Things are different this year."

That was an understatement.

As the wind whistled around the corners of her too-quiet house, Kate thought again of that empty stretch of altar at the Panther Junction church.

Her artificial Christmas tree was easy to replace. But that nativity? It was one of a kind. That congregation deserved to have its rare heirloom back in its rightful place. And the sooner, the better.

"The holiday season is just getting started." Kate gently set Charlie aside and got to her feet. "We have a few weeks, at least. Maybe we won't have much of a Christmas here this year. But what if I can help track that nativity down? If nothing else, it might raise my spirits to try."

* 5 *

Melinda studied the next row of evergreens, then shook her head. "You know, I think these are too tall." She eyed the Douglas Firs again as she took a sip of her hot chocolate, then turned to Kate. "You have high ceilings, but we'd still have to get it in the house."

Kate grinned. "Are you offering Lizzie as a transport service?" Melinda Foster had inherited a battered old farm truck when she bought her own acreage a few years ago, just west of Prosper.

"Lizzie can barely chug her way around the mile section." Melinda shook her head. "I wouldn't try to bring her over here. We're over halfway to Charles City."

Karen Porter had another idea. "My work truck would do, I'd just have to pull my vet stuff out of the back. I guess the bigger question is: Do you see anything you like? Something smaller would be just fine. Or even, no tree at all. Who says you have to have one, if you aren't feeling up to it?"

"There's always a fake tree," Melinda put in. "Cheap and easy. No needles to sweep up. And there's no rush to decide; tomorrow is only the first of December."

Kate had to smile at her friends' thoughtfulness. She'd had a rough night, as painful memories from the past battled with worries about the future to keep her tossing and turning.

Hazel had finally decided the foot of Kate's bed wasn't a restful place, and decamped to her overstuffed pet bed across the hall.

Despite all the commotion, Charlie had refused to give up his post on one top corner of Kate's mattress. Kate wanted to believe that was a show of solidarity, but it was more likely Charlie didn't want to forfeit his access to the side of Kate's pillow.

Melinda, Karen and Kate had organized this trip to the local Christmas tree farm a few weeks ago. But after yesterday's unexpected twists and turns, in events as well as emotions, Kate was especially glad she'd had the foresight to beg off an early round of cookie baking with her mom and sister-in-law, Anna, to spend the afternoon with her friends.

She needed to clear her head, think about something other than the challenges this Christmas season could bring. And to pack her bittersweet memories of Ben back into the mental box where she usually kept them these days.

The Scotch Pines in the next row weren't as tall. Or as expensive, for that matter. Even so, Kate hesitated. Live Christmas trees had their charms, but did she really want the hassle this year, along with the expense?

"Fresh trees are lovely," she admitted. "But I can get a decent synthetic one for this price, or less. And use it over and over again."

"You could always go super-cheap and natural," Karen suggested, "and cut down a little evergreen bush in your pasture."

Kate laughed. "That seems about my speed right now. Well, let's head up to the country store. The reindeer are supposed to make their appearance at three."

The tree farm was relaxing and serene on this sunny afternoon, despite the crush of visitors. Children ran from tree to tree, taking sides on which one their parents should purchase this year. Couples strolled the wide, snow-dusted earthen walkways between the orderly rows of evergreens. Laughter and conversation filled the air, along with the faint echo of sleigh bells from where wagon rides were being offered through the stand of oaks and maples down along the creek.

The main building, which was covered in cherry-red metal siding and white trim, was designed to look like an old-time general store. A welcoming porch stretched the length of its front, and the white railings were encircled with yards of colorful lights and fresh evergreen garland. The invigorating scent of pine was matched by the sweet and salty aromas that drifted out every time the store's front doors were opened.

"I could use some of that caramel corn." Kate spotted a recently vacated table on the porch. "And a cup of cider. But I'll grab us a spot, first."

"There are no calories between Thanksgiving and Christmas," Melinda declared. "I'll run in and get our snacks."

Kate leaned back in her metal porch chair and took a deep breath of the fresh, crisp air. The reindeers' appearance was a relatively new event at this tree farm, but she'd visited this place several times as a child.

She and her brother, Bryan, had dashed up and down the rows just like these kids were doing today, shouting and laughing and filled with anticipation for Christmas and all the excitement the season offered. How many of these trees had been here, albeit much shorter, the last time Kate visited this special place?

She pondered how the years had flown by, and the challenges and joys they had brought into her life. Maybe she couldn't muster up the exuberance of the children dashing around the yard, but Kate decided she needed at least a little Christmas this year.

It had been a tough time, full of stress and change, so keeping things simple was the way to go. Besides, the fewer decorations she put up in her farmhouse, the less she'd have to wrestle down in the new year. But she did need a tree, she decided. And Karen had some excellent ideas for helping Hazel learn to leave the decorations alone.

As soon as Melinda returned, Karen scooped up a generous handful of caramel corn. "So, what's up with this stolen nativity? Bev says it's gone for sure, huh?"

"That's the word." Kate shrugged. "Until someone comes up with a better explanation, that's all they have to go on."

Bev had called Kate after morning services to report the nativity was set up on Friday, just as Gladys had promised, and all the pieces were still in their rightful place when the last of the decorators left the church around five. No one in the congregation had taken the nativity home or otherwise disturbed the display. Or at least, no one had admitted as much so far.

Melinda couldn't help but chuckle. "Can you imagine those sweet church ladies lining up, one after the other, to be grilled by the sheriff or one of his deputies?" Then her tone changed. "Seriously, though, this is really sad. Who would do such a thing?"

"You never know what people are capable of, I guess." Kate shook her head. "Half of them are crazy these days."

Karen sipped her warm cider as she considered the situation. "This being a holiday weekend and all, I doubt too many people have heard about this yet. But come tomorrow, it's going to be the talk of the county. I'll keep my ears open while I'm on my rounds, and at the clinic, too. Someone has to know where it is."

The congregation's members were now on the hunt for a decent photo of the nativity, Bev had said. Snapshots from past children's Christmas programs were probably their best bet, and several people had promised to check their family photos for anything that could be used for the case.

"Bev told me something else of interest." Kate lowered her voice so those around them couldn't hear.

"The church has a broad insurance policy that covers the structure and all the congregation's possessions, of course. But no one ever thought to get the nativity insured separately. That would have meant detailed photos of the set would be on file, and an appraiser would have been called in to determine its value."

Melinda sighed. "Oh, that's too bad! But I can see why the congregation never bothered. I mean, who would have thought something like this would happen? I guess it's a good reminder to look around at home and take stock of what you really have."

"Someone must be desperate for money." Kate frowned. "But then, what's the black market on nativity sets? Where would you unload it, other than online?"

Karen and Melinda stared at each other for a second. First in confusion, then in recognition.

"Vicki!" Melinda finally said. "She might know."

Vicki Colton operated Meadow Lane, a Prosper gift shop that carried home accessories and specialty gifts. But in a nod to the area's rural roots, it also offered a carefully curated selection of antiques and vintage pieces.

No one would try to sell the nativity to Vicki, the ladies agreed, since it was such an unusual piece and Meadow Lane's proprietor wouldn't hesitate to call the authorities. But Vicki might have an idea of the set's value, and where it could turn up.

"She has a network of dealers and sellers all over the Midwest." Melinda was proud of her friend's accomplishments. "The store's only been open for just over a year, but she has people coming from all over to see what new gems she's uncovered."

A woman wearing an elf's hat exited the store with a basket of leafy-topped carrots over one arm. When she paused at a nearby table, the helper was swarmed by children eager to snag a critter snack.

"Treats for the reindeer." Karen was all smiles. "That must mean they'll be here any minute."

Melinda leaned sideways to get a better look down the driveway and up the gravel road. "I see a truck and trailer. Here they come!"

Kate could hardly contain her excitement as she and her friends helped themselves to carrots from the basket. And it wasn't all about the reindeer that were about to make their appearance. She'd yet to visit Meadow Lane, but here was the perfect excuse to make time to stop at the gift shop on her next day off.

Surely she could cross some names off her Christmas-shopping list. But if Vicki was able to offer any theories on the nativity's disappearance? Even better.

Monday morning was nothing short of controlled chaos at the post office, but there were sweet treats in the break room to make things a little easier.

"Mae's famous pecan rolls." Randy pointed toward the tray and motioned for Kate to help herself. "I'd say we're starting the week off right."

The buns smelled delicious and looked even better, but they weren't the sort of snack that traveled well. They required a sit-down and two free hands, along with a fork and several napkins.

Kate yawned as she hoisted one onto a paper plate. "And it's going to be a long week, I think."

Even with Thanksgiving Day and yesterday off, Kate felt like she'd been on the run for days. Good thing she had chicken tortilla soup simmering in a slow cooker on her kitchen counter, as she'd be too tired to do more than fill a bowl when she got home. Because once she punched out this afternoon, Kate intended to head to Swanton and select a fake tree from the superstore.

She forked up a bite of nuts and caramel, and closed her eyes in bliss. "This is amazing. Good thing I have a town route today; maybe I can walk some of this off."

Her regular gravel-road runs had been a challenge since the weather began to change. Jogging Chicago's sidewalks had been tough enough in the cold, but Kate wasn't sure how she'd huff and puff her way down a wide-open country road covered in ice and snow. Forget the dishwasher; Kate really needed Santa to bring her a treadmill.

Bev wandered in just as Randy was on his way out. "I see Roberta has the last of our holiday decorations up."

She gestured at a single strand of clear lights swagged over the break room's chipped porcelain sink, and the miniature wreath backed by a magnet that now clung to the refrigerator's door.

"She had the lobby done Friday afternoon," Kate said around a mouthful of pecan roll. "The public space always takes priority, I'm sure."

"It sure does." Bev reached for a plate. "And she says Thanksgiving needs to come first. I think your grandpa felt the same, from what I hear. Just because the holiday stamps show up in October, doesn't mean we have to rush the season otherwise." She gave a small sigh. "I just hope I'm up for whatever the next month brings."

This would be Bev's first holiday season as a carrier. "I'm sure we'll get through it," Kate said, "one way or another."

Jared and Allison wandered in to get their pecan rolls. As soon as they left the break room, Kate seized the opportunity to speak to Bev alone.

"We need to start sorting, but I want to show you something." Kate set her half-eaten roll on the laminate counter. "Be right back."

She soon returned with her mail-carrier parka over her arm. "When I was at the church on Saturday, I found something." She tossed the jacket on the table, reached inside one of the front pockets, and pulled out the burgundy button. "I snatched it up because I was worried Hazel would try to eat it. I forgot all about it, with everything else going on. Until this morning."

Bev frowned, put down her pecan roll, and wiped her hands on her jeans. "Goodness gracious, let me see that."

She turned the button from side to side under the glow of the break room's ceiling light. The fastener was shiny, and had variegated whorls on both surfaces. "It's quite large, isn't it? It must be from a coat. No blouse or shirt would have one this big."

"That's what I thought, too. It's pretty; I mean, as far as buttons go. A little unique. I would guess it's from a woman's jacket. Men's coats aren't this stylish."

Bev chortled. "Yep. Because if they were, most guys wouldn't go near them. I have a hard enough time getting Clyde to trade his brown chore coat for his navy parka when we leave the farm. Where exactly did you find this?"

Kate explained how Hazel had been sniffing the carpet near the altar steps, then zeroed in on the floor below the decorative railing.

"I know several of the ladies were in the church late last week," Kate said. "I'm sure it just came off one of their coats. It's certainly been too cold to go without."

Bev carefully set the button on the table. "You're right, it's probably not important. But what if this has anything to do with the nativity's disappearance?"

"I think I need to turn it over to the sheriff's department. I have errands to run in Swanton after work, I could stop in. Maybe it's nothing ..."

"But what if it's something? I think you should."

Although she could easily swing by the courthouse, Kate still felt a little reluctant. She had chatted with Deputy Steve Collins a few times, but had yet to meet Sheriff Preston or any of the county's other law-enforcement officers.

"Tell you what." Bev grinned. "I'm on for just a half day today. The perks of being a part-timer! I have errands to run, too. How about I meet you over there, and we go in together?"

Kate was instantly relieved. After all, Bev definitely had an inside track with Sheriff Preston. "I'd love that!"

Bev shrugged and picked up the rest of her pecan roll. "If Jeff's not in, we'll just leave it at the desk or with one of the deputies. Let's meet there at four. This shouldn't take long, I don't think we need to call ahead."

"I should have called." Bev fanned herself with one of her gloves. The sheriff's waiting room was uncomfortably warm, between the iron radiators clanging away under the windows and the snow-melt steam rising from all the coats and boots. "We've been here for half an hour already."

Kate held her breath as an angry-looking man shuffled past. One leg of his dirty jeans bumped the purse on Bev's lap but he didn't glance their way, much less offer an apology. If Kate's nose was correct, he hadn't seen the inside of a shower stall in at least a week.

"I think every disgruntled resident of Hartland County is here this afternoon," Kate muttered to Bev. "The office was closed Thursday and Friday, so they've had plenty of time to stew about their grievances."

Two women in the next row began to argue in whispers that quickly escalated into shouts. Something about "Rodney" and "those kids" and "the judge is really going to throw the book at him now!"

Afraid to accidentally make eye contact with either of the sparring women, Kate turned away and studied the clock on the far wall.

Good grief, was that a jagged crack down the side of its face? It was seven feet up, at least. Who had smashed the clock, and with what?

"Hey!" The stern-faced woman at the receptionist's desk pounded its metal top with one hand, as the other was stuffed with a stack of papers. "Knock it off, you two!"

"When can we see the sheriff?" the older woman yelled across the room.

"Maybe five weeks from Saturday, if you don't stop that nonsense right now."

"But he's not here on Saturdays!"

"Exactly. That's why you both need to shut up."

Without missing a beat, the receptionist adjusted her headset and punched in her call's destination as snickers and jeers filled the room.

"Wow." Kate was impressed. "And I thought we had trouble with the public."

"Leona's a rock." Bev nodded her approval. "She's been running this circus for twenty years, at least. After he got elected, Jeff joked he wasn't sure he could handle being sheriff if she ever retired."

Leona now wore a small smile, and she aimed it at Bev. A nod followed.

"We're next." Bev stood up so quickly she nearly dropped her purse. "And not a moment too soon."

Sheriff Preston waved them into his office and motioned to the two chairs across from his desk. "Why hello, Bev! Kate, it's good to finally meet you."

When the sheriff nodded in her direction, Kate instantly felt at ease. Even though he was the top law-enforcement officer in the county, Jeff Preston had an easygoing way about him.

But his exhausted expression told Kate that keeping the residents of this county safe and within the confines of the law took considerable hours and effort. If the interesting mix in the waiting room was any indication, he'd already had a very trying day.

"I want to get an update on that grandbaby." Bev started

with the familiar as they took their seats. "But first, Kate and I have something for you."

"What is it?" Jeff nudged his keyboard to the side and leaned forward.

While Kate and Bev certainly had the sheriff's full attention, he exhibited a wait-and-see attitude that Kate surmised had served him well over the years. If he overreacted every time someone said they had something of interest to share, he would have burned out in this career years ago.

"It's about the missing nativity, out at the Panther Junction church." Kate reached into her purse and pulled out the button, which was now sealed in a plastic sandwich bag.

"I was delivering in the area on Saturday, and I had my dog with me. Hazel noticed the church's side door was open and, well, you know the rest of it already. Hazel found this at the front of the sanctuary."

Kate hadn't expected a round of applause, or even profuse thanks for sharing what Hazel had found, but Sheriff Preston's neutral expression was impossible to read as she slid the button across his desk.

"Clyde and I go to that church." Bev jumped in when Jeff didn't say a word. "Kate and I talked it over this morning. We don't know if it's anything important, but we thought you should have it, just in case."

More silence.

"I'm glad you came in," Sheriff Preston finally said. "Especially because this is the first I've heard about it."

It was Kate's turn to be speechless. She had half-expected a call from the sheriff's office yesterday, given that she and Hazel had been the ones to stumble across the situation, but assumed the deputies had made it a priority to talk with Pastor Thorne and perhaps some of the congregation's members. Staffing had to be tight on a holiday weekend, she knew; some of the interviews likely had to wait.

She stared at Bev, and noticed the color had drained from her friend's face.

"But," Bev sputtered, "Pastor Thorne was going to ..."

"I have nothing on this, I'm sure of it." Jeff slid his keyboard back into place and turned toward his screen. "We had a busy weekend, but just the usual stuff for a holiday. Drunk and disorderlies, domestics ..."

"On a holiday weekend?" Kate was surprised.

"That's one of the worst times for those, unfortunately. And we had a few thefts, break-ins. A guy west of Mapleville swears his neighbor stole his inflatable Santa out of his garage. Still in its *deflated* state." A wry grin formed at the corner of Jeff's mouth but quickly disappeared. "But, no. Nothing about a nativity."

He turned back to the ladies, who were still in shock. "Wait a second. Is that the one that was hand-carved by one of the early settlers?"

"Yes." Bev blinked as she tried to regain her composure. "There are a dozen characters, at least. And the barn has a thatched roof."

"That's it! I had an aunt and uncle who attended Panther Junction, back in the day. We often went with them to Christmas Eve services." The sheriff's expression darkened. "That is an amazing piece of folk art, one of a kind. But it's missing, you're sure about that? No one from the church took it home, or ..."

"It was the talk of services yesterday." Bev leaned forward in her chair. "Some of the ladies set it out on the altar Friday, when they were decorating the church, but no one has seen it since that afternoon." She huffed with exasperation. "The pastor said he was going to report it. He promised! I don't understand!"

Kate held up a hand. "What he told me late Saturday afternoon was that he *would look into it*. Maybe that's not the same thing."

Sheriff Preston raised an eyebrow.

"I'd heard the same." Bev crossed her arms. "I assumed that meant ... What in the devil is going on here?"

Kate was stunned that Oliver Thorne hadn't already reported the missing nativity. Waiting until Sunday morning to make sure this wasn't a misunderstanding might have made sense.

But he'd had all the rest of yesterday, and all of today, to reach out to Sheriff Preston. And he hadn't.

She thought of the footprints Hazel found in the snow. Kate couldn't even be sure that's what those were, much less how long they'd been there. But none of that mattered now. The freezing and thawing of the slush over the past two days would have destroyed them, anyway.

"I'm not the expert on this," Kate told Sheriff Preston, "but I'd think so much time has now passed that it would be difficult to collect any evidence at the church. Dozens of people were there yesterday morning. For example, how many of them used the side entrance? Or touched the railings on the altar steps?"

"Too many, I'm sure." Sheriff Preston's shoulders were tense with frustration. "Maybe we wouldn't have been able to get any good prints, but you never know. Are there any security cameras?"

"No." Bev put her head in her hands. "We don't have the money for things like that. Oh, I don't know what's worse! The fact that the nativity is missing, or that our new pastor has let us down!"

Jeff's expression softened. "Now, Bev, please don't get yourself so worked up. We'll get on this as quickly as we can. You did the right thing coming in today." He nodded at Kate. "Both of you."

"I'm sorry." Bev took a deep breath and wiped her eyes with one hand. "I don't know how much monetary value the nativity has; and right now, I don't care. Because to me, and everyone at our church, it's priceless. I'm sure you have bigger things to worry about these days, but ..."

The sheriff leaned back in his chair. "That nativity is an important piece of local history. But it's not just that. If the set were to be appraised at fifteen-hundred dollars or more, and I'd say that's a possibility, we're looking at felony-level charges."

Bev and Kate stared at each other in surprise.

"Felony theft." Kate digested this news. "As in, maybe more than just a fine, or community service?"

"Yep." Jeff nodded. "That would be for the courts to decide, of course. But there's the potential for jail time here." He turned back to his computer. "Let's back up for a moment. We need to start a case file. I'll need you both to tell me everything you know."

Bev hesitated. "I don't know if I should speak on behalf of the church. I took my turn as president of the women's circle, but that was several years ago."

Jeff gave a sarcastic snort. "Well, so far, you're the only member of the congregation who's taken the initiative to let us know that a valuable artifact has likely been stolen."

"You're right." Bev raised her chin. "I don't know what's going on, but something has to be done."

"And that's why we're here." Sheriff Preston tapped away at his keyboard. "Let's get started."

* 6 *

Every window of Peabody's restaurant was decked out with a cheerful, lighted wreath, but Kate's mood was rather gloomy when she pulled into the parking lot the following morning.

She hoped a hearty meal and an hour chatting with Grandpa Wayne and his breakfast buddies would help her turn that around. This was Kate's weekday off, and also her best chance to get a chunk of her holiday shopping done. Extra hours were expected at the post office this time of year, and the following weeks were likely to pass in a rush and a blur.

She had several stops to make today. But first, she needed coffee. Lots of coffee. And if she got lucky, Kate might learn more about the Panther Junction nativity and gather a little gossip about what could have happened to the vintage display.

Everyone at Peabody's was sure to have an opinion, even if their insights might not be worth much in the end. But Harvey Watson, one of grandpa's friends, had farmed near Panther Junction before he retired and moved into Prosper. Kate couldn't be sure, but she thought Harvey and Carmen may have attended Panther Junction Christian Church.

And Harvey was known to have a bottomless supply of stories to share.

Kate would be expected to give a first-hand account of Hazel's search of the church, of course. But she had already decided not to discuss her interaction with Pastor Thorne. Or share details of the discussion she and Bev had with Sheriff Preston yesterday.

Kate's decision wasn't based on trying to protect Oliver Thorne. She agreed with Bev that the new pastor had failed his flock. And his standoffish, strange behavior on Saturday afternoon still made Kate cringe. She didn't know where he fit into this situation, but the last thing she wanted to do was get on this guy's bad side. And Sheriff Preston had asked both ladies to keep mum about the button Hazel found under the altar steps' railing.

"I won't say a word about Pastor Thorne," she reminded herself as she got out of the car. "Or how long it took someone to file a report with the sheriff." She shook her head in disgust. "Or the fact that it took Bev and I driving over there ourselves before anything was done at all."

As soon as Kate opened the restaurant's front door, she was greeted with holiday tunes playing softly in the background and the aromas of fresh coffee, spicy bacon and sausage, and sweet pancake syrup. Suddenly, her mood was greatly improved.

Peabody's main section was filled with small tables that were easily pushed together for lots of visiting as well as eating. "Good morning!" Joan Murray brushed past Kate with two platters of steaming food. "What can I get started for you?"

Kate thought she knew what she wanted. But a glance at one of the plates changed her mind. "I'll have an omelet, for something different. Sausage, peppers, mushrooms. Pancakes on the side."

"Got it!" Joan nodded confidently. Even though she was in her sixties, she didn't need to write it down. "Coffee's there on the table."

Grandpa Wayne was deep in discussion with Chris Everton, the proprietor of Eagle River's pharmacy, which doubled as the town's grocery store and flower shop.

"I'm telling you, we can't stop the state from repaving Main." Chris paused for a sip of his coffee. "It's part of their highway system, after all. It'll happen for sure, sometime next year. We'd better plan on it."

Grandpa gave Kate a quick wave and went back to his discussion. "The worst section is up by the auction barn. It's all those stock trailers coming and going, I'm sure. It'll be tough on the businesses while it's being redone."

"It'll be tough on everyone," Lena Wakefield said. "Main Street is the only way to get over the river, since they closed the old bridge on the east end of town. It's sure going to be a mess when they repave."

"Bah humbug!" Harvey started on his scrambled eggs. "Let's talk about something, I don't know ... more Christmassy."

Grandpa Wayne winced. "Oh, yeah, like how that antique nativity was stolen out at Panther Junction? I heard someone broke in and swiped it right off the altar."

Kate decided she might as well share her carefully edited story right now. Besides, there was one bit of gossip in Grandpa's statement that she knew to be wrong.

"As far as I could tell, no one broke into the church." She glanced around the table to be sure everyone heard what she'd just said. "There was no damage to the side door, I checked. And of course, several people have access to a key."

Joan delivered Kate's omelet and promised the pancakes were on the way. With her recap completed, Kate dived into her breakfast.

Max Sherwood groaned. "So it was an inside job, then." He had served as Eagle River's mayor for several years before retirement. His son, Roland, now ran the family's furniture store. "But why would someone do such a thing?"

Harvey glanced around the dining room, which was only about half full, then lowered his voice. "I shouldn't say anything, but I can't help it. I know you'll keep this to yourselves." He stared right at Grandpa Wayne, then went on before his friend could protest his innocence.

"Carmen and I attended that church all those years we were on the farm. We're still members, technically. I heard Panther Junction's having money trouble."

Eyebrows went up around the table.

"You don't say?" Max was intrigued. Kate shoveled in wonderful, cheesy bites of omelet, and waited for what might come next.

"But they just hired that new pastor." Lena wasn't convinced. "So many small congregations are sharing these days, can't afford to do otherwise."

"Maybe that's the problem." Chris added jam to a triangle of toast. "Is it?"

Harvey didn't offer more details, but his tone was certainly convincing. "All I know is what I heard. And you're right, Lena, about the pastor-sharing debate. Some at Panther Junction wanted to do that very thing. But they were outvoted."

Grandpa Wayne chewed on that along with his French toast. "So there's dissension in the ranks. Sounds like a recipe for trouble." He turned to Kate. "What did you think of Pastor Thorne? I haven't met him yet, myself."

Kate shrugged and chose her words carefully. "He seemed nice enough, I guess. Upset, of course, But who wouldn't be?"

"I've never seen the nativity," Lena said, "but I hear it's beautiful. It has a ..." she searched for the right word. "A presence to it, I guess. It's awe-inspiring. But it wouldn't be worth anywhere near part of a pastor's salary."

"The cash could go a long way toward something else, though." Harvey reached for his phone. "For those of you who've never seen the thing, you're in luck."

Kate almost dropped her fork in her eagerness to lean over the table. A few congregation members had been fortunate enough to find pictures that included the nativity, and one of them had been shared with Harvey. The photo's colors had faded some over the years, but the shot of the church's altar during the holiday season indeed had the fabled set front and center.

There were more than a dozen pieces, just as Bev had said. Given the nativity's humble origins, Kate had expected a collection of rustic figurines with similar faces and simplistic lines. But even in this picture's dim light, the craftsmanship Gustav had put into his work was on full display. And that attention to detail extended beyond the human and animal figurines.

The barn-shaped backdrop had an elaborate framework of dark-stained timbers with cream plaster in between, a clear nod to Old World architecture. Strips of wood whittled to resemble sections of thatched roof topped off the backdrop, and an angel perched on the peak gazed upon the scene below.

"Wow." Kate struggled to find the words. "It's incredible." She handed Harvey's phone to Lena. "Magical, just like you said. I can't imagine what it's like to see it in person. Harvey, do you know anything about the artist himself?"

"I want to hear this." Chris leaned in.

Harvey chuckled. "Oh, there's more than a few rumors, from what I've been told. Not sure if they're all true, but it's a fascinating story."

Gustav Weigmann left the Black Forest region of Germany in the early 1860s, Harvey said, and first settled in Illinois.

After he served in the Civil War and married, he brought his bride, Caroline, to the Panther Junction area. They were among the first families to settle there, and founded the church with their immigrant neighbors in 1868.

They had several children, as was common back then, and lived in the area the rest of their lives. Gustav passed away around the time of World War I, and Caroline a decade later.

"In many ways, Gustav's life was typical for his time. It's his artistic talent that sets him apart from the rest." Harvey paused for a few bites of his scrambled eggs.

"Now, all of what I just told you is pretty well-known in Panther Junction. It helps that the congregation has always kept meticulous records, and the cemetery's right there behind the church. But beyond the biography, that's where things get a little murky."

Along with farming, Gustav's father and an uncle had apparently been well-known artisans in their region of Germany, and their wood carvings were in high demand. Gustav had carried on the family tradition, and found whittling to be a welcome respite from tending crops and livestock in a new land.

His earlier creations, which were mostly animals (domesticated and otherwise), were cherished gifts to his friends and family. But sometime in the late 1870s, he decided to tackle his biggest project yet.

"Now, here's the good part. This is all hearsay, this far out, but Gustav allegedly claimed the idea for the nativity came to him in a dream, just a few days before Christmas."

Once the holiday passed and the long, dark winter nights closed in on his farm, Gustav went to work.

One of his oak trees had been struck by lightning in a late-summer storm, and he and his sons had harvested every bit of the strong, beautifully-grained wood that hadn't been damaged. Many people said Gustav took the fallen tree as a sign that he was supposed to turn that wood into something special.

A few even claimed that, if you looked carefully, you would spot a flaw on one of the camel figurine's flanks that could have been a scorch mark made by lightning.

Wayne had to laugh at Gustav's supposed frugality.

"My grandpa was of 'good German stock,' as he used to boast. Nothing went to waste. Growing up, I thought that just meant he was cheap."

"Even so," Chris shrugged, "Gustav would have had plenty of pieces of wood to choose from."

Then he nodded slowly. "Oh, I see. Maybe the camel was a reflection of how no one is perfect, yet we are all valuable. Or something like that."

Max chuckled. "That's pretty deep for this early in the morning. How many cups of coffee have you had?"

"I never saw any marks on the camel," Harvey admitted to his friends. "But see, this is what I'm saying. This nativity inspires so many feelings in people. Its subject matter, along with its age, captures the imagination."

Besides the barn, Harvey said, fourteen characters made up the display. Along with the Holy Family, the shepherd and the three Wise Men, Gustav included an angel, a donkey, a camel, a cow, a lamb, and two sheep.

His family raised sheep for their wool, which Caroline and the girls spun into yarn that brought in a bit of side income for the family, but that wasn't the only reason the sheep received preferential treatment.

Without the second ewe, the display would have had thirteen figurines.

"Gustav was a man of great faith," Harvey told his friends, "but he was superstitious, too. Why press your luck, right? The nativity's been in the care of Prosper Junction Christian Church for about a hundred years now. No one seems to recall exactly when it was donated, though."

Max topped off his coffee, eager to stay a while longer. He was retired, after all, and this was a fascinating discussion.

"What a story! So we have some facts to go along with the potential fiction, at least. I hate to sound crass, but does anyone know what the display is worth these days? I mean, that might help ferret out who would go to the trouble of stealing it."

It was difficult, but Kate kept silent. Sheriff Preston's take on the nativity's potential value, and the weight of the theft charges that would come with it, would be of great interest to Grandpa Wayne and his friends. But while they meant well, they weren't always the most discreet bunch. And besides, the men at the next table were hanging on every word of this conversation.

"I bet it was those stupid kids." One of them leaned across the aisle with a knowing glint in his eye. "Something needs to be done about that, either way. I don't care how young they might be. Stealing is stealing."

Kate recalled what Sheriff Preston had told Bev about the burglaries. "It sounds like they've been picking off easy stuff," she said casually. "Tools and such. Nothing like this."

"That's true," one of the other men admitted. "But once they get started, it's too easy to keep going. The thrill fades, and they start looking for bigger stuff to swipe."

He was in earnest, but his comments still brought a round of laughter.

"You seem to know all about it," Max joked with the guy. "Are you sure you don't know more than you're letting on?"

The chatter then turned to other topics, and Kate decided she wasn't going to get any more leads this morning. Which was just as well, because her mind was now as jam-packed as her happily stuffed stomach. Harvey knew more about the nativity than Kate had expected, and it had been a thrill to finally get a glimpse of the display.

"Have you started your shopping yet?" Lena asked as they finished up their meals. "I feel like I'm already behind. All those grandchildren, and my music students, too!"

"I'm going to start today." Kate checked her ticket and reached for her purse. "And while I don't know if I can stick to it, I plan to only shop locally this year."

Grandpa Wayne gasped in mock horror. "Does Roberta know about this?" He turned to Chris with a grin. "That's a good thing for folks like you, but it's bad for the post office. This is their ..."

"Most-profitable time of year," Kate finished Grandpa's thought. "I know, I know. But being back home, it just feels like the right thing to do."

"We got in a small selection of housewares last week," Chris reported with a smile. "Coffeemakers, blenders, that sort of thing. If you need anything for your new place, I mean."

Kate laughed. "What makes you think I'll be shopping for myself, too? But you're right, I will be."

* 7 *

Kate snagged a few gift cards from Peabody's before she left town. Her parents visited the restaurant frequently; and Grandpa Wayne was a regular, of course, between his buddy breakfasts and enjoying lunches and dinners with Grandma Ida.

"I'm off to a good start." She grinned and cranked the holiday tunes as she drove west toward Prosper. "With my shopping, and with the nativity, too."

Harvey prided himself on being an unofficial local historian, but he certainly wasn't the only one. Who else had insight about this one-of-a-kind artifact? Word of its disappearance had surely spread across the county by now, and Kate vowed to keep her ears open as she ran her errands.

There was always the possibility that some bit of lore about the nativity's past could be a clue to its current location. But beyond that, Kate was simply fascinated by the tale of this long-ago immigrant farmer and his amazing talent, and a nativity that still captured people's imaginations over a hundred and forty years after it was created.

Her day was certainly looking up, Kate decided as she snagged the last open parking spot in front of Prosper Hardware. She was glad to see so many shoppers gathered inside, even though it was a weekday.

"Family owned businesses like these are what keep a small town going." She pulled off her sunglasses and reached for her purse. "Eagle River's the same. If the drug store closed, or the restaurant or coffee shop, I don't know what we'd do."

Prosper Hardware's front door was flanked by a pair of large plate-glass windows. Through one, Kate spotted the vintage sideboard around which the coffee-group regulars gathered six mornings a week. The other front window served as a merchandise showcase, and Melinda, who served as the store's marketing director as well as one of her aunt and uncle's few employees, had it decked out with evergreen garlands encircled with colorful lights.

This was a practical establishment, just like its clientele. Rather than aspirational gifts, an array of sturdy, warm work clothes took up most of the display. But there was a toy tractor parked temptingly close to the window, and a plastic, light-up snowman nearby beamed with holiday cheer.

"I need boots," Kate reminded herself as she pushed open Prosper Hardware's heavy oak front door. "But I may not be able to resist getting something else. That snowman is so cute!"

A little bell above the door announced her arrival, and Kate was greeted by the aroma of lemon polish and the gleam of the store's original hardwood floors.

She hadn't stopped by Prosper Hardware since she'd moved back to Eagle River, but the store had been a must-visit destination when she was a teen and Grandpa Wayne was Prosper's postmaster. After all, the post office was just next door.

The white-haired woman tidying a display of knit stocking caps was obviously in a holiday mood. Kittens in Santa hats frolicked across the front of her red sweatshirt, and tiny snowflake earrings completed her festive ensemble. "Why, hello! What brings you in today?"

Before Kate could answer, Melinda waved her on from behind the counter, which was a vintage oak showcase with a glass front.

"Esther, this is Kate. Wayne Burberry's granddaughter. She's here to try on some boots."

"Oh, wonderful!" Esther beamed and pointed to a rack in the first aisle behind the display window. "We keep them right over here."

"The ones we set back this morning," Melinda whispered to Esther before she turned back to ring up a woman's purchases.

Esther picked up a tote hidden behind the counter. "We have quite the sale going on, and they're going fast. Size nine, right?"

"This is extraordinary service." Kate grinned. "Right in line with the best boutiques along the Magnificent Mile."

"This way, my lady." Esther steered Kate toward a full-length mirror bolted to the far wall. "We may not be able to outfit you for your next ball, but if you're going to be clomping around in the dirt and the snow, I'm confident we have just what you need."

"And the mud," Melinda said over her shoulder. "We have two insulated options, and then there are our rubber boots, too. Sorry, but yellow is all we have left for those."

Then she shrugged. "I'm partial to mine, actually. Why go boring when you can go bold?"

Esther took over the counter so Melinda could spend a few minutes helping Kate try on boots. Sure, she could have found some over at the Swanton superstore, but none of them would be half as sturdy as these. Or last as long.

Kate settled on a pair of yellow galoshes and a set of steel-toed winter boots. Then a display on the end of one row caught her eye.

Melinda's marketing degree had been put to good use with a line of branded merchandise, which featured a vintage-looking logo in white on a dark-green background. There were tees and sweatshirts, ball caps and a few cozy knit hats. The idea had been to give the store a little free publicity, and keep the coffee guys stocked with grounds. But the line had quickly become so successful that it was now a nice addition to the store's profit margin.

"I'll take a sweatshirt and a knit cap." Kate's arms overflowed with goodies, but she didn't care. This was more enjoyable than any trip to a nondescript mall. Besides, the closest one was a forty-minute drive away. "Looks like I'll have to come back another time if I'm going to buy gifts for anyone but myself. I have so many errands to do today, I'd better keep moving."

"Have you heard anything more about the nativity?" Melinda asked as she rang up Kate's purchases. "The coffee guys are running wild with their theories, but no one has a lead on where it went. Not yet."

"Give Auggie a few days." The owner of Prosper's co-op was known for his nosy ways. "His farmer-gossip network covers most of this county. He'd be my bet for the one to track it down."

Kate filled Melinda in on her breakfast with Grandpa Wayne's friends and Harvey's fascinating, if perhaps not totally factual, stories about the display's origins.

"I've heard the same," Esther said as she joined them at the counter. "I think. Or something close to that." Then she lowered her voice.

"I'm not sure that Gustav had a premonition about the nativity. See, my neighbor's cousin married into one branch of that family. She's certain he started to whittle the pieces after one of his children died as an infant." Esther sighed dramatically. "Gustav was awash in grief, of course. It helped keep his mind busy as well as his hands."

"I'd believe that." One woman paused near the counter, her shopping basket in hand. "When my sister had a miscarriage, she took up knitting. We all got mittens for Christmas the next year."

A man with his arms full of boxed Christmas lights couldn't resist joining the conversation.

"It wasn't just to keep himself busy," he told the ladies with conviction. "Immortalizing Baby Jesus in the manger was a way to remember the other little boy, if you get my meaning." Then he frowned. "I'm not sure, Esther, but I do believe it was a *grandson* who died young."

"Everyone's an expert," Melinda said after both customers drifted away. "Who knows what the truth is? I just hope the nativity turns up, and before Christmas Eve."

She glanced at the clock above the sideboard, then gave Kate a knowing smile. "Meadow Lane opened just a few minutes ago."

"That's my next stop." Kate picked up her canvas tote bags. "I'm eager to see what Vicki has in stock. And get her professional opinion on this nativity."

※　※　※

If Prosper Hardware sported a practical, understated holiday style, Meadow Lane was the opposite.

Strings of delicate white lights and faux greenery were draped across the tops of the wooden bookcases that served as the shop's wall displays, and velvet bows and glittering ornaments highlighted the front of the ornately carved counter.

More lighted garlands circled the former porch railing that set off the store's small snack area, whose fresh-brewed coffee and flaky pastries make Kate's stomach rumble despite the breakfast she'd packed away at Peabody's not long before.

Meadow Lane was a winter wonderland, but there was no sign of the traditional red-and-green palette. Instead, the colors were soft shades of blue and gray, with a touch of peach mixed in for contrast.

These hints of understated luxury were matched by the light-blue cashmere twinset worn by the woman behind the counter. Given her sophisticated style and the just-right caramel highlights in her dark hair, Kate knew that had to be Vicki. By comparison, Kate felt like she'd just dropped out of a haymow in her faded jeans and well-worn sweatshirt.

Vicki's smile as she waited on another customer, however, was genuine and kind. After the woman had found her just-right gift, Vicki glided over to where Kate studied a tasteful display of woolen scarves.

They were hand-knit by an artisan in the northwest corner of the county, according to the delicate script on the nearby placard, with fibers spun from the woman's own sheep. Meadow Lane's gift selection was carefully curated; there was no mass-produced junk here.

"I think my mom would like this one," Kate told Vicki as she fingered a waffle-knit scarf in a soothing shade of slate blue.

"Does she prefer cool colors, or warm? This is another option." Vicki picked up a fawn-shaded scarf and draped it elegantly over her arm. "What brings you in today, anything other than a little holiday shopping?"

Kate quickly introduced herself, then reached for another scarf in rich notes of olive green. Anna would love it.

"Oh, Melinda's told me all about you!" Vicki gasped with glee. "I hope you're enjoying being back home, especially now that the holidays are here."

"Yes, I certainly am." Despite the bustle around them, Kate had Vicki's full attention. Being so present with people was an admirable quality, and one that likely drew confidences as well as sales.

No wonder this little shop did so well, even in a town this small. Between the selective offerings and its perceptive proprietor, Kate saw why its good reputation continued to spread.

Kate decided to take both scarves, but she needed something else from Vicki. "I was making deliveries west of Eagle River Saturday, and came upon, well, the incident at Panther Junction church. Melinda and Karen said you're our resident antiques expert these days. Do you have any idea what it might be worth?"

Vicki smiled. "You're not the first person to ask. Let me wait on this customer, and we'll chat."

They soon settled at a little table in the back of the shop while Vicki's assistant watched the counter. "I can't imagine how upsetting that must have been for you." Vicki offered Kate a cup of coffee, free of charge.

"Who likes to drink alone, huh?" She laughed as she poured one for herself, too.

"Now, this nativity ... I've yet to see a photo, I know the church is working on that. But I've heard a bit about what it looks like. And some of the history of the set."

"Or its alleged history." Kate took a sip of her coffee. Harry and Eloise Peabodys' bottomless supply was strong and hot, but it couldn't hold a holiday candle to this fresh-pressed brew. "I wonder how much of what I've heard is true."

The women compared notes and decided that, given the impressive age of the nativity, the truth about its past would continue to be a mystery.

"And that is part of the package, when you look at an item's monetary value." Vicki paused momentarily to wave at another shopper and inquire after the woman's dog.

"Provenance, appraisers call it. They like to nail down a piece's age and who created it, of course. The quality of the work is important, as well as its current condition. But beyond that, historical context is key."

The Panther Junction nativity was the sort of thing appraisers and collectors loved to stumble across, Vicki said. It was elaborate, yet relatable. Its pieces were likely the only items created by this master craftsman to survive to modern times; or at least, the only ones that could be reasonably attributed to Gustav Weigmann.

The rumors about how it came to be, and the apparent artistic choices Gustav made as he worked on his masterpiece, only added to the nativity's value.

"But not every item is as rare and expensive as people want it to be." Vicki gestured at a whimsical display of mismatched china teacups on a nearby wooden table. "People come in with things they want to consign, swear on the family Bible that their great-great-grandma received some dishes as a wedding present, only to find out they were mass-marketed in the seventies and aren't worth much more today than they were back then."

Kate nodded in understanding. "Sometimes, it's the sentimental value that matters."

"Exactly. I remind people of that all the time. Only have things in your house that make you happy, don't worry about their cash value." Vicki shook her head in awe. "But this nativity, though. This is the real deal. If it's half as lovely as what I've heard, it could be worth a significant amount of money."

"Like fifteen-hundred dollars? Or more?"

"I see you've done your homework. It's very likely, I would say. If Gustav's nativity makes it out of our little corner of the woods, and ends up at an auction house in one of the larger cities or turns up online ... the collectors will start a bidding war."

"We can't let that happen." Kate stared into her mug. "It belongs here, in Panther Junction. Not on display in some wealthy collector's home, or even in a museum."

"It may already be long gone." Vicki rubbed the side of her face and sighed. "I hope not; I hope it's not too late."

Sheriff Preston called last night, Vicki said, looking for leads. She passed along contact information for several auction houses in Chicago and the Twin Cities, and promised to call him right away if she heard anything that could be useful to the case.

"Criminals aren't always very bright, but I doubt any of them would be stupid enough to bring it here." Vicki gave a wry smile. "There's been lots of talk, though. For instance, you've heard why there are fourteen characters. But some man yesterday tried to tell me there were initially fifteen."

Kate leaned forward. "What?"

"Yeah." Vicki shrugged. "He swears Gustav had also whittled a chicken, most likely a rooster. It was a small piece, of course, and it was lost many years ago."

"And that is how a story gets started." Kate drained her cup and handed it to Vicki with a thankful smile. "I'll take the two scarves, and I might be back for more."

It was after three by the time Kate unlocked her back door and was welcomed by the quiet warmth of her kitchen. She'd been in and out of the cold for hours, and her cheeks were raw from the wind. Charlie's meows said he'd been awaiting her arrival, and not with a great deal of patience.

"Yeah, I'm late, I know. So much shopping to do!" But the second her several sacks hit the linoleum floor, everything was forgiven.

"That has the chicken and hamburger." Kate quickly snatched up one of the bags. "You can sniff the cereal and bread, if you're bored. But this one's just for me."

Hazel trotted into the kitchen, and she and Charlie created an unofficial security team. "You two could work at an airport! Let me put the groceries away, and then I'll show you the cool stuff I bought."

Before she unpacked, Kate took a second to peek through the opening into the dining room. Much to her relief, the artificial Christmas tree was still standing. She'd put it up in a hurry last night, weary from a long work day and rattled by her trip to the sheriff's office, and hadn't bothered with any garland, lights or ornaments.

If Hazel managed to leave it alone for another day or two, Kate would consider that a victory and proceed with a few carefully curated decorations. Nothing breakable, and no precious mementos.

"One step at a time, we'll get this place looking at least a little festive."

With the food put away, it was time to unpack the gifts. Charlie had settled inside one of the now-empty canvas bags on the kitchen floor, but he couldn't resist joining Hazel to see what else Kate had brought home.

"With all this talk about nativities, I decided we needed one of our own."

She unrolled a ball of bubble wrap to reveal a humble stable backdrop made of molded plastic. It was only about eight inches tall at the apex of the barn roof, and not of the highest quality. But its paint was still colorful.

"Look here." She slid the barn across the linoleum so Hazel and Charlie could inspect it. "I think there used to be a star glued to the eave of the roof, but it's missing. Maybe we can rig something up."

She revealed the first figurine, one of the wise men, and set it next to the stable. "Here's one of the characters." Then she eyed Hazel's snout, and shook her head.

"Choking hazard. I wondered about that." Kate snatched up the wise man and the barn. "I think the mantel's the only safe place to set it up."

Two new nativities had been on display at the superstore, jammed in with the boxed ornaments and snow globes, but neither offering had captured Kate's fancy.

A quick stop at Swanton's bargain-priced consignment shop had netted several options, however, and Kate chose this one for its five-dollar price tag and slightly rundown condition.

In every way, it was the opposite of the ornate, vintage nativity missing from Panther Junction. But Kate had decided this set's knicks and scuffs were an appropriate reflection of her holidays this year, and its plastic people and animals needed a home.

Once the characters were displayed on the mantel, Kate stood back and gave them a good look. She had to laugh. "It's kinda tacky, right?" Charlie was already stationed by the fireplace, his tail flicking in irritation because the new arrivals were now out of his paws' reach. "But it works, somehow. And it's a good reminder of the reason for the season."

The Christmas tree was still bare. And her biggest decorating effort so far was a kitschy nativity that had probably been bought at a five-and-dime store fifty years ago. Kate looked around her farmhouse, and let out a long sigh. From what, she didn't know. Regret? Resignation? Maybe it was just a little too quiet around here.

And then, she had an idea.

"I think we need a little more Christmas," she told Hazel. "And I don't just mean more decorations." Kate nodded slowly as she thought her plan through, and a smile soon spread across her face. "Why not?"

* 8 *

Roberta stared at Kate for a second, then began to laugh.

"Are you sure?" The boss gave the idea some thought. "Well, that would be a big change. And a good one," she added quickly. "We always go to Peabody's by default."

"I'd really like to host the holiday party this year. And I promise," Kate pledged as she held up one hand, "there will be no fancy appetizers, no orchestra, no dress code. Hazel and Charlie will provide the entertainment, if they decide to hang around. Everyone brings a dish to share, and that's it."

Mae, who'd been listening in, jumped on the idea. "Put me down for a dessert, I'll think of one today while I'm on my route. Oh, this will be fun! And we'll get to see your new place."

Kate rolled her eyes. "In its natural, unaltered state. I haven't had the time or money to do a thing, other than make a few necessary updates to the bathroom."

If only she'd been able to afford to have the kitchen pantry transformed into a half bath, as she'd hoped. Someday she'd be able to swing it, but it wouldn't happen in time for this party.

Everyone would have to go upstairs, which meant they'd get the full tour along the way ... fluffy carpet, fussy wallpaper and dated paint included.

But Mae didn't mind. "From what you've said, it reminds me of my grandparents' house, which was stuck in the seventies and eighties for way-too long. I bet it's charming, in its own way."

"*To Grandmother's house we go*," Roberta sang as she continued to sort parcels.

"Thanks for volunteering. I've thought about it, but it always seems like the kids have so many holiday activities going on. I have a hard enough time getting to our office gathering, much less trying to host it."

The truth was, this would benefit Kate as much as the rest of the staff. Planning a holiday gathering at her farmhouse was just what she needed to boost her spirits.

She couldn't get any major updates done in only a few weeks, but she certainly could put up more holiday decorations.

And maybe new curtains. Kate had been trying to wait until she found the time to do some painting, at least, but simple panels were inexpensive and easy to hang. If she didn't keep them long-term, they could always be donated.

What about fresh towels for the bathroom? Maybe new mats at the front and back doors? And throw pillows for the couch ...

"Just don't make too much of an effort on our account." Roberta's spot-on request made Kate almost laugh out loud. If her boss only knew! "We'll show up with plenty of food and drink, behave ourselves, then clean up before we head home. Let's talk about it at our staff meeting this afternoon, try to pick a date."

"Hey!" Randy called to Roberta from across the room. "There's no way I can get all these parcels in the truck. I'll have to come back at least three times today. That's going to put me over hours."

"Be right there," Roberta told Randy. "We'll sort out the overtime in a minute."

She turned back to Kate. "I know you have Jared's shift today. But can you watch the counter over my lunch break? I have an appointment."

"Sure. What time do you need me to come back in?"

The lobby of the post office was usually a madhouse this time of year, and the queue to mail packages was still long when Kate arrived. But as the clock ticked toward twelve, the crowd thinned to a manageable number. And once snow started to fall thick and fast outside the plate-glass windows, the rush came to a halt. The shop was still peaceful when the boss returned.

"Oh, I love when it's quiet like this." Roberta shook the snowflakes off her knit cap. "This weather should keep folks at home, at least for most of the afternoon. The roads aren't too bad, if you're wondering."

"I was," Kate admitted. "And I was also thinking I'm sort-of glad to be here right now, instead of out there. Hopefully it won't turn into much."

Either way, Kate needed to get back to Jared's route. Just as she was about to hand back the counter's reins, an older car pulled up out front.

Even with her parka's hood pulled up against the driving snow, the woman looked vaguely familiar.

"It's Candace," Kate whispered as her former schoolmate approached the front door. "Where is her pile?"

Roberta reached into the first cubbyhole below the counter. "Right here. I'm glad it's bundled and ready to go; it'll save her time."

After some bickering between Jack and Roberta, the postmaster had decided to give the Taylors a few days' grace to have their mail dropped at their door. And Jack had finally agreed, as it would have been nearly impossible to get someone out there to fix the mailbox around Thanksgiving.

But as of Monday, their mail had been held at the post office per federal regulations.

Roberta had called the Taylors Friday afternoon to break the news. They still had a landline phone, and Wyatt had answered. He'd been angry and defensive, but Roberta held her ground. The carriers would drop packages if any came through, as usual, but none of the Taylors' regular mail would be delivered until the situation was resolved.

"Well, if she's here to get the mail, Wyatt must have been sober enough to pass your message on," Kate muttered just before Candace opened the door. "I wish there was a better way around this, but ..."

"Hey, Candace!" Roberta tried her best to sound cheerful. "Here's your stack."

Candace pushed back her parka hood and barely nodded. "Thanks."

Kate smiled, and her old schoolmate smiled back, but this didn't seem like the right time for mindless chatter. Kate regretted the foolish promise she'd made that afternoon on Candace's porch, and it wasn't just because she lacked the authority to grant such an exception.

She'd given Candace false hope, and the resulting about-face by the post office wasn't likely the first time this young family had been let down.

"I'm so sorry you have to come all this way," Roberta said gently. "I know you and your husband both work in Charles City. I wish we could keep bringing it up to the house."

"I understand." Candace swallowed hard and looked away. "We don't need charity. It was a nice idea," she told Kate with a grateful nod. "But if it's against the rules, then, well, we don't need any more trouble."

Roberta looked out at the wind-driven snow. "Here's what we will do. If anything looks important, or hints that it has time-sensitive information, I'll give you a call. Otherwise, please don't make a trip into town just on account of us."

"We can't open anyone's mail." Kate quickly warmed to her boss' idea. "But we can certainly keep an eye on what comes through."

"Would you do that?" Candace's tired eyes lit up, just a bit. "That would be a big help! If there isn't anything important, maybe I can let it sit for a week or so. Wyatt has a buddy who's handy, they've talked about trying to get the box fixed, but ..." She rolled her eyes. "I have no idea when that's going to happen."

"We'll do what we can to help." Roberta reached for the candy dish kept on the end of the counter. "Now," she said brightly, "we have candy canes and chocolate Santas in stock. Why don't you take a handful home for the kids?"

"For you, too," Kate added, then reached for a pad of scratch paper kept near the register. "What's your cell? Like Roberta said, we'll call if something important shows up."

Candace nodded with relief, and rattled off her personal number. It was better to communicate directly with Candace, Kate decided, as calling the farm meant Wyatt might answer. He didn't seem like the most responsible person. It would be terrible if important mail arrived, and he didn't pick it up or pass the message on to his wife.

With a small smile, and a handful of candy now tucked into her purse, Candace wished Kate and Roberta "Merry Christmas" and hurried out into the snow. After she was gone, the ladies could only look at each other in sympathy.

"You know it'll be weeks before they can get that box fixed." Kate sighed. "I know it has to be this way, but this is so much more work for her."

Roberta leaned one elbow on the counter, and dropped her head into her hand. "I just hope this doesn't drag on until spring. A few more weeks of weather like this, and it'll be too cold to set the post properly."

Kate crossed her arms. "I shouldn't have made a promise we couldn't keep."

"You did the right thing." Roberta patted Kate's shoulder. "That's exactly how I would have handled it. If Jack hadn't protested so much, I might have let it slide. But it's just as well. If we make an exception for the Taylors, other people will want one, too."

Bev burst through the door from the back of the shop. "Kate, I have good news!" She stopped in her tracks. "What's wrong?"

"Candace was just here." Kate gestured out at the snow. "This is just one more hardship for her."

"I've half a mind to take it out there myself. After work," she added for Roberta's benefit. "But I promise I won't."

"If what I heard yesterday is true," Roberta said quietly, "getting the mail isn't even the biggest worry Candace has right now."

Wyatt had apparently been pulled over late Saturday night for driving while intoxicated. All the details would appear in the crime blotter in the next edition of the Swanton newspaper. If the charges held, he was facing steep fines and the loss of his driver's license for several months.

"Oh, that's terrible." Bev shook her head sadly. "Poor Candace."

Decades of teaching school had taught Bev how difficult it could be to know when to intervene in people's personal lives. If a child was struggling at school, or possibly in danger at home? Well, Bev said, that was a no-brainer. But something like this? As hard as it was, there wasn't much anyone could do other than offer Candace emotional support.

Roberta agreed. "We do more than deliver the mail. Often, we're people's first, and only, contact with anything close to social services or the law." Then she sighed. "Although from what I heard, Wyatt's already interacted with the sheriff's department."

"It could have been the Eagle River police that pulled him over." Kate remembered Candace's disparaging comments about Paul's Place. "Depends on where he was stopped."

Bev huffed with frustration as she and Kate exited into the back room.

"It's bad enough when a mailbox is vandalized. You may never know who did it, so you can't make them pay for the damages. You just fix it, and move on. But when it's your own husband?" She grimaced. "I don't know what I'd do in her shoes."

"Yeah, you do," Kate teased. "You'd have Clyde, stone-cold sober, out there in the snow, fixing it up while you stood by with a tape measure to ensure it meets federal guidelines."

"You got that right."

Now that Roberta was back at the helm, Kate needed to return to her route. "You were pretty chipper when you came in," she said to Bev. "What's going on? Have you heard anything from Jeff? Or anyone else, for that matter?"

Two people had unearthed decent photos of the nativity, and those had been handed over to the sheriff's department. Several members of the Panther Junction women's circle were interviewed yesterday, Bev shared, and more expected to get a call from a deputy today.

The church's grapevine indicated there were no good leads at this time, but Bev had one she was confident could widen the pool of possible informants.

A cousin's adult daughter was fascinated with genealogy, and had conducted some research at the Panther Junction church over the summer. A review of the church's founding families might turn up a few helpful sources outside the immediate area, Bev said. They probably wouldn't have any leads on who'd taken the nativity, but might be able to shed some light on its mysterious past.

Kate gasped. "Are you related to Gustav Weigmann?"

"Oh, no, not as far as we know." Bev laughed. "But that's exactly where Chloe comes in. I called her last night, and what luck!"

Chloe Peterson was a sophomore at a private college about an hour away, but she was coming home to her parents' place in Elm Springs tomorrow afternoon to spend the long weekend studying for semester finals. When Bev explained the situation in Panther Junction, Chloe eagerly agreed to meet up at the Eagle River library.

"Oh, I want to join you!" Kate was thrilled. "Can I?"

"Absolutely! I hoped you would. Tomorrow night, at seven. But I know it's late notice, so if you're busy ..."

"I'll be there."

"Who knows what we'll find?" Bev started to sort boxes, as her afternoon duties included organizing parcels so they could be loaded quickly when the other carriers needed to refill their trucks. "At this point, we may be better off reaching out to people who aren't current members of the church."

While everyone was upset that the nativity was missing, people were beginning to debate who had taken it, and why. Before long, Bev predicted, some in the congregation were likely to suspect their friends or neighbors had a hand in the theft. And a few had confided to Bev they were embarrassed that such an incident happened at their church.

"One woman told me, it'd be like if someone swiped the Mona Lisa while you were on guard duty. She said we look like a bunch of rubes because we don't have any security cameras at the church and the nativity wasn't insured."

"That's absurd! And it doesn't do any good to fuss about that now. People need to focus on finding the thing, not pointing fingers."

"I certainly agree." Bev sighed. "But I think we need to tread lightly with the locals. Because our little group is getting restless in the glare of the spotlight."

✳ 9 ✳

Kate debated her options as she left the post office the following afternoon. She had to be back in town at seven to meet Bev and Chloe at the library, and she needed to fit in critter chores and her own supper before she returned.

"I don't have time to get coffee," she told herself as Eagle River's lone stoplight approached. But at the last second, she decided to head south and stop at The Daily Grind.

"That's exactly why I have to go there first," she reasoned as she piloted Bertha down Main Street. "I need the caffeine. There's so much to do at home, I have plans for tonight, and I have to start prepping for the post-office party."

Kate had exactly ten days to get her house sparkling and ready to host the crew and their guests. Not enough time to make major upgrades.

But scrolling through a few websites could net some stylish housewares that would be dropped on her front porch within the week.

"So much for shopping locally." Kate parked in the coffee shop's back lot, as all the spaces along Main Street were full. "But I only meant to do that for gifts. Not for other things I need. Want," she reminded herself as she started for the back door. "I want this to be the most memorable party in the history of the Eagle River post office."

Plenty of holiday cheer was on display inside the coffee shop, which was housed in a historic red-brick storefront. Strings of colorful lights and faux greenery now festooned the entire space, and Kate had to laugh when she spotted owner Austin Freitag sporting a Santa-style hat.

He'd gone to school with Bryan, and hanging out with her brother's quirky friend always made Kate smile. "Are you going to wear that all season long? Because you have three weeks to go, at minimum."

"I planned to," Austin admitted. "But probably not. It's only tolerable for a few hours every day." He leaned on the counter. "What'll it be, same as the last time? Peppermint mocha with whipped cream, seems like."

"Yep, that's right." Now, this was good customer service, small-town style. When Kate had more time she needed to give the merchandise display a good look. Surely she could check some names off her gift list at The Daily Grind. Along with take-home coffee beans and branded hats and apparel, the store offered colorful, insulated mugs that'd be perfect for Melinda and Karen.

"Candy sprinkles, too?" Austin gave his pom pom-topped hat a flip. "You know you want those."

Kate sighed. "Why not? The sugar will be as helpful as the caffeine. Pile them on!"

She moved down to allow the next customer to step forward, then fought back a yawn as she waited for her drink. But Kate was instantly more alert when she spotted a familiar face at a table next to the Christmas tree.

Alex Walsh blended into this casual crowd with his faded jeans and gray fleece pullover, but his muscular frame and coffee-brown eyes made him stand out to Kate. Along with being one of the handsomest men in this little town, he owned one of Eagle River's well-established businesses. Paul's Place wasn't the most highbrow of locales, but the bar's come-as-you-are vibe continued to be popular with local residents.

Including Wyatt Taylor, who, according to his wife, liked to drown his sorrows and drink away his payday windfalls at the tiny pub on the east side of town.

During the past several months, Kate had discovered that Alex was more than good-looking; he was also funny and a quick study of people's personalities and quirks. She was still debating whether to stroll by Alex's table on her way out when he nodded at her from across the room.

Of course, he'd managed to scan the entire coffee shop while appearing to keep his focus on the laptop screen in front of him. Kate caught Austin's eye, gestured in Alex's direction, and moved away from the counter.

"Hey." She dropped her purse on the other side of Alex's table and took her seat. "Do you always sit so your back's against the wall?"

"Excellent observation." He smiled and slid his laptop to the side, but didn't answer her question. "I wondered if you might join me, or if I was going to have to flag you down. What's new?"

Kate was about to launch into some mindless chatter about holiday decorations and shopping, but quickly gave up on that idea. Alex was nothing if not direct, and something important was certainly on Kate's mind. She might as well jump right in.

"Candace Taylor came in yesterday to get her mail." Kate eyed Alex's half-eaten cherry turnover, and wished she'd ordered one for herself. "We can't deliver out there right now, because their mailbox was damaged over a week ago. She knows who did it, though."

Alex's neutral expression was accompanied by silence. If he knew where this conversation was headed, he wasn't about to let on. This was probably Kate's only opportunity to put in a supportive word for her old schoolmate, and she wasn't about to let it pass her by. She took a deep breath, and tried her best not to sound accusatory.

"I hear Wyatt likes to hang out at your bar. And that he likes to overdo it."

This elicited a raised eyebrow.

"If someone else had hit the post, she'd have filed a complaint with the sheriff. That might be hard to prove, but there would be at least a small possibility the responsible person could be tracked down and made to pay for the damage."

"But since it was her husband, she's out of luck." Alex crossed his arms. "So she's trying to find someone to hold responsible?" He leaned over the table. "Or is the post office?"

Kate's jaw dropped. "I didn't say that!"

"Well, then, say what you mean." Alex seemed more hurt than angry. "Out with it, Detective Duncan."

"Just keep an eye on him, OK? If he's getting out of line, cut him off. Because it's not just the mailbox. I heard he got picked up Saturday night, pulled over for driving drunk. If he keeps this up, who knows what might happen? Worst case, there's an accident."

Kate leaned in until their faces were only inches apart. "I went to school with Candace. They have three kids, and money's tight. She doesn't need any more trouble."

Alex looked away, then back at Kate. "Did she ask you to talk to me?"

"No." Kate was emphatic. "In fact, she'd probably ..."

"Tell you to stay out of it?"

Austin suddenly appeared at their table. "Peppermint mocha with whipped cream and sprinkles!" he chirped as he slid the to-go cup under Kate's nose. Then he pointed at Alex. "Dude, you need a refill?"

"Not now, thanks."

Austin widened his eyes at Kate before he moved on.

Kate took a sip of her drink. "All I'm saying is, keep an eye on Wyatt, OK? Please."

Alex nodded. "You know, I don't let people get really

wasted, anyway. It's a dive, sure, but we keep things pretty low key."

Kate recalled the baseball bat tucked behind the bar's counter, but said nothing.

"The people that come in are pretty responsible, I make sure of that. They sober up, or they get a buddy to drive them home, or whatever." He laughed. "We may not have ride-share services here, like they do in Chicago, but we still look after our own."

"Good, glad to hear it. Especially because there are laws about over-serving customers."

"Been reading Iowa Code lately?" Alex said archly.

"Most federal employees have a handle on what their state's rules and regulations are," she countered. "Especially anything having to do with safety."

He shrugged. "Well, Wyatt wasn't even in on Saturday night."

"He wasn't?"

"I usually don't run around telling tales about my patrons, but no. He wasn't there." Alex lowered his voice. "Look, everyone knows Wyatt has a problem. We cut him off, and we do it earlier than he'd like. He's not the only one." Alex thought for a moment. "The night he took out the mailbox; did Candace say what time that happened?"

"Hmm, I think she said around three."

"We stop serving at one-thirty, all the places around here do. Even if he'd been at my bar that night, he definitely went somewhere else before he showed up at home. He may have gotten more booze and parked down some field lane to drink alone. The worst ones like to do that, you know."

"Well, either way, it's a mess." She shook her head. "I don't know what Candace is going to do, or how best to help her."

"Just be her friend," Alex said gently. "It sounds like she needs one, badly. Is she OK, do you think?"

Kate relayed how she'd pulled Candace outside that afternoon to have a heart-to-heart away from the children. That made Alex smile. "Way to go! Like I said, we look out for each other around here. So, what are you hearing about the Panther Junction nativity?"

Kate nearly choked on her mocha. "You're quick to switch gears."

"Well, I bet you need to get going. But I heard about you and Hazel, and I'm sure you're on the case." His eyes lit up with interest. "Anything to share?"

Kate summarized what she knew so far, minus the button Hazel had found, and skimmed over her face-off with Pastor Thorne. Alex was intrigued by Bev and Kate's plan to track down descendants of the church's founding families.

"People get emotionally attached to things. And places, too. That might get you a few leads, it's worth doing."

Kate had already shown her cards, or most of them. And Alex was right, she couldn't linger for long. "So, any good tidbits down at the bar?"

Alex nodded slowly, then looked her square in the eye. "Those descendants are worth looking at, but don't forget about the current members of the congregation."

"What have you heard?"

Alex gave a slight shake of his head. "Money is always a huge motivator. Where there's money trouble, you'll find trouble in general."

Another observation that backed up Harvey's theories. As Kate pondered this tip, Austin came back to their table. "I seem to recall you really enjoyed being in the chorus in high school," he said to Kate. "Musical productions, too."

Another hairpin turn in this conversation. Austin caught Alex's eye, and both guys grinned.

What was this all about?

"Well, yes," Kate said slowly. "It's been years, but ..."

"We need a few more people for the historical society's

strolling chorus." Alex, at least, got right to the point. "For the holiday festival."

Kate frowned at him. "You sing?"

"I sure do."

"The first practice is tonight, at the high school." Austin adjusted his Santa hat. "Your cousin Stacy is going to do it, she's friends with the head music instructor."

"Peer pressure, then." But Kate was smiling now. She'd taken her turn at the post office during the town's Halloween celebration, so Roberta wouldn't need her that night. Kate had assumed she'd take in the sights with her family, but this sounded like fun.

And the perfect chance to spend a little more time with Alex. And her cousin and Austin, too, of course.

"I'm busy tonight." Kate reached for her purse. "Which means I need to hurry home. But, yeah, I'll think about it."

"We'll see you Tuesday at six, then," Austin said before Kate could even retrieve what was left of her drink. "Practice is twice a week until the festival."

As the president of the town's chamber of commerce, Austin was an expert at talking people into getting involved. But given the look of triumph he now exchanged with Alex, Kate wondered how long this plan had been in the works.

"Just the standards," Alex promised. "You already know the words. Easy-peasy." He closed his laptop. "I'll take that refill on my way out," he told Alex, and the two of them wandered off toward the counter.

"What did I just agree to?" Kate muttered as she hurried out to the car. "Guess I have less time to prep for this party than I thought."

※　※　※

Fueled by her peppermint mocha and her excitement over joining the community chorus, Kate powered through her chores at home and still made it to the library on time.

The Classical Revival-style building was grand and beautiful all year long, but it really shined during the holidays. Lighted garlands and wreaths were everywhere, and the high ceilings on the first floor left plenty of room for a towering artificial tree next to the circulation desk.

Kyle Gibson, who'd been the head librarian since spring, was tidying up as Kate came in. The building was open until nine on Thursdays during the school year, but the crowds tended to thin out after suppertime. There were just a handful of patrons browsing the shelves, and one older man was engrossed in his newspaper in an overstuffed reading chair by the fiction section.

"I'd almost forgotten how wonderful the library looks during the holidays," Kate told Kyle as she removed her coat. "It's breathtaking!"

He laughed. "Yeah, I got a workout going up and down that ladder a few weeks ago. All the staff helped out, as did my wife and kids. It took some effort to dig the boxes out of storage, but it was fun."

Kyle gestured to the far corner, where several computers were set up on long tables. "Bev's already here, with her cousin. This should be interesting, what the three of you might dig up. I'll be over in a bit to see how it's going."

Kate didn't know if this deep online dive would net anyone with specific knowledge of the nativity, but it was worth a try. Either way, she was eager to get a crash course in genealogy research.

Kate's knowledge of her own family tree stopped at her great-grandparents; of the eight, three had still been alive when she was growing up. Beyond that, the waters were certainly murky. Maybe once the holidays had passed, and Kate could find the time, she'd use what she learned tonight to strike out on a personal quest.

Given the way her blue eyes sparkled behind her retro-cool glasses, Chloe was eager to share what she knew. Her curly, ginger-hued hair, which was held back in a low ponytail, was in stark contrast to Bev's short white locks.

"Do redheads run in the family?" Kate asked.

"Not really." Bev laughed. "Most of us are a shade of brown. At least, when we're young."

"I blame my dad." Chloe grinned. "I'm sure I got it from his side."

"I was just telling Chloe about our little office party," Bev said to Kate. "I'm so glad you're going to host! When Roberta said they always went to Peabody's, I briefly considered volunteering, myself."

"Well, we'll see how it goes." Kate set her purse and notebook on the end of the table. "That might be a one-and-done for me." She turned to Chloe. "Thanks for helping us out! I'm so glad you were willing to drive over from Elm Springs tonight. I hear you're quite the expert on Panther Junction and its members."

Chloe swapped a bright-pink laptop into her other hand to meet Kate's handshake.

"Well, some of them. I'll do what I can to help. I got into genealogy a bit in high school, but an assignment for my American History course last spring really kicked things into high gear. Once you get going, you want to keep going. There's always one more name to find, one more date to uncover."

"Like pieces of a puzzle." Bev took a seat at the closest monitor. "Oh, this should be fun! Where do you want to start?"

The library carried subscriptions to a handful of online genealogy and historical newspaper databases, and Kyle had provided Bev and Chloe with details on all the free opportunities that were available through the internet.

Genealogy research was popular with local residents, and the Eagle River library's collection of on-shelf and online resources meant people in this far-northeast corner of the county didn't have to travel to Swanton to access the county historical society's collections.

"I have our family's details here." Chloe held up her laptop. "The Thurbers, which is the line that Bev and I are part of, were some of the founding members of Panther Junction church. So that's one part we already know."

Kate was instantly intrigued. "How cool is that? I asked Bev if she was related to Gustav Weigmann, but she didn't think so."

Chloe shrugged. "Not that I'm aware of. I've been able to take the Thurbers back to Johann and Magdalena, who were my great-great-great grandparents. They settled in the Panther Junction area around the same time as the Weigmanns."

Based on their surname, it was very likely the Thurbers were from Germany. Chloe had found a few hints that they may have settled in Illinois before coming to Iowa, a migration pattern followed by many German immigrants.

But that's where the trail had gone cold. Some records from other countries were available online, but without a parent's name or a hometown for someone's birth, it was often difficult to trace those family connections across the ocean.

"But I do have most of our family's recent descendants figured out." Chloe began to scroll through her notes and charts as Bev and Kate leaned in for a look. "That's easier to do, since, well, people are alive."

Kate laughed. "Makes sense."

"Going way back is harder to do," Chloe admitted. "But the process I used to establish our family line can certainly help us research the other founding families of the church."

Bev held up a small booklet with a faded blue cover. "This is from the centennial celebration, which was in 1968. Thank goodness my mom had the foresight to save our copy, and it's in good condition."

Given Pastor Thorne's odd behavior, Bev hadn't felt comfortable asking to browse the congregation's historical records. Kate had agreed it was best to keep their efforts off the church's radar, especially given the rising tensions within the congregation. Any inquiries would likely be brushed off as invasive, or even suspicious.

Chloe set her laptop aside and carefully turned the pages of the church booklet. "When you said you had this, I knew we could get somewhere," she told Bev. "Panther Junction has done an impressive job of preserving its history; I'm confident what's in here is accurate. It's the perfect place to start."

With the Thurbers already sorted out, the ladies divided up the rest of the founding families. As the most-experienced researcher in the trio, Chloe offered to take the Weigmann ancestral line. While she logged in to one of the online search engines, Kate pulled Bev aside to share Alex's observations from that afternoon.

"He thinks it might be an inside job?" Bev pondered that idea for a moment. "Well, that's not surprising; but it is disappointing. I'd love to think this was the work of some outsider, instead. Did he say anything else?"

"Nope." Kate sighed. "And you know how he is. Cryptic as can be. But I guess that comes from running a bar, and filtering all the gossip that flows through it. I don't think I could have weaseled it out of him if I'd tried."

"I'll talk to Clyde, see if he's heard anything more along those lines. They don't like to admit it, but the men gossip just as much as the women." Then she smiled. "But first, let's see what we can uncover tonight."

Kate was impressed with the wealth of information she found online. Along with names and dates, some other researchers had been generous enough to post old family photos, gravestone pictures, and document scans.

"Look at this," she told Bev. "Here's a copy of the ship

manifest for when this family came over from Germany." She shook her head in awe. "How fascinating."

The ladies searched for almost an hour, then huddled to share what they'd found. Chloe offered to start an online document where the three of them could pool their ongoing research. Because while these initial efforts had been productive, it would take more hours of work to uncover current family members and track down their contact information.

While she wasn't about to approach Pastor Thorne or any of the congregation's officers, Bev still hoped to make a few personal inquiries.

"I'm fairly certain at least three women's circle members are related to these original families. We're pretty good friends," she explained to Kate and Chloe. "I might be able to gather some contacts from them without ruffling the feathers of the whole church."

Chloe left soon after, as she had more studying to do once she got back to Elm Springs. But not before she made sure Bev and Clyde would be attending their extended family's holiday celebration on the last Sunday before Christmas.

Her parents were hosting this year, and the event drew dozens of relatives from around this part of the state. Three generations were often in attendance; it was a party no one wanted to miss.

"I'll see you then, if not before." Chloe gave Bev a hug. "And Kate, it was wonderful to meet you. Let's keep at it!"

"That went well." Bev logged out of the databases and powered off her monitor. The library would be closing soon, and Kyle was sorting returned books to be reshelved in the morning. "Chloe's really interested in this sort of research, and I can see why. It just makes you want to keep going, doesn't it?"

Kate had admired the library's main artificial tree on her way in that evening, but she now noticed a modest-sized one near the children's department decorated with round paper ornaments. "Is that new?" she asked Kyle.

"It sure is. That's a giving tree, part of a program we've set up with the elementary school."

Kyle had participated in similar projects in Cedar Rapids, and was glad local school leaders had been willing to start one in Eagle River. Counselors, with help from the classrooms' teachers, had identified children who weren't likely to have much of a Christmas this year. Genders and ages were listed on the paper ornaments, along with gift ideas, but no names or other personal information.

Kate perused a few of the requests with a sinking heart, as there were no dolls, toys, or other fun items requested for the children; just practical needs, such as socks and stocking hats.

The local fire and police departments were holding their toy drives as usual, Kyle said, so the giving-tree program had a different focus. "It's sad that some kids lack the basics, but that's where we step in."

"Is it hard to get the parents to sign up?" Bev wondered. "Even when it comes to helping their children have a better Christmas, I could see where pride might be a problem. People around here don't want to feel like they are taking a handout."

"You're right. The counselors said there were a few families who declined to participate. Even so, we hope to help about thirty kids this year."

Kate thought of Candace and Wyatt's children. If only there was a way to make their holidays brighter. But like Bev said, charity was a sensitive subject for many. Any obvious overtures of assistance might make Candace uncomfortable. Her youngest was only a baby, but as for the other two ... Kate hoped ornaments for them had been added to this tree.

She couldn't do much for Candace's kids, but she could help some other local children in need. She took three cutouts off the tree, and Bev did the same. Presents were due back by the sixteenth, Kyle said. "Wrapped, if you have time. Or we can handle that on this end."

"Not a problem," Bev promised. Then she turned to Kate. "What do you think? Does the post office need a community-service project?"

They would have to chat with Roberta first, but Kate and Bev thought the other carriers might be willing to pick up some of the shopping slack. If all the ornaments weren't taken in the next week or so, perhaps the post office could find a way to make sure none of those children were forgotten on Christmas morning.

"That would be wonderful!" Kyle rubbed his hands together with glee. "We're spreading the word on social media, of course. Hopefully we'll get enough participants. But this is something new, so you never know."

"We'll see what we can do." Bev picked up her notebook and her purse. "But for now, I'm eager to get home and do some more searching. If we can shake the right people out of these family trees, maybe one of them will lead us to the missing nativity."

* 10 *

Kate yawned as she tugged open the back door to the post office. It seemed heavier than usual this morning, but she knew why. She'd been up until nearly midnight following the leads she'd uncovered at the library.

Chloe had been right; the search was exponentially easier going forward in time. Kate's laptop uncovered a good number of potential sources, and she wondered which ones might be worth approaching. Every generation often had a storyteller in its ranks, or someone who was the family's unofficial historian. If she could match any of those people up with profiles on the genealogy sites, they might be the ones to contact first.

As she opened her locker, Kate's weary, wandering mind picked up on an unfamiliar voice within the usual chatter in the post office's back room. She turned to find a white-haired gentleman huddled with Allison, Jared and Bev around the closest counter. "Barney's here. Well, this could get interesting."

Barney Wilburn had retired fifteen years ago, but Roberta kept him on speed dial to help out when the team's roster was short due to vacations and illness, or the delivery volume was especially high. He couldn't walk a route these days, but he could still drive the back roads and run the front counter.

And tell long-winded stories, too, given the looks of feigned interest on the faces of his listeners.

As Kate started across the room, she gathered Barney's latest tale was about a rooster that had once chased him back to his mail truck.

"I'd run *afowl* of the law when I went up to the porch without his say-so." Barney's blue eye sparkled with mirth as he delivered the punch line. "His law, you see. Barnyard law."

Allison blinked twice and tried to smile, while Jared hid a yawn behind one hand.

The sight of Kate heading toward the break room gave Bev a chance to break away. "Thank goodness you're here."

"Something else come up last night, after we talked?" Kate was exhausted, but all ears.

"Oh, no. Not that. I just wanted to get away from Barney. He means well, but he's a chatterbox. I can't believe Roberta is going to let him run the counter."

"Maybe she thinks he'll be too busy to talk so much." Kate laughed despite the early hour. "Does he really despise Jack, like everyone says? This will be interesting."

"It's a mutual grudge, I guess, tended carefully over the years." Bev eyed Kate and shook her head in a sympathetic manner. "So, how late were you up last night?"

"Too late." Kate yawned again as she filled her coffee thermos, then her to-go cup. "I went down the rabbit hole, couldn't help it."

"It's addictive, isn't it? One thing leads to another, then you look at the clock and see it's almost two. I couldn't keep my eyes open any longer, I had to quit."

Then Bev sighed. "This is fun, and I love that Chloe's willing to give us a hand. But I don't know, maybe this is a wild goose chase."

Kate had to agree. She was eager to learn more about the nativity's history, but was starting to think its past had little to do with its present location.

While the set was well-known and admired in this neck of the woods, she wasn't sure knowledge of its existence went much beyond that.

And its monetary value, as murky as that was, seemed to be the only motivation for someone to steal it.

"So the criminals are local folks, and they need cash." Kate tossed up her hands in defeat.

"That's all I have. I'd love to believe that the founding families' descendants who moved away have stories to share, or otherwise care about the nativity, but they may be too far removed from the situation to be much help."

"I think you're right. We may be barking up the wrong tree." Bev filled her travel mug, took a sip, then coughed. "Good Lord, Barney must have made this. Be careful. It's strong enough to strip paint."

Kate took Bev's advice, and dumped part of her coffee into the sink before diluting what was left with hot tap water. "It's Friday again, which means the nativity has been missing for about a week already. And we both have so much to do. Maybe we need to narrow our focus?"

"I'll keep searching online, I won't be able to help it. But I'm too old for too many late nights." Bev yawned. "I think I'll start with those three ladies from the women's circle, instead. See if anything turns up there."

"Good idea." Kate's phone beeped, and she pulled it from her back pocket. "Oh, it's from Auggie."

Come by when you can. I have something for you.

Bev leaned in for a look. "Do you think it's a lead?"

"Could be. I chatted with him a few days ago, he knows we're looking into this. I should be able to get over there after work. I'll let you know what he has to say."

Jack and Randy were coming in the back door as Kate and Bev exited the break room.

"Hey, Randy," Barney called out warmly, then simply gave the other newcomer a level stare. "Jack."

"Barney." Jack barely nodded. "So, how long do you plan to be around this time?"

Marge widened her eyes at Bev and Kate, then popped a bite of caramel corn into her mouth as if she were watching a movie.

"Through Christmas Eve, at least." Barney squared his shoulders. "Roberta wants me here every day, if I can manage it. I might be in the following week, too, as the returns start to pile up."

Jack's face was certainly devoid of holiday cheer.

Randy clapped Barney on the back, but he was gentle about it. "Well, it's good to have you around."

Randy was no spring chicken himself, but Barney had almost two decades on him. "That chair at the counter is pretty comfy, if only in the short term. But then, you'll be on your feet quite a bit."

"Oh, I brought my lumbar cushion." Barney pointed toward the row of lockers. "And Roberta says I might as well take up my usual cubby, just like before, since we have a few empties over there."

Barney had name-checked the boss twice in as many minutes, and Kate suspected that was all for Jack's benefit. And then, her foggy mind settled on something else: Barney and his wife would probably want to come to the department's holiday party.

Kate could easily find room for two more guests inside her farmhouse, but throwing Jack and Barney together for even a few hours could be a recipe for disaster.

✳   ✳   ✳

Prosper Feed Co. had been on the far-west edge of town for a hundred years, and its grain-storage towers were impossible to miss on the horizon.

But in the gathering gloom of a late afternoon, Auggie Kleinsbach's business was lit up like, well, a Christmas tree.

A massive metal sculpture in the shape of a star blazed brightly from a catwalk on the largest grain tower, and the modest one-story shop's front windows were wrapped in colored lights.

Inflatable shapes gathered on the snow-covered ground along the main drive, and strains of holiday tunes piped from a speaker in the parking lot reached Kate's ears the moment she opened Bertha's door.

"My goodness, he really goes all out. I guess if Santa gets lost on Christmas Eve, he can always point Rudolph toward all these lights. There's plenty of room for the real guy to land his flight crew on this lot."

Auggie's cryptic message from that morning had Kate wondering exactly why she was being summoned to the Prosper co-op. He wasn't adept at texting, and often claimed it was the downfall of modern society, so maybe this wasn't all that important.

While they'd chatted about the missing nativity earlier in the week, Auggie had also been eager for updates on Kate's barn kitties, and Kate had shared her pledge to shop locally this holiday season.

Maybe that's what this was about, she decided as she picked her way through the snowy ruts in the gravel parking lot. The co-op was in the midst of a massive sale, if the generous ad in the Swanton newspaper was any indication of its scope.

Maybe Auggie had received a shipment that included perfect gifts for some of the folks on Kate's list. She was especially stumped when it came to Bryan and their dad.

"I will not resort to only gift cards," Kate pledged for the umpteenth time as she neared the shop's front door. "There has to be something more meaningful I can give them."

The newspaper ad was posted in one front window, and Kate decided to give it another look before she went inside. Maybe it would spark some shopping inspiration.

And then, she noticed another oversized flyer in the next window. Its focus was a scan of the nativity photo the sheriff's department had shared publicly Wednesday.

Have you seen us?

A young couple on their way home from Bethlehem has been missing since Nov. 28. They were last spotted in the vicinity of Panther Junction.

They are accompanied by their infant son, who is someone of great significance in this area and worldwide, and several farm critters. Their group may be traveling with three wise guys and a camel.

Anyone with information regarding their whereabouts should contact the Hartland County Sheriff's office.

Auggie made this flyer, Kate was sure of that. The manual cut-and-paste of the poster told Kate he'd printed out pieces and taped them together to craft this bulletin. And the witty wordplay? That was exactly his style.

"Oh, Auggie." Kate didn't know whether to roll her eyes or laugh. "You put some serious thought into this. I wonder if it's generated any leads?"

The holiday tunes continued inside the store, and the aisles were full of shoppers stocking up on items for their animals, both indoors and out. Kate sighed with disappointment when she saw Auggie at the register. She'd hoped to talk to him alone, not around dozens of pairs of eavesdropping ears.

But Auggie had already spotted Kate, and he motioned for Dan, his assistant manager, to take over the counter.

"That's quite the sign you have in the window." Kate followed him into the co-op's office and took the seat in front of the desk. "Is it doing any good?"

"Well, it's stirring folks up." There was a glint of triumph, as well as humor, in Auggie's brown eyes. "Exactly what I wanted." Then he frowned. "But no specific leads. At least, not yet."

Mr. Checkers, one of the co-op's two shop kitties, had been napping on a pile of papers on Auggie's desk. The buff-and-white cat quickly decided Kate's lap was a superior location.

"I like the poster, it's catchy," Kate told Auggie as she scratched Mr. Checkers' chin. "But I didn't see anything about the angel, and the barn backdrop. They're missing, too."

Auggie shrugged. "I tried to come up with something cute for that, but ran out of steam. Angels fly, as you know; and barns don't travel at all. The whole thing was getting awkward. I decided to quit while I was ahead."

"True." Kate nodded. "So, what's up? If you don't have any specific leads, what are you hearing, at least?"

There had been a few more break-ins at rural properties in the last week, Auggie reported, and the items being stolen were apparently increasing in both size and value. A snowblower was the latest casualty, swiped overnight from a farm north of Swanton. More power tools had gone missing, as well as expensive horses' tack and animal supplements.

"Aren't some of those drugs used on people, for dubious reasons?" This was more serious than what Kate had last heard. No wonder Auggie wanted to share his findings.

"Yep. It's scary, and those are tough to trace. Even for the rest of it, it's alarming. There's always a market for swiped stuff. But word is the stolen-goods market in our county, and this part of the state, is far-more sophisticated than what many realize. When things disappear into the system, if you will, they aren't likely to be recovered."

"Like the nativity." Kate was intrigued, but skeptical. "You really think the same criminals who are breaking into sheds and barns took it? Seems a little high-brow compared to their usual targets."

Auggie agreed, but pointed out the vintage set's apparent value. Or rather, that it was basically priceless and would be a fought-over item once it hit the antiques market. And these folks needed, or at least wanted, money. The fact that the Panther Junction church was a sacred space would mean nothing to them.

It was easy to get inside the church, Auggie mused, and it was unoccupied most of the time. Far-less risky than sneaking up to a farm, even in the middle of the night, where there was certain to be a dog or two and maybe security cameras.

Kate knew that all made sense. But it wasn't enough to steal such a work of art. The criminals would need to unload it. "They'd have to go out of the area for that. And I can't imagine these people have accomplices at high-end auction houses in major metropolitan areas."

"Exactly." Auggie glanced around Kate's shoulders to make sure his office door was tightly closed. "They'd need a contact to do that for them. Someone local, someone they know."

"Don't tell me you think Vicki Colton's wrapped up in this. She's ..."

"Not on the radar." Auggie was clear about that. "Meadow Lane would never get mixed up in such a thing. But there's another place that might be."

A business just outside of Eagle River bought and sold items on consignment, including entire estates' worth of goods. While the owners sometimes held public auctions, most of the pieces were sold individually from the large warehouse on the family's property. Kate had maybe been there once as a child, if ever.

Auggie said that in addition to the main building, the company had several structures on its rural property that were packed to the rafters with items bought outright or taken on trade.

"They're hoarders, you mean," Kate said.

"Well, no." Auggie shrugged. "OK, maybe the husband is. But he's a legit businessman, too." He leaned over the desk.

"I know you're looking to get some more furniture for your new place, so when Steve Collins said ..."

Kate's jaw dropped. "Deputy Collins? What does this have to do with him? Or with me?"

This was all off the record, of course, but Auggie claimed the sheriff's department suspected the estate-sale company might be involved in the area's burglary ring. Kate had never heard a bad word about that family, but had to admit someone in that line of work would have the ability to unload stolen items as well as those acquired through legal means.

"He sells *everything*," Auggie said with a shake of his head. "Household stuff, tools, yard items, farm goods, you name it. He's way out there in the country, down by the river. He has regular business hours and is open to the public, but people are so impressed with the main building's vast collections that they never think to ask about what might be out in the sheds."

Auggie gave Kate a knowing smile. "But you're good at asking questions."

"Am I?"

"Sure you are. And playing dumb, when it's required. And you're getting really good at tracking stuff down."

Steve Collins and his family lived in Prosper, and he'd stopped in yesterday afternoon to get more feed for their pet chickens. Deputy Collins wasn't breaking any laws; the birds had been legal in the city limits as long as anyone could remember. But as he and Auggie chatted, their conversation drifted toward the recent criminal activity around the county.

"And this is where you come in," Auggie told an astonished Kate.

Someone needed to head out to the estate company and wander around a bit, do a little window shopping, then report back if they noticed anything suspicious on the property. None of the deputies could do it, nor could their immediate family members. Too many people in Hartland County, well, knew too many people.

Kate took a deep breath. "So what you're saying is, the sheriff told Steve he'd like someone to go out there and snoop around, and then Steve told you, and you volunteered me for the gig?"

"Well, yeah." Auggie threw up his hands. "You've been gone for, what, at least a decade? Practically a stranger, these days. I'd go myself, but everyone around here knows me. That wouldn't work."

"Everyone around here knows you're *nosy*," Kate corrected him. She couldn't believe Auggie had nominated her for something like this, but the plan itself made sense.

"You don't have to go. But, why not?" Then Auggie grinned. "Take Bev along, make it a fun outing. Who knows, you might find some stuff for your house. Just keep your eyes open when you're there, that's all I'm saying."

"Well, I don't think the nativity is going to be out on a shelf, with a festive bow looped over the top of the barn."

Auggie heartedly agreed that would be too obvious and very stupid. But Bev and Kate could check the business' inventory for some of the other, everyday items that had been reported stolen.

"If this guy has any of those, they'll be hiding in plain sight." Auggie reached into a desk drawer and pulled out a sheet of paper, then slid it across the desk.

Kate leaned around Mr. Checkers to study the handwritten list. Makes and model numbers were listed for various tools, as well as specific brands for the other shop and barn items. There were colors and lengths listed for insulated extension cords, and so on.

"All you need to do is wander around, then let us know what you see. If this thing has any legs, the sheriff's department will take it from there. You can do the community some good, and shop for yourself at the same time."

"I 'do the community some good' every day I'm at the post office," Kate reminded Auggie. "OK, I'll think about it. Can I tell Bev what the real deal is?"

Auggie considered this. "Yeah, she's in the clear."

Kate glanced at the calendar on the wall of Auggie's office, and counted the days until Christmas. Only twenty to go. If there was any chance the nativity was still in the area, or someone local knew what had happened to it ...

She nodded, even though she wasn't quite sure yet what she was agreeing to. Auggie was right. Kate didn't say that out loud, since she didn't want it to go to his head, but this was a lead that needed to be followed.

"Oh, and there's more." He reached under the desk and pulled out a navy canvas tote stamped with "Prosper Feed Co." in sharp white script.

"You're going green? No more plastic bags?" Then Kate laughed. "Oh, I get it ... it's a *feed sack*, like back in the day. Just a modern one."

"Brilliant!" Auggie hooted. "I hadn't thought of it that way. We still offer the other kind, of course. But maybe Melinda can help me market these like that, get some of the stick-in-the-mud folks to give up their plastic."

He handed the tote across the desk. "Why don't you see what's in there?"

Kate peeked inside, as did Mr. Checkers. "What's all this? Treats, toys ..."

"There are a few things for Charlie and Hazel, and the rest are for the Three Mouseketeers." Auggie's expression turned contemplative, then sad. "Milton would want them to have a little something extra, for Christmas."

"Yes, he certainly would. Thank you. I'm sure they'll love all of this."

"But there's more." Auggie rolled his office chair around

to point at the cat tree next to the window. "Do you think you can get that in your car? I mean, if I take it apart?"

Kate blinked. "Um, yeah." She looked down at the cat still purring in her lap. "But Mr. Checkers and Pebbles ..."

"Are bored with it," Auggie said quickly. "You know how finicky they can be. I'm sure you can find a place for it out in the machine shed."

"The shed?"

"Of course! Unless Scout has moved himself into the house and brought the other two along. Wouldn't put something like that past him, but I doubt Charlie would put up with it."

Kate loved her barn kitties, but she had never thought to install a carpeted, multi-perch cat tower in one of her outbuildings. It would quickly be covered in bits of straw and muddy paw prints, and the trio had all the real trees they could ever want out in the yard. But Auggie was serious. More than that, he was eager to do whatever he could for his deceased relative's cats. Sure, he and Milton had been distant cousins, but family was family.

Kate finally smiled and nodded, and Auggie let out a whoop. "Good deal, because I ordered them a new one and it's coming tomorrow." He lowered his voice, even though no one else was around to hear. "I'm having it shipped here, to the co-op. Didn't want Jane to have to fuss with it coming to the house."

"Does she even know about it?" Kate was smirking now.

"I'm not replacing the two upstairs in the weather lab. Just this one." He reached for a screwdriver and hustled to the window before Kate could ask more questions. "Bring that tote over here, I'll put all the hardware in it."

Half an hour later, Bertha was loaded down like Santa's sleigh. The cat tree's sections took up most of the back seat, and two economy bags of food were in the trunk along with the bag of treats and toys.

It was quite the haul, but Kate knew better than to object. Auggie wanted to give a little this holiday season; she wasn't about to deny him that joy.

"And I might as well head out to the consignment place," Kate muttered to herself as she drove through Prosper. "Bev should be down for this. In fact, she'll think it's a hoot."

The car was packed with gifts, but Kate realized something was missing. She slapped the steering wheel, and had to laugh at herself.

"I was so busy getting the lowdown from Auggie, I forgot all about my holiday shopping. Well, I guess Hazel and the kitties take priority today."

11

There was a box on Kate's front porch when she turned up the lane the next afternoon. "Delivery two of three. No, four, I think. Depends on how they packaged stuff. I'll have to check my messages."

Then she laughed. "There's Scout on the lookout! No one would dare steal my stuff with such an imposing-looking kitty on watch."

The big, fluffy cat had turned into a love bug, but his supervisory ways were still on display now that he belonged to Kate. Or more like, she belonged to him. So did this little acreage and the house, and everything else. That included deliveries dropped while Kate was away.

Porch pirates weren't much of a problem in rural areas. Kate liked to think this was because small-town folks were more honest, but she didn't quite believe that. Too many miles of gravel meant too much effort to snag something that may, or may not, be worth stealing.

Hazel was the one with the security training, albeit rudimentary, but she seemed to prefer hanging out with Charlie indoors to clocking all the comings and goings in the yard.

"Some guard dog Hazel is," Kate good-naturedly told Scout. "I'm so glad you're here to keep an eye on the place."

Scout put his paws up on Kate's pant leg, and she set down her things long enough to pick him up for a cuddle. "I'm glad you're here, every day. And Maggie and Jerry, too. I'll bring that box in off the porch. Your work is done for now."

The kitchen was warm and cozy, as always, but Kate inwardly groaned as she came in the back door. The more she pored over decorating ideas online, the more restless she was to update her surroundings. The post office's holiday party was a week from tomorrow night, and Kate was determined to make her home shine.

"I know, it's the fun that'll matter," she told Charlie as he trailed her through the foyer to the front door. There was no worry about him trying to escape. He hated the cold; and besides, the yard was Scout's domain. "The camaraderie will be what's important, not the curtains."

Then she grinned. "But if my online alerts are correct, that's exactly what's in today's delivery. Wait until you see what I found!"

Hazel came down from upstairs, and the three of them gathered next to the coffee table for a peek. "Oh, these are perfect!" Kate ripped the plastic bag off the first curtain panel, not bothering with scissors in her haste. "A soft gray, see? With a little blue."

Hazel wagged her tail. Charlie, however, was only interested in the box. "Let me get the rest of them out," she told the cat, "and then that's all yours."

Kate held the first panel up to one side of the picture window, and the mauve, pinch-pleated draperies temporarily vanished. "Oh, that's a thousand times better! This will make a big difference until I can paint."

With the first curtain draped over one arm, Kate hurried into the kitchen's small pantry to retrieve yesterday's shipment.

In a burst of creativity and overconfidence, she'd ordered several rolls of wallpaper for the dining room. Not the old-fashioned, paste-up kind; but the modern, peel-and-stick stuff that went up in a flash and came down with a gentle tug on one corner. Or at least, that's what the bloggers and home-improvement websites promised.

"I can still back out," she muttered as she carried the box to the dining-room table. "I can return these. Besides, if they don't look right with the curtains, I won't want them, anyway."

Shopping online was quick and easy, but there was always a chance that an item's color was off, or the quality wasn't what it appeared to be.

But these hues were spot-on. The wallpaper's light-gray background was offset by a cream-hued geometric pattern that reminded Kate of garden paths. It was neutral and subtle, and would make a beautiful backdrop for the deeper gray-blue shade of the curtain panels.

"This wallpaper is going to change everything," Kate promised Hazel while she studied the faded cabbage roses that still covered the dining room walls. "We'll start after supper, and see how far we can get tonight. Everyone's using this stuff these days. It can't be that hard."

When she purchased this farmhouse, Kate's first instinct had been to strip the old paper from the dining room's walls, along with whatever other layers that were likely hiding beneath. But that would be a tedious, messy process. Why not smooth over the old stuff with a fresh look instead, and one that could easily be undone later?

Kate had never expected to work with wallpaper again. But then, she also hadn't planned to get divorced, move back to Eagle River, and buy a farmhouse that was more shabby than chic.

Charlie was intrigued when the stepladder emerged from the pantry, and he made a perch out of its tray while Kate dusted down the first wall. The instructions insisted clean surfaces were key to making the adhesive-backed strips stick.

Hazel supervised from the floor beyond the far end of the table while Kate spread out the first roll of paper. "I'll hold down your end with books, since you can't reach," Kate told her dog. "Measure twice, cut once, and we're ready to go. As long as I get this first strip straight with that pencil line on the wall, the rest will be easy."

Except it wasn't. The back of the wallpaper was sticky, all right. So sticky that, once the backing was removed, the paper clung to everything in its path: the wall, the trim, Kate's hands. Worst of all, itself. Thank goodness it was removable. But she had to pull slowly and gently, reposition the paper without getting more wrinkles in it, and then smooth it with a plastic trowel.

Kate went up and down the ladder so many times that Charlie soon tired of the disruption and decamped to the living room. Hazel was nearly asleep in the corner by the tree, her head on her paws. Apparently, watching Kate hang wallpaper was as boring as watching paint dry.

After twenty minutes of sweating and swearing, Kate finally had the first piece wrestled onto the wall. "It's pretty," she had to admit as she stepped back to admire her hard-fought work. "And I think it's straight. Or as straight as I'm going to get in a hundred-year-old house. But this is going to take forever."

The next time, she peeled the backing off in pieces from one side, rather than from the top down. That seemed to help. But once this strip was on the wall, Kate had to trim it to fit around the corner of the cased opening.

Before long, the shag carpet disappeared under strips of smooth backing and chunks of adhesive-coated wallpaper. The rustling scraps were too tempting for Charlie to ignore.

Measure, peel, stick. Adjust, smooth, trim. She'd followed the instructions online, of course, but had she really ordered enough? And why had she thought this was a good idea?

A howl came out of the scrap pile on the floor. "Charlie?"

Kate turned on the ladder so fast, she nearly lost her balance. "Are you in there somewhere?"

More rustling and yowling, and then a cream-and-brown fluff ball trailing scraps of patterned gray paper shot out of the debris and disappeared through the cased opening.

"Oh, no!" Kate hurried after Charlie, Hazel at her heels. "It's stuck in his fur!"

There was no sign of the cat. "Where is he?"

Hazel stuck her nose under the couch's pleated skirt, and was greeted with a growl. Kate received the same reaction. "You have to come out," she pleaded with Charlie. "I can't help you unless you come out of there."

Treats, more begging ... nothing worked. Finally, Kate took a deep breath and reached under the couch. The scratch was expected, but the bite was not.

As Kate pulled back her stinging hand, an agitated Charlie dashed out from under the couch and ran for the stairwell. The rattle of the paper strips stuck to his fur only added to his fear. Something had ahold of him from behind, he was sure of that!

"Let him go." Kate put a hand on Hazel's back, and the dog obediently settled on the carpet. "Wow, look at that. Charlie freaking out makes it easy for you to be the well-behaved one, huh?"

Kate's thumb was bleeding, and Hazel padded along as she fetched the first-aid kit from the kitchen. After she applied the antiseptic, Kate closed her eyes against the sting as well as her defeat.

"We have to quit for tonight," she told Hazel. "Somehow, I have to help Charlie. And I obviously can't wrestle that wallpaper alone. I think it's going to take another set of paws to get this done."

❋   ❋   ❋

Headlights swept up the drive just before six the following evening. "She's here!" Kate checked the take-and-bake pizza's progress, then wiped her hands on a dishtowel. "The calvary has arrived. Or at least, the decorating deputy."

She shook her head sadly at Charlie, who glanced up from his supper long enough to give her yet-another disgusted look.

"I know. It's terrible, and I'm sorry." His fur was still thick and silky, but the two cut-out clumps on his right rump couldn't be missed. "It'll grow back. Somehow, I think you'll stay out of the fray tonight."

There was a knock at the kitchen door, and Gwen blew in with a gust of cold air. "Whew, it's windy! Glad the snow is going to hold off until morning, I think."

"I'm so glad you could come over." Kate took her neighbor's coat and added it to the pegs by the back door. "My first two assistants weren't much help last night, and I'm pretty sure one of them has quit."

Gwen couldn't hold back her laughter as Kate pointed out Charlie's woeful haircut. "Oh, my, I bet that was a tussle." The more Gwen stared at the cat's coat, the harder she laughed. Charlie was not amused.

"He's mortified." Kate reached into a cabinet and pulled out plates. "And I don't blame him."

The sound of a second voice brought Hazel in from the living room, and she eyed the oven with a hopeful expression.

"None for you," Kate said gently, then pointed at Hazel's dishes. "There's plenty over there."

Gwen gasped again when she peeked into the dining room. But this time, it was from admiration. "Wow, what a transformation! Even if it's still in progress. I'm excited to see what it's like when it's done. And it goes with the new curtains, right?"

"Yes, perfectly." Gwen's enthusiasm was contagious, and Kate decided her impulsive decision to wallpaper the dining room had been the right one. They'd tackle this together, and the finished project would go a long way toward sprucing up this farmhouse in time for the post-office party.

Gwen carried the veggie tray and dip into the dining room while Kate plated the pizza. There was only soda tonight, no wine; the ladies had agreed they'd need every ounce of focus to get this job done.

As they chewed and chatted, they came up with a plan to tackle the rest of the wallpaper.

"Once we turn that first corner, we'll be golden," Gwen promised as she worked through a slice of pizza. "I think we should trim it off just past the bend, like we used to do with the old stuff, then hang a fresh strip that's square."

"I was thinking the same." Kate heaped a generous spoonful of sour-cream dip on her plate. "The pattern's optical illusion will be in our favor. And we need to get it as straight as we can before we continue on, because you know these walls certainly aren't."

"Oh, old houses." Gwen shook her head with an admiring smile. "They're just full of character."

The wallpaper was just as sticky as the night before. But a second set of hands, and no furry assistants, made everything easier. Charlie had retreated to the adjoining room and curled up on his bed by the fireplace, but Kate noticed he was awake enough to keep an eye on all that rustling paper. Hazel watched with interest from the couch.

Another wall was soon covered in fresh paper. It was time to pull out the fully loaded Christmas tree, another chore that would have been difficult for Kate to tackle alone. "I couldn't finish this without your help," she told Gwen. "You get in a bind like this with a project, just let me know, and I'll come over."

Gwen shrugged. "Oh, it's not a big deal. The boys have been at their dad's all weekend, they aren't back until tomorrow after school."

Despite her neighbor's smile, Kate picked up on the hint of loneliness in Gwen's voice. Especially because she understood the feeling.

"It must be hard," Kate said as they sidestepped toward the ladder with the next strip in their hands. "I mean, it's your first holiday season since the divorce. What with the boys going back and forth ..."

"Maisie and I sit by the tree and read at night, when they're gone. Well, I do," she quickly added with a laugh. "Maisie loves to look at the lights." She tipped her head toward the next room, where Hazel now snored on the couch. "When she's not asleep, that is."

"It's been hard for me, too," Kate admitted as she started up the ladder. "But I don't have kids, of course."

"That doesn't matter." Gwen held the bottom of the strip away from the wall while Kate positioned it at the top. "Things are still different for you, in so many ways. Do you miss Ben?"

"Well, sometimes." Kate sighed. "We had so many plans. But I guess plans change sometimes, huh?" Then she laughed. "I can't imagine the two of us hanging wallpaper without things getting ugly."

The more pieces the women put on the walls, the faster their work went. By the time they rounded the last corner, Gwen and Kate felt like professionals.

Even so, they agreed there would be no more wallpaper parties anytime soon.

"I've been tempted to try it, myself," Gwen said as they admired their work. "It looks incredible, and it was the perfect solution for this room. But I think I'll stick with paint."

As Kate watched her neighbor's taillights disappear down the dark lane, she felt blessed to have someone just up the road who was willing to help out. Not just a new neighbor, but a new friend.

Since all the paper scraps were now tucked away in trash bags, Charlie couldn't resist touring the renovated dining room. "The coast is clear," Kate promised him. "You can move around freely and don't have to worry about being attacked. I left you some treats in the kitchen."

Her phone began to ring, and Kate frowned at the screen. "Why is Bev calling at this hour on a Sunday night? Oh, I hope everything is okay."

But Bev was as cheerful as ever. "This is so exciting, it can't wait until tomorrow morning! Are you sitting down?"

"I am now. What happened? Did someone find the nativity?"

"No, sorry. But this is almost as good. I just got off the phone with Chloe." Bev took a deep breath. "Kate, you're related to Gustav Weigmann."

Kate couldn't speak. *What?!*

"Are you still there?" Then Bev laughed. "You didn't faint, right?"

"No." Kate was laughing now, too. "But I'm glad you told me to sit down, first. I can't believe it! Wait, how am I ... tell me everything you know!"

Chloe had intended to spend most of her weekend studying for finals, but tracking down descendants of the church's founding families was an assignment she hadn't been able to resist. One of Gustav's and Caroline's daughters had married a man named Josef Stiefel, and one of their daughters married into another area family ... the Duncans.

"You're telling me that Great-Grandma Duncan was Gustav's granddaughter?" Kate tried to piece it all together. "Well, the Duncans have been in this part of the county for a long time. Maybe not as long as the Weigmanns, but ..."

"That's right. People didn't get far from home, back in the day." Now that she'd shared her big news, Bev was back to business as usual. "And when women married, their maiden names were all-but forgotten."

"That explains why I've never heard anyone in my extended family talk about the Weigmanns. The surname is buried too far back in my family tree."

"Exactly! Which brings me to another piece of exciting news."

Helping Bev and Kate had spurred Chloe to pick up the loose threads of her own research, and she'd circled back to the Thurbers and their journey to America. Bev wasn't clear on all the twists and turns, but one of them had ended with a breakthrough discovery: Magdalena Thurber was Gustav's sister.

Magdalena Weigmann and Johann Thurber were married in Germany, which meant her maiden name had been obscured since before their boat docked at Castle Garden in New York City.

During the 1860s, Magdalena, Gustav, and one of their brothers, Heinrich, had all brought their families to Panther Junction. Two other siblings stayed in Illinois, and there were at least three more that remained in Germany.

"So you both are related to him, too? This is crazy!" Kate had wandered into the kitchen, and reached for the cookie jar on the counter. Charlie wasn't the only one who needed a snack right now.

"Wait! That means ..."

"You got it!" Bev shouted with glee. "Kate, we're cousins!"

Fourth cousins once removed, officially. But for these friends, it was the connection itself that mattered.

"It took some digging," Bev said, "but our Girl Friday was able to put the puzzle pieces together. She's updating our online file now; give her another hour or so, she said, and it'll all be there."

Still dazed by this news, Kate went into the living room and stared at the dime-store nativity on her mantel. It had never crossed her mind that Gustav Weigmann might be one of her relatives, much less her great-great-great grandfather.

Kate thought of how she and Hazel had been the ones to stumble upon the scene at the church. How she'd felt so compelled to help search for the nativity, and even to purchase this second-hand set so she'd have one of her own.

It was all a coincidence. It had to be. But was something else at work here?

Kate had no way of knowing, couldn't begin to wrap her mind around all of it. But one thing was certain: she was more determined than ever to track down her ancestor's masterpiece.

"One way or another, we're going to get to the bottom of this," she told Bev. "And given what we've found out, I can't think of anyone better than the two of us to scope out that estate company for the sheriff."

* 12 *

Kate's Monday assignment was the perfect backdrop for her jumbled thoughts, which were still more focused on the past than the present.

Aaron was sorting packages at the post office, which meant she had his west-side town route where many of the streets were lined with historic homes.

Her first neighborhood was one of the oldest in Eagle River, with many homes dating back to the 1870s. Even the two-story structures were small, with narrow windows and steeply pitched roofs.

These houses huddled close to their streets, as they'd been built long before sidewalks were added to this area. Many of their front walkways were crooked and uneven, which made them tricky due to the half-heartedly cleared ice and snow. Add in the fact that Kate's arms were often overflowing with mail, and she was thankful for her new, high-traction work boots from Prosper Hardware.

Most of these porches were as neglected as their front walks. This was, and had always been, a working-class area of town. But here and there, Kate still spotted signs of the season: a lone string of lights wrapped around a sagging porch railing, or a wreath with just one small bow fastened to a weathered front door.

The worn-down appearance of these homes reminded Kate of the Taylors' farmhouse, and she wondered how Candace was managing as the days counted down toward Christmas. That made her think of Alex, and his observations about Wyatt's alcohol problem.

"Alex is right about the secrecy part," she reminded herself as she refilled her mailbag from the back of the truck. "Some people prefer to drink alone. Unless, of course, Wyatt's with someone else."

Kate cringed at the memory of when she'd discovered Ben's cheating. For Candace, a busted mailbox was certainly a nuisance; but her husband's possible betrayal was a hurt that would be much harder to heal.

With that neighborhood's deliveries finished by late morning, Kate moved the truck into a nearby area that was also historic but exponentially more grand.

By the late 1800s, most of Eagle River's prominent families had built new homes along and near Oakland Avenue. Whether through land speculation, railroad investment or a booming business along Main, those residents had greatly improved upon the previous generation's idea of wealth and success.

Not all the properties were in home-tour condition these days, as the upkeep of historic houses was as expensive as it was time-consuming, But many places had been handed down within a family, or purchased by people eager to pour cash and effort into one of these genteel homes.

Kate had forgotten how this neighborhood shined during the holiday season. Garlands encircled front porches up and down her route, and lights glowed along the outlines of many of the rooftops. Inflatable characters dotted some of the yards as well, and one corner property featured a sizable herd of light-up reindeer sculptures.

Given the comparative wealth of these homeowners, a majority of the parcels in Kate's truck were destined for their porches. By the time she was halfway through the district, her arms ached and her shoulders burned. But Myrtle Bradford's house was in the next block, and it offered Kate a welcome chance to catch her breath.

Myrtle's now-deceased husband had managed a profitable insurance business, meaning she was one of the wealthiest folks in town as well as one of the oldest. She refused to comment on monetary matters and other such nonsense, but was proud of the fact that, at ninety-two, she still lived in her own home.

While Myrtle's extended family visited her on occasion, most of its younger members had moved away for different scenery and better employment opportunities.

Myrtle spent most of her daytime hours with Patty, her health-care aide. Percival, Myrtle's little terrier, kept track of the neighborhood's comings and goings from the generous bay window that looked out on the front yard.

It wasn't common practice to take residents' letters and parcels inside their homes, but Eagle River's mail crew often made exceptions for those who were elderly or otherwise housebound.

Myrtle was as eager for visitors as she was for her mail, and was known to linger on her front porch around the time the carriers reached this part of the route. In-home delivery at Myrtle's place, especially during the winter, made it much-less likely the elderly woman would take a tumble in her eagerness to get a letter or enjoy some much-needed social interaction.

Kate was glad to see the snow and ice had been cleared from Myrtle's brick-herringbone pathway. Two neighbors usually took turns shoveling the walk, but Aaron occasionally did it himself.

Percival was already at the front window, barking out news of Kate's arrival, by the time she pushed the button on the home's antiquated doorbell.

"No wi-fi cameras here, that's for sure." Kate admired the carved-oak door's fresh, overstuffed evergreen wreath, whose branches were entwined with purple ribbon and topped by gilded pinecones.

There were just two envelopes today, both of which looked to be holiday greetings, and Kate hoped their arrival would bolster the elderly woman's spirits. Kate expected to be invited in for some cookies or even a cup of tea. And after a few hours of tramping around in the cold, both would be welcome.

There was more barking inside, and then Patty came to the door. "Kate! Come on in." Patty's brown hair was held back in a French braid, and flour dusted her cheeks. "I'm in the middle of some gingerbread cookies, but there's a batch that's already out of the oven."

The grand old home was filled with the scent of cinnamon and cloves, and its sudden warmth soothed Kate's chilled cheeks. The foyer's stair railing was festooned with greenery and more purple bows, and the stained-glass window in its halfway landing glowed in the late-morning light.

Kate didn't have much chance to admire the house's holiday decorations, as Percival insisted on sniffing her boots and receiving some attention. Myrtle remained in her lift chair by the already-lit fireplace in the front parlor, but her eyes glowed with excitement when she spotted her visitor.

Along with a live evergreen tree decked out in shades of purple and gold, three Christmas stockings were fastened to the fireplace mantel: one each for Myrtle, Percival, and Patty.

"How is she today?" Kate quietly asked Patty as she unlaced her boots. She wasn't about to spread slush on these inlaid-oak floors.

"Oh, she's been better." Patty frowned. "But it's not her mind," she added quickly. "Yesterday's Mason City newspaper really stirred her up. It's all that fuss about the Panther Junction nativity."

"Yes, of course. Everyone's talking about it."

The Swanton newspaper's coverage of the case had been brief, and mostly focused on Sheriff Preston's pleas for the set to be returned before the holidays were over. But one of the region's larger publications had picked up on the missing nativity's story, and its Sunday edition included a detailed profile of the Panther Junction church, some of the rumors attached to its prized possession, and the announcement of a hefty reward being offered for the set's safe return.

Kate read the article online yesterday morning. And late last night, after she learned of her family's ties to Gustav Weigmann, she had studied every word again through a new emotional lens. The monetary reward, in particular, caught her attention. If the Panther Junction congregation was as cash-strapped as gossip claimed it to be, how had its members come up with the money?

"Did you bring me anything?" Myrtle's thin voice rose with hope as Kate entered the sitting room, Percival at her heels.

"I sure did." Kate's heart soared to see how the mail's arrival brightened this woman's day. It was one of her favorite parts of her job. "And there are two!"

"Oh, my dear, thank you!" Myrtle carefully placed the envelopes on her lift chair's side table and gave them an affectionate pat. "I'm sure those will be wonderful to read this afternoon."

While Kate enjoyed her occasional visits with Myrtle, she wished the older woman would move to an assisted living facility. There, a few pieces of mail wouldn't be the highlight of her day. But Myrtle had apparently refused all efforts to sell her grand home, where she'd lived for seventy years. Besides, she could afford to hire help to come to her.

"Here are some cookies." Patty returned with a small dessert plate, and a cup of tea. Now it was Kate's turn to beam with gratitude.

"What's it like out there today?" Myrtle was eager for news from the outside world. "It looks rather nice. They are saying we might get more snow tonight."

"I heard the same. It's pretty decent, for early December." Kate bit into a gingerbread cookie, and nearly groaned in delight. Patty's baking was legendary. "The sidewalks are in good shape, at least on your street. People around here do a pretty good job of keeping their paths clear. The carriers really appreciate it. So, how are you?"

Myrtle harrumphed. "Well, I've been better." She lifted a section of carefully folded newspaper from her side table, changed her mind, and dropped it with a look of disgust. "That silly woman at that big-city paper, she's up to no good."

Kate raised her eyebrows but kept chewing.

"I've been telling Patty, those things she wrote about the nativity are all wrong." Myrtle's thin lips set in a hard line, and Percival barked his apparent agreement. "It's lies, I tell you. All lies."

Kate merely nodded. "I see." Then she decided to come clean. Sort of. "You know, I made a delivery at the church a day or so after the nativity went missing. It had been on the altar, but then it was gone. I don't think anyone misplaced it."

How Kate wanted to share her news about being related to the nativity's creator! But Myrtle was already so agitated, and Kate had no idea what exactly had the elderly woman so upset. Best to keep that revelation to herself, at least for now.

"That's not what I meant." Myrtle braced her veined hands on the padded arms of her chair and leaned forward. "It's been stolen, I'm sure of that." Her eyes snapped with anger. "And not for the first time! No, I'm talking about how the church ended up with the nativity, all that nonsense about the family donating it. That's hogwash."

Kate glanced at the clock. She shouldn't stay long, but something told her a few more minutes could prove to be very interesting. Kate wasn't sure how sharp Myrtle's cognitive function was these days, but she was eager to hear what the old woman had to say.

"So they didn't donate it, then?" She took a sip of her tea. "How did it end up at the church? Everyone says that ..."

"They don't remember." Myrtle raised her chin in defiance. "But I do. I may be ninety-two, but I remember exactly what my parents told me."

"How do you ..."

Myrtle held up one wrinkled hand. "Just listen. You can ask questions later."

Gustav and Caroline Weigmann always displayed the nativity in their home during the holidays, a practice that continued when their oldest son, Karl, took over the home farm and began to care for his aging parents. Karl and his wife, Augusta, kept up the tradition after Gustav, and then Caroline, passed away.

The nineteen twenties were hard on farm families across the Midwest, Myrtle told Kate with a sad shake of her head. By the time the stock market crashed in the fall of 1929, the rest of the country was just starting to get a taste of what rural folks had been coping with for years.

While the Weigmanns had once been prosperous farmers, the family's finances were now dire. Karl felt the weight of responsibility on his shoulders. His immigrant parents had sacrificed so much to rebuild their lives in this country and, as their oldest son, he had been urged to expand on their success.

"But it was too much," Myrtle reported. "Karl's heart was bad, always had been. Some childhood illness, I guess, and then the stress got to him. He'd taken out a mortgage to make some improvements on the homeplace, you see, and then fell behind on the payments."

Percival jumped into Myrtle's lap, and she paused to give him a few pets. "One day, Augusta rang the front yard's bell to call Karl in for dinner and, well, he didn't show."

Karl had collapsed in the barn's main aisle. He was only forty-six, but a heart attack had taken his life. Augusta was now a widow with five children. Their oldest daughter was seventeen, and Karl junior, fifteen. While they could help their mother with the farm, neither was mature enough to fill their father's shoes.

"How terrible!" Kate blinked back a few tears. These were her ancestors Myrtle was talking about; and until last night, she'd had no idea they even existed.

Patty came in from the kitchen, a dish towel still in her hands, and took the other spot on the sofa. "Can you imagine?" Patty shook her head. "Augusta had all those children to care for, and a note on the farm to pay, too."

"She sure did. And it wasn't long before the Eagle River Savings Bank's president came to call." Myrtle's voice was now filled with fury and contempt. "My uncle, Oswald Baxter, in case you didn't know."

At Kate and Patty's stunned expressions, Myrtle went on. "Oh, yes, I'm related to that rascal." She tipped her head toward the picture window, in the general direction of Main Street. "And the rascals that run the show these days, too."

Kate was now on the edge of her seat. She'd had an account at that bank, which was Eagle River's only financial institution, since her elementary-school years. But an odd conversation with an employee a few months ago had caused her to take her mortgage application elsewhere.

She now wondered how many locals gave Eagle River's lone bank their business out of habit or even social obligation. The Baxter family founded the bank in the 1870s, and its members were proud of the fact that five generations had been at the business' helm.

Some of its members, at least. Because Myrtle, like Kate, apparently wasn't impressed.

Augusta hadn't had the cash to make the loan payment, Myrtle said. Like most people in those days, her family struggled along on what they raised in their garden, and bartered with neighbors for their other needs.

Oswald Baxter was aware of the handcrafted nativity, as Gustav had whittled and sold small items to area residents for a bit of extra income in his twilight years. A child's toy, or perhaps a small bird statue. But never anything that came close to the size and scope of the magnificent display he'd created for his family years ago. That was a true work of art.

"Aunt Amelia liked nice things," Myrtle said acidly. "Antiques, art, jewelry. She always sent off to Chicago for her clothes and such. Nothing here was good enough for her. Uncle Oswald liked nice things, too. Pretty young things, if you know what I mean. Amelia turned a blind eye to his carousing, a trick that was easier to manage if her husband spoiled her with expensive gifts."

So, a bargain was made. Oswald took the nativity, and the Weigmanns got to keep their farm. The Baxters proudly displayed the set in their home that holiday season, told their wealthy and well-connected friends they'd purchased the one-of-a-kind artifact from Augusta Weigmann. Desperate to keep her farm and save face in the community, Augusta never corrected the tale. After all, Oswald Baxter was the richest man in town.

But in the end, it didn't matter. In the spring of 1930, the Eagle River Savings Bank foreclosed on the Weigmanns' farm.

"What?" Kate gasped. "After he took the nativity, he still pushed them off their land?"

Myrtle didn't know the details of the agreement between Augusta Weigmann and Uncle Oswald, if the trade was meant to wipe away all the debt or only a portion of it. "But he was a nasty person," she said simply. "Money meant everything to him. Which certainly explains what happened next."

The Great Depression worsened as the months went on and, despite Oswald's ruthless management, the bank began to falter. It wasn't long before Oswald Baxter found himself in the exact-same predicament Karl Weigmann had faced: the possibility of being the one to run his family's finances into the ground, become the weak link in the chain.

"Uncle Oswald started drinking, more than he had before," Myrtle said. "My mother was his sister, and she and Father had stopped speaking to him after he'd tried to swindle them out of some money right after their marriage. But Eagle River's a small town, and everyone knew he and Amelia were in serious money trouble."

The nativity was packed away in a spare bedroom closet at the Baxter house, tucked inside the wooden crate Gustav had crafted for his masterpiece.

But even though the nativity was no longer on display, Oswald couldn't stop thinking about the set and what he'd done to acquire it.

"He started to think it was cursed," Myrtle said in a whisper. "Or more likely, that he was cursed. He'd swindled Augusta Weigmann out of her family's prized possession, just like he'd short-changed so many others."

"Do you think it was?" Kate was mesmerized by this story. "That the nativity had some sort of power attached to it?"

"Well, anything is possible." Myrtle gave a small shrug. "There's so much in this world that we don't understand. Of course, everyone was in dire straits by then. Many of the other banks around here failed. So many families lost their farms and their homes, businesses were going under right and left. My uncle didn't need to be cursed by Gustav Weigmann to find himself going broke. It was just the way things were."

What mattered, though, was what Oswald believed. And he started to think that Gustav was reaching out from beyond the grave to punish him for what he'd done.

The Baxters had to sell their fine home, which was the three-story Queen Anne down at the next corner, and move into a modest house on the north end of town. In a desperate bid to get enough cash to save the bank, all their artwork, fine china and the other expensive baubles they'd collected over the years went to an auction house in Chicago.

Oswald Baxter set only one item aside before his family's riches were packed up and taken to the train station.

Augusta Weigmann and her children had already moved far away, to a big city where they could find work to support themselves. But it was just as well. Oswald was too proud, and now too broken in spirit, to face Augusta and beg for her forgiveness.

But the extended Weigmann family had been prominent in the Panther Junction congregation for several decades by then. All his life, Oswald Baxter had cut deals to get ahead; now, he hoped that donating the nativity to the church might balance out his past transgressions and cause the cloud of doubt and fear that plagued him to disappear.

"Did it work?" Patty wanted to know.

Myrtle chuckled, then rolled her eyes. "Maybe, maybe not. Uncle Oswald saved the bank, as you surely can guess. It continued to struggle through the depression, and almost went under again in the late thirties, but he managed to keep the doors open."

There was no doubt in Kate's mind that Myrtle was telling the truth. Or at least, the truth as it had been told to her. Because for many of the elderly, the past was just as clear, if not more so, than the present.

While Kate tried to process a second revelation about the nativity in as many days, Patty was focused on more practical matters.

"So, what about the church's members?" Patty called from the kitchen as she pulled the next batch of cookies from the oven. "I mean, they knew who donated the nativity, right?" Then she laughed. "Did your uncle leave it out on the steps, or something?"

"Goodness, no!" Myrtle gave a snort of disgust. "He was going broke, but his ego was as big as ever."

Oswald wanted, and received, recognition for his generous donation to one of the area's iconic churches. And given Augusta's silence about how the nativity changed hands to begin with, the congregation accepted his version of events. Publicly, at least.

"Of course, some of them had to know what really happened." Myrtle pulled her brown-wool cardigan closer over her plaid blouse, as if fighting off a sudden chill. "That's how my parents found out about it. But the nativity was finally in good hands, in a place where it would be honored and respected. And it's been at the heart of the church's Christmas season ever since."

"Details can be lost over time." Kate thought of how her ties to Gustav had unraveled through the generations.

"The Weigmanns were a founding family of the congregation, the nativity was donated to the church fifty-some years after the set was created ... I can see how the narrative everyone now takes as the gospel got started."

"But I know the truth," Myrtle said proudly. "And now, both of you do, too."

✳ 13 ✳

Kate had to gobble her sandwich in the truck to make up time, but her head-spinning visit with Myrtle was worth every minute. She'd been tempted to talk about her link to Gustav Weigmann before she left the older woman's home, was eager to share her own story. But something gave her pause and, in the end, she kept her silence.

As she continued her route that afternoon, Kate pondered what she'd learned and what might happen next. She was glad she'd heeded her intuition and left her personal connection out of the conversation. After all, her best chance to find the missing nativity likely stemmed from her perceived neutrality about the case.

As far as other people knew, Kate was simply curious about the missing artifact. And who wasn't these days, especially following that blockbuster article in Sunday's newspaper?

Late that afternoon, Kate pulled Bev aside in the post office's break room and shared Myrtle's shocking story. Kate would have preferred an immediate phone call, given the revelations she now had in hand, but both ladies had been racing to complete their rounds and there was no time to waste until their shifts ended.

Bev was floored, to put it mildly. She'd never heard a

word about Oswald Baxter's shameful role in the nativity's history, even though she was a lifelong member of the Panther Junction congregation.

Who else knew the truth these days? What else might people be hiding?

"We're trying to get to the bottom of things," Bev whispered to Kate. "But sometimes, I guess, you need to be careful what you wish for. Because given what we've learned from Chloe and Myrtle, I feel like we've opened a Pandora's Box. The question is: What do we do with all this information? Does it matter, or not?"

"I have no idea." Kate closed her eyes, suddenly exhausted. "Because I've been blindsided twice in less than twenty-four hours."

Bev was right; Kate could feel the weight of all these secrets on her heart as well as her mind. "We need to tell the sheriff, I guess. At least about what Myrtle said."

"I'll call tonight," Bev promised. "I can't imagine there's a lead in there anywhere, but you never know. And from what I'm hearing, Jeff and his deputies are hitting dead ends everywhere they look."

Word was that while law enforcement officials continued to interview members of the congregation, none of those conversations had turned up anything of significance.

Bev and Clyde had each chatted about the situation with a few close friends from church, but no one seemed to know who had put up the money for the reward. The person apparently wanted to remain anonymous, from what Jeff had told Bev, and she knew her former sweetheart would keep his promise.

One of the church ladies said a deputy asked her if anyone in the congregation had lost a button off their coat.

What an odd thing to say, the woman had grumbled to Bev; how could that possibly have anything to do with the nativity? Bev had feigned ignorance, joked that maybe the deputy had taken on too many hours of overtime, then quickly changed the subject.

"I agree we need to keep our connection to Gustav quiet," Bev told Kate as she washed out her coffee thermos in the break room's sink. "Let the focus be on the nativity, not ourselves. At this point, I feel like I know too much as it is."

Jack wandered into the break room, and his sharp gaze zeroed in on Bev and Kate at the counter. "What's going on?" He frowned. "You two are thick as thieves over there."

Kate almost laughed. Jack was certainly on to something, even if he did have the wrong end of the stick. "Just talking about the office party. What are you bringing, by the way?"

That threw Jack off the trail. "Uh, I don't know."

"Maybe Audrey can bring her homemade cinnamon buns," Bev suggested. "I hear they are fantastic."

"Sounds good. I'll ask her."

If Bev and Kate didn't have any good gossip to share, Jack was eager to move on. And head for home. "Morning seems to come earlier every day, doesn't it?" He dumped the accumulated debris from a long day in his mail car into the trash can by the refrigerator. "Christmas Eve can't get here fast enough, in my opinion. Only sixteen days to go!"

After he left, Bev shook her head sadly.

"Sixteen days." She sighed. "Why do I think that's not going to be enough?"

One of Kate's favorite holiday movies was on television that night, and she hoped getting lost in the comforting world of Bedford Falls for a few hours might quiet the questions in her mind.

As she microwaved a bag of popcorn before the movie started, Kate almost wished she hadn't caved into Austin and Alex's good-natured peer pressure about joining the festival's community chorus. She'd already missed the first rehearsal, so she certainly couldn't bail on tomorrow evening's practice at the high school.

That meant the earliest she and Bev could stake out the estate company was late Wednesday afternoon. Between extended shifts at the post office, as well as their everyday chores that were now compounded by holiday tasks, the ladies were finding it hard to fit in their mission.

Kate had grudgingly accepted Auggie's offer (or was it a challenge?) to scope out the business' buildings. But now, she couldn't wait to get over there and give everything a good look.

Charlie was quick to join Kate in the kitchen, as he knew she would toss him a popped kernel or two once the microwave beeped. He was the only cat Kate had ever known that liked popcorn.

"How about you and I and Hazel just enjoy this movie, and try to forget about the nativity until at least tomorrow?" She glanced at the clock. "The show's about to start."

The beloved holiday film was easily accessible through streaming services these days. But tonight it was being shown on a major network, just as it had been for many years and all through Kate's childhood.

There was something special about watching it this way, Kate decided as she settled on the couch, knowing that countless others around the country were doing the very-same thing at this very moment.

Years ago, Kate and Bryan had always counted down the hours until their favorite holiday movie came on the screen. Maybe he and Anna were watching it tonight, too. She could text one of them to find out, but decided not to bother. Because if she was going to give into the nostalgia, she needed to leave her smartphone out of easy reach.

Hazel had already settled into her plush pet bed. "You're not in the chair tonight," Kate observed. "You must have spent most of your day running around outside. I bet you won't even be awake by the time George Bailey meets his guardian angel."

Charlie nudged his way into Kate's lap, which meant her soda and the popcorn bowl had to move to the end table. She brushed his coat to meet his high standards while the movie's opening credits rolled. After he got the other thing he wanted, which was a few more kernels of popcorn, Charlie opted for his own bed near the warmth of the fireplace.

That left Kate to enjoy her snack and take comfort in the movie's familiar scenes and lines of dialogue. This story never changed, even as the decades of Kate's life flew by, and the questions surrounding the missing Panther Junction nativity were soon forgotten. That is, until Mr. Potter made his appearance.

The cranky industrialist took on a new layer of meaning for Kate this time around. He had a massive ego to match his overflowing bank accounts, and zero compassion for the other residents of his small town.

"Sounds like Oswald Baxter," she said to no one in particular, as Charlie and Hazel were both asleep. "But from what Myrtle said, Oswald would have been in the prime of life when he took the nativity. And dapper enough to draw the attention of several younger women who weren't his wife."

For a fleeting moment, Kate wondered if Augusta's seventeen-year-old daughter had been unfortunate enough to catch Oswald's wandering eye. She cringed as she hoped Oswald hadn't tried to make a very-different sort of bargain for the Weigmanns to keep their land.

"Poor Augusta." Kate wiped away a tear. "How scared she must have been, how desperate. No wonder she handed over the nativity, and never let on about how the Baxters got it in the first place."

Charlie was awake again, and soon settled in Kate's lap. "And I believe it; I believe every word," she told him. "Myrtle was crystal-clear about every detail. There was no confusion about names and dates, no stalling as she recited the nuances of her story."

And what a story it was. A family down on its luck, struggling to hold on to their farm. Their one valuable possession their only chance to keep a roof over their heads. A betrayal by someone who held all the power in a little town. Someone known for his unscrupulous behavior; a man who, as his success started to slip away, began to doubt his own choices.

Another bargain made, a last-ditch attempt at redemption passed off as a gesture of goodwill. A series of events that evolved over time as the story was told, and retold. The truth fading away as the years marched on.

"You could make a movie out of it." Kate shook her head in wonder. "And I knew nothing about any of this. Until today."

While Kate didn't doubt Myrtle's story about how the nativity changed hands long ago, there was a possibility the older woman's harsh opinions about the contemporary Baxter clan might be skewed.

Myrtle had been raised to distrust that branch of her family tree, and for good reason, but maybe the family's current members ran a tight ship. After all, it was no longer realistic to barter possessions in lieu of a loan payment. There were too many regulations in the modern banking era, so much oversight that wasn't in place a hundred years ago.

Kate's chewing slowed, and she set her bowl of popcorn aside.

"Maybe they don't cut those sorts of deals out in the open, but what might be happening under the table? Even criminals have bank accounts. I mean, look at Potter."

George Bailey was in the crotchety old man's office now, begging for mercy, and there was none to be had.

"What about the people involved in that burglary ring? Hiding your stack of hundred-dollar bills in a shoebox under the bed is only cool for so long. Most people want their money somewhere safe, eventually."

Illegally obtained money could be flowing in and out of accounts at the Eagle River bank, and none of its officers would be the wiser. To be fair, they weren't responsible for how their customers earned a living.

But this was a small town; there was always the chance that someone knew something. Or, at the very least, had suspicions they didn't share with authorities.

But what about the nativity itself? Was there a chance anyone in the Baxter family felt Oswald had been wrong to hand the set over to the church? That the one-of-a-kind artifact had been obtained by their ancestor through appropriate means, and never should have left the family?

Given how long ago the nativity was donated, Kate didn't think such a scenario was likely. Oswald's descendants were too-far removed from the situation.

Compared to luxury cars and vacation homes, a wooden nativity whittled by some long-dead farmer probably held no value for current members of the clan. And then, there was the specter of that curse ...

"My imagination is getting the better of me." Kate yawned and reached for her popcorn again. "I need to just watch the movie, and enjoy it. Because I know exactly how this story is going to end."

✳   ✳   ✳

"I can do this." Kate locked her car and hurried toward the high school's closest entrance. It was a bitterly cold night, and the robust wind blowing in across the empty fields on the southwest edge of town only made it worse. "It's just like Alex said; I already know all the songs. It can't be that hard."

While Kate had attended a few home football games in the fall, she had yet to explore the inside of the district's new secondary-school campus. It was actually a few years old, but this was far and away more modern and spacious than the historic facility on the east end of town that now housed only elementary students.

"Wow." She paused to peek into the lunch room, which was now dubbed the "community social center." It looked like a big-city coffee shop multiplied several times over, with chrome-legged round tables and chairs, and modern pendant lights.

"Wonder what they did with the old metal-and-laminate picnic tables? Times certainly have changed."

Laughter and the tinkle of piano keys told Kate her real destination was down this hallway. While the high-school and middle-school students stayed in separate wings for most of their classes, the lunch room, gym and music departments were clustered in the center of the campus.

"Kate, in here!" Her cousin Stacy grinned and waved, and Kate suddenly felt so much better. She hadn't done one note of public singing since high school; but so what? No one else here was a professional, either. Other than Lauren Davis, the choir director.

And Austin and Alex had promised Kate that Lauren would take it easy on her band of volunteers. While a few of the faces appeared to be those of high school juniors and seniors, eager to add another community-service note to their college applications, Kate saw a wide range of would-be singers in the group.

At least a few were seniors of another sort, and Kate wondered which of them were members of Eagle River's historical society. While she doubted that any of Oswald Baxter's descendants had a hand in the nativity's recent disappearance, Myrtle's story had Kate curious about one of the town's early families. If she asked the right questions, she might get a crash course in local history along with enjoying some traditional holiday tunes.

"We're just about to start." Stacy hovered nearby as Kate

pulled off her parka and other layers of winter gear. Kate's cousin was the school's creative writing and literature instructor. "I'm so glad you're able to join us. Don't worry, you didn't miss much on Thursday. We'll really get rolling tonight."

"We do have three practices left." Kate took a big gulp from her water bottle. "That should be enough to get us in tune with each other."

"Exactly. Lauren's going to show us some harmony parts, but don't worry. If you aren't comfortable with that or, quite honestly, don't want to bother, just follow the main melodies."

The pressure was off, that was for sure. And Kate was relieved. There were twelve people in the chorus, more than enough performers to cover for each other if someone hit an off-key note. "Sounds easy enough. This should be fun!"

Stacy wore a wide grin. "I was so excited when Lauren told me the costumes came in yesterday! We get to pick them out tonight."

"Costumes?" Kate nearly dropped her water. "What ..."

"Come on." Her cousin pointed toward a small room off the main practice area. "Wait until you see these. They're spectacular!"

Community carolers had strolled through the town's holiday festival for several years now, Stacy reminded Kate as she unzipped a garment bag, but this would be the first time the singers would be decked out in historical finery. Thanks to Milton Benniger's generosity, the local historical society now had the cash to rent costumes from an online theatrical shop. The styles echoed the looks of the mid- to late-1800s, with hoop skirts for the women and waistcoats for the men.

"Isn't it divine?" Stacy ran one hand over the heavily embroidered black trim on the hem of the first dress, which was a regal shade of deep blue. "There are bonnets and top hats, too. And capes to keep us warm."

Kate could only imagine the drafts that would sneak inside those capes on a night like tonight. And given the close fit of this dress' bodice, she wondered how many warm layers she could get underneath it.

"We don't have to wear corsets, I hope." She took a step back. "Because if we do ..."

"Oh, no." Stacy was adamant about that. "Everything is really adjustable." She wrestled the dress out of its protective bag and turned it over. "See?"

Sturdy lacing ran down the back of the bodice, and there was a substantial inner panel meant to bridge whatever gap was needed. The skirt had a similar flexibility, as well as a generous stretch of elastic in the back. No wonder there was a cape for each outfit; they would hide a multitude of adjustments.

"When they recruited me, Austin and Alex conveniently left this part out," Kate told her cousin. "But it's only for a few hours, I guess."

Now that the shock had worn off, she could see how the costumes would greatly add to the authenticity of their choral group. Eagle River was a town steeped in history, and its holiday celebration was full of beloved traditions. Why not start another one?

But one of those traditions might prove problematic this time around.

"We just can't stand too close to the bonfire wearing these hoop skirts." Kate lifted the hem to study the tiers of ruffles hidden underneath. "The fire department will be there, of course, but we'll need to be careful."

Kate had always thought a bonfire was more in line with a fall festival, but a big burn had closed out Eagle River's Christmastime event for decades. Although the revelers weren't allowed near the flames, members of the fire department roasted marshmallows and stacked them inside s'mores that were handed out for a free-will donation.

While the carolers spent most of the festival strolling along Main Street, their last few songs were always performed at the bonfire ceremony.

"That's the other surprise." Stacy ushered Kate back into the main room just as the choir director clapped her hands to get the group's attention. "Lauren has created a special arrangement for our final number."

"What is …"

Stacy handed Kate a faux-leather songbook. "You'll find out later. Now, the sopranos are hanging out over there, on the end."

Kate decided it was useless to ask any more questions. Stacy, like Lauren, was in full-on teacher mode. They were running this show; everyone else needed to fall in line and follow instructions.

Alex's face lit up when he spotted Kate coming his way, and she couldn't help but smile back. But when he tipped the imaginary brim of his top hat in her direction, that made her stop in her tracks.

"Hey! You said nothing about costumes. I thought we'd just put on warm coats and walk around as, you know, modern, comfortable people."

Alex laughed, a mischievous twinkle in his brown eyes. "Would you have shown up tonight if I had?" He didn't wait for an answer. "Austin told me not to mention it. You know how ruthless he is about getting people involved around here."

"You're backpedaling."

"Yeah, so what?" He leaned in closer. "I heard you sang soprano in show choir, and took first place in solo vocal competitions not once, but twice, during high school. Look around. We need you."

Kate had to admit that, while her previous choral accomplishments weren't exactly noteworthy, she probably had more on-stage experience than many in the group.

She sighed. "Fine. So, who in this crowd is part of the historical society? I have some questions about ... our town's past."

Alex studied her carefully. "What angle are you working now?"

It was difficult, but Kate kept her mouth shut.

"Fred Winthrop's your guy." Alex pointed out a white-haired man in the tenor section. "When we take a break, hit him up."

"Places, everyone!" Lauren clapped her hands again, then took a seat at the piano. "This will be our last night with accompaniment, then we'll switch to the pitch pipe. Let's start with 'Jingle Bells.'"

It didn't take long for Kate to get into the spirit of things. One of the other sopranos was a retired beautician, and the second handled the books for her husband's auto shop, but they all managed to stay in tune.

Kate found herself listening for Stacy's alto off to the right, and harmonized with her cousin just as they had around Grandma Duncan's piano at family gatherings. And was that smooth, clear baritone coming from Alex? It certainly was. He seemed to really be enjoying himself, and Kate decided her best bet was to do the same.

At the first break, Kate introduced herself to Fred. A retired teacher, he was also the historical society's vice president.

"It's so good to be home, and I'm trying to shop locally this year. As I go around town, I can't help but notice how many of our businesses have been here for decades. Like the bank, for instance. Someone told me it's been run by five generations of the same family. Is that true?"

Fred was a fountain of information, just as Kate had hoped.

Adolphus Baxter was born in Ohio in 1833, and piloted a river ferry out East before he came to Iowa in his late twenties. He switched to running a stagecoach line, made a few smart investments in the area's early railroads, and used his cash to open Eagle River Savings Bank in 1871. Oswald had been Adolphus' grandson; and Oswald's grandson, Leonard, now ran the institution.

Kate didn't know Leonard, but recalled that two of his sons were close to her in age. She remembered them as brash and entitled, but kept that observation to herself.

"What a fascinating story! I guess we're honored to count people like the Baxters as part of our town's past. And its future, too."

She was laying it on thick, but hoped such a gushing statement would elicit some sort of reaction, either positive or negative, from Fred.

"Oh, that's the truth! They've given so much to this town. Do you know, this very campus was in danger of not being built? The district was short on cash. But Leonard stepped up with a sizable donation and saved the day." Fred shook his head in a show of admiration.

"The school board wanted to put the Baxter name on something, either the stadium or the auditorium, but he wouldn't hear of it. He said he wanted it to be all about the kids."

"Really." Kate couldn't match Fred's enthusiasm. Somehow, she suspected the family mostly relished the opportunity to throw some money around and gift themselves with a hefty tax deduction. Before she could press for more details, Austin came over.

"It's time to pick out our costumes," he told Fred and Kate. "Better be first in line to get what you want."

Lauren promised the carolers they wouldn't have to wear their costumes for the next two practices, only for the festival performance. But it was important to claim outfits that were roughly to size, then figure out the best way to dress warmly within the confines of this period-appropriate gear.

Kate came away with the dark-blue dress, and a gray bonnet trimmed in velvet ribbon. Lauren insisted Kate take the blue-plaid cape and, when Kate spread her ensemble out on the nearby risers, she had to admit it was rather pretty.

Once the singers made their selections, Lauren brought them back together for the last half-hour of practice.

"Every one of you is doing a fantastic job!" She gave the group a big thumbs-up, and Kate guessed the choral director's chipper praise was her go-to way to keep dozens of teenagers under control. "So much so, in fact, that we've come up with a special twist for our final number."

Stacy stepped forward from the alto section. "This is so exciting! Our last song will be 'We Wish You a Merry Christmas,' as you all know." Her gaze landed on Kate. And then, Alex. "And we'd like two of our very-best performers to lead this tune."

Kate stared at Alex in disbelief. Unlike the costumes, it was clear by the expression on his face that this development was news to him, as well.

"Come on!" Stacy urged them forward as they reluctantly stepped away from the group. But apparently, that wasn't enough.

"Here, get together." Stacy motioned for them to stand side-by-side.

"How close? Do we need to hold hands?" Alex joked.

Lauren clasped hers together. "Actually, that's perfect!" She hurried over and placed Kate's hand in Alex's, as if they were sixth-graders at their first dance. "No, wait. Face each other, and hold *both* hands."

What is going on? Kate mouthed to Alex. He only widened his eyes in response.

"Everyone," Lauren announced to the group, "Alex and Kate are going to sing solos to start off this song."

"To each other!" Stacy could hardly contain her glee.

It didn't help that this announcement brought a round of

cheers and claps from the rest of the performers. Kate wasn't sure if they liked the idea that much, or were just relieved they hadn't been singled out.

"A solo? No way," she protested. "I haven't sung in public in years."

"My bar-band era doesn't count." Alex shook his head. "I can't ..."

"Nonsense." Stacy's schoolmarm attitude quickly took over. "You can do it. Both of you can. Just think positive, OK?"

The plan was for Kate to sing the first line to Alex, substituting "I" for "we." He'd do the same. And then, they'd turn partway toward the crowd and sing the greeting a third time using the standard "we." Holding hands the entire time.

"The rest of you join in starting with 'Good tidings we bring,'" Lauren explained. "We'll do a similar treatment for the rest of the verses."

"How many are there?" Alex asked.

"Oh, five." Lauren shrugged. "Well, it's really four, the last is a repeat. But whatever, it's easy."

Stacy crossed her arms. "This song is hundreds of years old. We had to zing it up, somehow." Then she smiled. "People are going to love it! Just imagine us all at the bonfire, in our wonderful costumes, maybe a few snowflakes in the air. It'll be so ..."

"Festive." Kate jumped in quickly before her cousin could utter the word *romantic*. "Got it."

She and Alex were still facing each other, and still holding hands. Kate had to admit it felt nice. They hadn't been given permission to let go yet, and given how determined Lauren and Stacy were to create a winter-wonderland moment for the group's final number, Kate decided it was best to play along.

Alex must have been thinking the same. "Do you think they'll give us detention if we refuse?" he whispered to Kate while the rest of the group received their staging instructions.

"I think their minds are made up. We'd better do as they say."

Behind Kate and Alex, the rest of the chorus was rearranged to better distribute the four voice types throughout the group. But Kate noticed no one else was commanded to hold hands, much less sing to a partner.

Stacy got engaged to her boyfriend over the summer, and her every free moment these days was spent poring over bridal websites and fussing about dresses and flowers.

Kate didn't see Stacy as often as she'd like, but maybe that was just as well. Because her cousin always asked Kate if she was dating anyone yet, as if there were hundreds of unattached guys Kate's age wandering around Eagle River looking for true love.

Even if Lauren came up with the idea of the solos and the lyric tweaks, the old-fashioned romance of this fabricated moment was all Stacy.

One of their aunts was supposed to draw names later that week for the gift exchange at the Duncans' holiday gathering at the end of the month; and Kate really, really hoped she'd get Stacy this year. Because after tonight, a lump of coal seemed like the perfect present.

* 14 *

Bev grinned as she buckled her seat belt. "My first undercover assignment! Not sure I'd sign up for something like this on my own. But if we're needed, I guess I'm game. Any pointers, pro?"

Kate and Hazel had been tapped to join a stakeout two months ago, when a string of arson fires terrorized the community. It was a thrilling experience, but one Kate never expected, or really wanted, to repeat anytime soon.

"Well, if you have no idea what you're in for, I guess you're on the right track."

Kate started her car and checked for signs of strolling cats, but she and Bev had the yard all to themselves. It was a chilly afternoon, the skies were heavy with the promise of more snow, and the barn kitties were tucked away in the warmth of their insulated shed.

Even the sight of Bev's unfamiliar truck arriving a few minutes ago hadn't been interesting enough to pull Scout from his perch inside the shed's nearest window. And what a perch it was! Scout often commandeered the third level of Auggie's four-shelf cat tree, which had soft carpet tucked around its platforms and a rope-wrapped center post perfect for sharpening a set of claws.

"I'm really curious to check this estate place out," Kate

said as they started down the lane. "I can't remember the last time I was out there, if ever. But I know it's down the last street on this side of town, and near the river."

Bev nodded. "We'll go about a block once we turn south, and the street will switch to gravel. Just follow the bend in the road. Or bends, I guess; there are several. But they'll lead us right to it."

A few worn-down houses crouched along the ladies' path, and then a rusted metal sign noted the next farmstead was the right place.

Along with a big old house, which was a bit on the shabby side, there was a sizable, modern, metal-sided building across the drive. But it was the three rustic sheds huddled behind the newer structure that caught Kate's eye.

"It's just like Auggie said, they have several places to store stuff here. Wonder if we'll be able to get inside all of them?"

"Well, we might." Bev seemed hopeful. "Looks like there aren't any other shoppers here right now. But then, it's late afternoon on a Wednesday. I think we can charm our way into a complete tour."

"Oh, you do? And how do you plan to accomplish that?"

"I need a lot of everything. Two of my daughters are getting an apartment in Cedar Falls, now that the last one's out of college. And my son just bought a house in Meadville."

Kate gave her friend the side-eye. "You have only two kids, and both are very married and very settled."

Bev guffawed. "Yeah, but these people don't know that." She patted the arm of Kate's parka. "I need to buy in bulk, you see. Christmas is coming, after all. And your house? Well, it's just about as empty as it can be."

That wasn't true. But Kate saw the beauty of this plan. "We're high rollers, then." She pulled into the parking lot, which was only a strip of wide gravel by the main building's door. "Ladies with cash to burn. Of course, we're looking for bargains to make our money stretch."

"Oh, my." Bev leaned toward her side window for a better look. "There are four of the famous kitties. Quite the welcoming committee!"

While the estate company was known for its wide-ranging inventory, it was also the home of a sizable colony of cats. After all, this place was a stray's dream destination. The property was patrolled by only one, feline-friendly dog; there was plenty of food and fresh water available in the barn, along with great mousing opportunities; and the assortment of old cars, lawn art and other items dotting the yard offered a variety of kitty perches.

The owners had welcomed dozens of homeless cats over the years, and made a good-hearted effort to get the kitties spayed and neutered. But as soon as they had a few fixed, more always seemed to show up. A visit to this rural business had inspired Melinda and Karen to start a trap-neuter-return program, which had since helped more than five hundred barn and shop cats from around the region.

"I think that big gray one is Queenie." Despite her nerves about this mission, Kate had to smile. "She's a legendary mouser, and likely the mama of several of the cats that live here. But lucky for her, she won't ever be pregnant again."

"I love to see Queenie, and the other cats, living such a good life." Bev tucked her detailed, if fictional, shopping list back into her purse. "While I'm confident we can get a good look around, this may turn out to be nothing more than a wild goose chase. I don't know these folks, but it seems like I've never heard a bad word against either of them."

"Auggie said the same. I guess it's the next generation the sheriff has his eye on."

The couple's son, who was in his late twenties, had quit his regular job a few months ago to work for his aging parents and eventually take over the business. If there was a weak link in the chain, someone who was up to something shady, it had to be him.

"I know how you feel," Kate admitted as she cut the engine. "Who knows what's going on, but I'm not convinced the nativity is here. Or, what if it was last week, but it's been hustled off to somewhere else already? What if we're too late?"

"Well, we have that list of stolen items, too. If nothing else, maybe we'll come across some leads there. Those poor farmers." Bev shook her head in sympathy. "I can't imagine how upsetting it would be to go out for morning chores and find that someone's busted the locks off your doors and pawed through your stuff."

While the yard was a haphazard mix of rusted-out cars, old farm machinery and tarp-covered building materials, the main business building was immaculately clean and very organized.

The store's inventory was cleverly arranged by room, and the wide aisles made it easy to stroll from one section to the next. Older cabinets marked "not for resale" showed off the current crop of smaller goods.

The prices were just as nice, and Kate decided it wouldn't be hard for either of them to pose as an eager shopper. They weren't likely to find what they were really looking for, but this mission was going to be a piece of cake.

And that cut-glass dessert stand with the delicate floral design was only five dollars. She could arrange Christmas cookies on it for the party ...

"Anything specific you're looking for today?" A young man in a faded Minnesota Vikings sweatshirt and jeans met them partway up the main aisle. His light-brown hair was matched by a two-day scruff of a beard, and his eyes lit up with interest as he greeted his newest customers. "I'm Travis, by the way."

"Oh, I'm sure you can help us." Bev smiled warmly and reached into her purse. "I just have so many things on my list, I don't even know where to start!"

Bev went into mother-hen mode as she gushed over her fictional children's life changes and exclaimed over all the wonderful items on display in the front of the store. The more she talked, the more interested Travis was in her plight. As he steered Bev toward several rows of sofas and loveseats, Kate took her cue to wander off on her own.

She soon saw several other items she wanted, along with the cake plate, and reached into her purse for paper and a pen. For Kate, at least, this wasn't an act; it would be smart to take notes and photos, narrow her wish list, then come back another day.

There was much to see beyond the furniture and dishes, including knick-knacks and area rugs. There were even a few quality home-improvement materials, such as insulated exterior doors and runs of salvaged kitchen cabinets, but Kate couldn't find what she was really looking for.

She didn't spot any tools or yard items, other than what was clearly visible outside. And while one corner was stuffed full of second-hand holiday garlands, ornament boxes and light-up Santa figurines, there certainly was no sign of the nativity.

When Travis hustled to the front counter to answer the building's old-school corded phone, Bev made a beeline for where Kate was poking through china sets stacked in cardboard boxes.

"Any luck?" Bev whispered, then answered her own question. "It's not here, is it."

Kate briefly shook her head, but smiled anyway. Travis was still on the phone, but he was watching them out of the corner of one eye.

"And I don't think it will be, not out in the open and for sale. Do you think we can get him to take us into the other buildings?"

"Clyde said they used to be open during regular business hours, but who knows? I've mentioned them in passing a few times. He's been friendly, of course, but I can't seem to get him to take the bait."

"Maybe he's just busy, and they don't have any other help today. He probably doesn't want anyone poking around, unattended." The idea that a guy with possible ties to a burglary ring was worried about people stealing his stuff was ironic, to say the least.

"How about you keep him busy, and I'll see if I can slip out?" Kate suggested as Travis hung up the phone. "Do you think you can?"

"Oh, certainly. Susan and Maria collect salt-and-pepper shakers." Bev jerked her head toward a display. "I'm sure I can trap him by asking him to help me choose some sets."

While Bev and Travis debated the merits of animal shapes versus bird designs, Kate roamed toward the back of the shop. Just as she passed a section of shelves filled with clocks of all shapes and sizes, a big orange tabby cat slid out from under a nearby table to rub against her jeans.

"Hey there, you're so friendly." Kate crouched down to scratch the cat's back. "You remind me of Sunny, one of Melinda's barn babies."

But this guy wanted more than a little attention. He strutted over to a nearby side door, stared at its handle, then meowed for Kate to join him.

"You want to go out?" Kate didn't hesitate to follow. "I'm sure I can do that for you."

As the cat slipped through the open door, Kate got a glimpse of a wooden-board shed that wasn't ten feet away from the main building. There were two, four-pane barn windows in the nearest wall, and down the way was a steel door that likely replaced the original years ago.

Kate expected the orange tomcat to saunter off, despite the light snow that had started to fall in the past few minutes. But he waited in the walkway between the two buildings, his golden eyes fixed on Kate.

"What?" She frowned at him. "You wanted to go out, so, there you are."

She glanced over her shoulder and saw Bev and Travis deep in debate over a set of end tables. The cat was still there when she turned back, one ear now flattened in annoyance. Kate checked behind her again, slipped out the showroom's door, and quietly pulled it closed behind her.

That was what Mr. Kitty wanted. He hurried over to the wooden shed and meowed at Kate again. She couldn't believe her luck. It was the perfect excuse to wander off: The property's cats had free roam of the place, and she was just helping this furry guy out.

"I don't know why you want in there so badly, but I do, too." Kate's shoes crunched through the skim of snow on the packed-down ground between the buildings. "Let's go."

The door was unlocked. Kate took a deep breath and let herself in, along with the cat. He gave a chirp of triumph, then began to sniff the dusty concrete floor.

"You come in here to hunt mice, I bet. I'm sure there are enough to keep you busy."

Kate found the switch for the two overhead bulbs, and listened to the wind moaning around the corners of the shed while she gave her eyes a few seconds to adjust to the gloom. The unheated building was packed nearly to the rafters with layers of furniture, boxes and crates, and had only a narrow path through the middle.

Deep shadows filled the gaps between the items, and Kate wondered what might be hiding in the dark spaces along the floor. A scampering sound came from somewhere off to the left, and Kate hoped it was only the cat on his rounds.

This shed was creepy and beyond dirty, but Kate's mind lit up with excitement. If you had stolen stuff on your property, this was the perfect place to hide it.

She crept down the makeshift aisle, dodging cardboard boxes and stray chairs and tables along the way. An area stocked with rusted, metal milk crates caught her attention. A coiled garden hose nested in one basket; two more held drills and a few small power tools.

"Meow!" The orange cat suddenly appeared atop one of the crates, and Kate jumped back.

"Hey!" But she gave him a pet anyway. "No mice yet, huh? I'm probably scaring them off."

The cat started an impressively agile climb over scraps of lumber and a teetering stack of battered house shutters to reach a large dresser shoved against the side wall. Or at least, that's what Kate guessed it to be given the dust-coated drawers that peeked out through the jumble of stuff.

She leaned forward into the gloom, and wished she'd brought her small flashlight from the car. "You can get back there easily," she told the cat," but I can't."

There was a line of stuffed-full black garbage bags on the dresser, and the corners of several license plates peeked out of one of the bags. Many of the plates were vintage and rusted, but some looked nearly new.

That was strange. But the next bag quickly grabbed Kate's attention. It was over on its side, right on top of the dresser, its opening loose and wide. By the shape of the sack, Kate guessed it held a large box.

A wooden box, from what she could see. Timeworn, to be sure, but its stained and varnished finish was still intact. There appeared to be a seam near the top, indicating where a lid would lift away. Kate's heart pounded in her ears, and her fingers itched to push back the plastic and wrestle the box until it opened.

The cat had been watching Kate closely, his golden eyes glinting in the gloom. As she took a few careful steps forward around the items strewn across the floor, he jumped over and landed right on top of the half-concealed box.

"Are you trying to show me something?" she whispered. "Is that it?"

Kate once again experienced the strange feeling that came over her Sunday night when she learned Gustav Weigmann was her great-great-great grandfather: the sense that the coincidences piling up in her life weren't coincidences at all.

There had been several even before Kate heard Myrtle's startling story. And then, she and Bev came over here today, and this cat sidled up to her in the showroom. He guided her out here, to this box ...

The shed door's hinges screeched in protest, and Kate jerked her hand back as if she'd touched a hot stove.

"What are you doing in here?" Travis' boots crunched down the dust-covered aisle as he hurried in her direction. "This building is off limits to the public."

In her haste to beat a retreat, Kate nearly tripped over a pile of log chains. "Oh, I'm just looking around. The door was unlocked. Sorry, I didn't know."

She pointed out the orange cat, who'd since slipped away from the mysterious box and planted himself near a sack of license plates. "He asked me to let him out of the other building, and then let him in here."

The cat narrowed his eyes at Kate, and then at Travis.

"Yeah, this is one of Pumpkin's favorite hangouts." Travis' tone softened. "He's a champion mouser, and there's plenty to be had in this shed."

"Oh, there you are!" Bev chirped as she hurried through the open door. Behind Travis' back, she gave Kate a grimace that said, *sorry, I tried.* "Goodness, it's chilly in here."

"Yeah. There's no heat." Travis turned away from the women and gave Pumpkin a few distracted pets. "Just one more reason why you can't roam around in here."

Kate wanted to ask what the other ones were, but suspected she wouldn't get any answers. Or at least, any honest ones. With one last glance at the wooden box and Pumpkin, Kate followed Bev and Travis as they zigged and zagged their way toward the entrance.

Once they were all outside, Travis made sure the door was closed. "I'll come get Pumpkin in an hour or so. He'll be bored by then, and he'll want to come back into the shop for a snack that's easy to get his paws on."

They marched toward the showroom in awkward silence. Travis brought up the rear, as if he half-expected the ladies to attempt to circle back and was prepared to prevent them from doing so. Bev and Kate exchanged anxious looks, and then Bev raised an eyebrow at her friend.

Kate raised one back, and Bev's eyes widened.

"You have so many nice pieces here." Bev smiled at Travis as soon as they were back inside the shop. "I'll make notes on my favorites, talk to my family, and come back another day."

The showroom's light and warmth reminded Kate how dark, cold and dirty the shed was by comparison. The other building had been unlocked, and she hadn't seen a "no trespassing" sign. But given Travis' flash of anger in the shed, it was Kate's turn to play nice.

"I'm really impressed by the range of items you have. I mean, look at all this furniture. And the dishes, lamps, all of it. There are some nice primitives, too. And, wow, four buildings full of stuff! How do you keep track of it all? That must be some spreadsheet."

Travis said nothing until they neared the front counter. "We're closing a little early today." His smile was forced. "Looks like the snow is picking up."

"Oh, certainly." Bev nodded. "We'll need to head for home. I'll just take another gander at those salt-and-pepper shakers, and ..."

"You need to leave." This time, there was no mistaking Travis' intent. "I'm asking ... no, I'm telling you to go. We can't have people wandering around where they don't belong."

Kate was about to remind Travis about Pumpkin. But it wouldn't do any good. Based on his unfriendly gaze and how he nervously grasped one hand with the other, it was clear he wanted them gone.

"Thanks for showing us around," she said crisply. "Happy holidays."

"Yep, he's guilty," Bev proclaimed as she snapped her seat belt. "I couldn't tell you of what, exactly, but he is. Guilty as can be."

The cats had all headed for the barn, but Kate was still careful as she backed out and started down the lane. Because Travis was right; the snow was really coming down now.

"I can think of a few possibilities. Theft, for one. Aiding and abetting a criminal enterprise. Burglary and/or trespassing, depending on how directly involved he is."

Kate glanced in the rearview mirror. Travis still stood in the shop's half-open doorway, watching them leave. "He's going to let all the heat out of the building if he doesn't stop staring at us like that."

"What exactly did you find?" Bev was anxious to hear the details. "If you'd spotted the nativity, I don't think you would have been able to keep your composure like you did. That was impressive, by the way."

"I don't know, exactly." She explained about Pumpkin, the shed, and the mysterious wooden box hidden in a dusty trash bag. "You've seen the nativity's crate, right? Does that sound like it?"

"Maybe." But Bev wasn't convinced. "Such wooden cases were common back before plastic and cardboard and such. It's very possible that was something else." She shrugged. "An instrument, for example. Or an enormous set of silverware. I mean the real stuff, with the velvet-lined trays. You know what I'm talking about."

Kate did. Grandma Ida had a more-modest set that made an appearance at Burberry holiday dinners.

"I want to find that nativity." Kate gripped the steering wheel tighter. "But if Travis has it hidden at his parents' business, and I'm not sure that he does, it could be anywhere. That shed is packed to the rafters with stuff. And it's only one of many buildings on the property."

They reviewed the other items Kate had spotted, and Bev decided those were worthy enough to share with Sheriff Preston. The license plates in particular were interesting. There were several vintage vehicles on the property. But where did those newer plates come from? And some of the other items, like the tools and log chains, could have been stolen from barns and sheds around the county.

"I'm glad we came over here," Bev said. "Maybe what you found will help, after all." But then, she gave a long sigh of irritation.

"You know, I hope Travis doesn't have the nativity. I can't stand the thought of it packed away in one of those old sheds! They could have scrapped the wooden container, stuffed the pieces in a dirty cardboard box that the mice can chew their way through. You want to talk about curses? Whoever stole that nativity had better watch their back. Old Gustav has to be rolling in his grave."

"Myrtle said she didn't think that part was true," Kate reminded her friend. "That it was all in Oswald's head."

"Well, maybe. And maybe not. I mean, Gustav worked hard all those years to build a new life in this country. He made that nativity for his family, no one else, and it was practically stolen away. And then, decades after it finally landed in a safe place, some idiot swipes it right off the altar, just weeks before Christmas!" Bev crossed her arms over her purse. "If it were me? I'd come back and haunt people, too."

"The Ghost of Christmas Past." Kate considered this idea as she slowed for the next swerve in the snow-covered gravel. It would be dark soon, and she couldn't wait to get home. "But somehow, I don't think these criminals care to see the error of their ways."

* 15 *

"These are for the post office crew," Kate explained to Hazel as she packed a container with Christmas cookies the following morning. "We've had plenty of treats lately, but a few more certainly can't hurt."

Kate had only found the time to bake one small batch each of frosted cutouts and peanut butter-chocolate stars, but that was just as well. The old stove's oven was temperamental, which was merely annoying most of the time but could spell disaster for a tray of cookies.

"Sorry, there are none for you," she told Hazel. "You have your own treats."

Just before she put the cookie-storage containers back on top of the refrigerator, one of the few spots safely out of reach of both sets of furry front paws, Kate grabbed a storage bag from a nearby drawer.

"I don't need to eat all of these," she decided as she bagged an assortment of another dozen cookies. "And I can think of someone who might appreciate them more."

The post office was bustling as usual when she arrived, but several co-workers paused long enough to snatch a cookie for a post-breakfast snack. Kate set the container on the break room table, but kept back the last dozen.

Up at the counter, Bev was prepping for another busy day.

"Barney's running late," she explained to Kate. "He told Roberta he's still waiting for his neighbor to come by and clear the snow from his driveway. But then, he's practically volunteering. We should be grateful he'll work at all."

"I had about six inches overnight; had to get out my little tractor this morning."

Jared was out front, tackling the post office's sidewalk with a shovel and the vigor of a guy in his twenties. Just watching him made Kate tired.

"I'd rather Barney wait for help, rather than do it himself," she told Bev. "But don't let Jack know about Barney's supposed infraction." Jack was off today, and Kate had his route.

Bev chuckled. "I won't. You know, something's changed between those two in the past few days. Maybe they're going to bury the hatchet. But that's probably too much to hope for."

Roberta came up from the back, her cheeks still rosy from the wind. "It's a cold one out there! And the sun comes up so late these days, it's hard to get a move-on. I feel like a bear that wants to hibernate. But there's way too much to do."

Then she smiled at Kate. "I see you brought cookies. Those will help us get through the day."

"I'll take tomorrow's sweets shift," Bev promised. "I'm thinking cinnamon rolls. It's been a few days since we had those."

Kate needed to start sorting for Jack's route, but her first priority was the stack waiting under the counter. The Taylors' mail was piling up. Nothing too important had come through, or Roberta would have called Candace and let her know. But when an extra batch of parcels arrived yesterday afternoon, Kate spotted one with a familiar address.

"There's a box to drop off today, so I have to go up to the house anyway." She reached for the pile of mail. "And I brought some extra cookies."

Bev pulled a clear plastic bag out from under the other end of the counter. "I like that idea! Here, this will keep everything together and dry."

Roberta shook her head. "As postmaster of this joint, I'd like to state for the record that: a) I don't recall overhearing this conversation, and b) I had no knowledge of Carrier Duncan's plans."

"You're exonerated," Bev told their boss in a solemn voice.

"Thank you." Roberta gave an exaggerated bow. "Kate, tell Candace how sorry I am about all this. I wish there was more we could do. I'd ask you to add 'happy holidays,' but that seems like it'd just be salt in the wound."

Marge poked her head through the swinging door. "Where's the rest of the ice melt?" she asked Roberta. "I'll get the back walk salted down while Jared finishes out front."

After their boss left, Bev debriefed Kate on her call to Sheriff Preston. He was intrigued by what Kate discovered in the estate company's old shed, but cautioned it probably wasn't strong enough evidence to get a search warrant. And given Travis' on-guard behavior, sending a deputy out there anytime soon would backfire.

The last thing the sheriff wanted was for Travis and his associates to know they were on Jeff's radar.

"That is, if Travis is even involved. And we don't know that, for sure. But Jeff's really glad we went out there. Who knows what might come of it?"

"Well, I'm going to focus on something I can control today." Kate picked up the sack holding the Taylors' mail. "It'll be a slow go out on those roads. I'd better get moving."

"And you have choir practice tonight." The hint of teasing in Bev's voice was unmistakable.

"You'll need to work on that duet."

※　※　※

The snow started to fall again by late morning. It was light this time around, not much more than flurries, but the rising wind threatened to erase all the hard work the county snow plows accomplished before sunrise.

By the time Kate reached the Taylors' section of Jack's route, she was eager for her workday to be over. Not only because of the reduced visibility, but because she'd been debating whether her plan of action was the right one.

The parcel had to be delivered, of course, as it would never fit in a mailbox and therefore wasn't subject to those regulations. But Roberta had been clear with Candace about the rules regarding regular mail. Would the Taylors now start to hope, if not assume, that the Eagle River post office might be persuaded to make more exceptions until their mailbox was replaced? As Roberta had said, this could go on until spring if something wasn't done soon.

The cookies had seemed like a nice gesture this morning. But now, they felt more like ... what? An apology, or a show of pity? Kate wasn't handing out holiday snacks to any other customers today; or any other day, for that matter. She decided it was best to leave them in the car.

"Oh, look; the mailbox is gone, at least." As Kate slowed for the Taylors' driveway, she noticed the busted container had been removed. But the crooked wooden post was still there, its west side now coated with a sticky layer of wind-driven snow.

"I hope Candace is home." She gripped Bertha's steering wheel tight as she started up the lane. It had been cleared hours ago, but she had learned the hard way never to take a driveway at face value.

Kate parked Bertha close to the porch, then turned her back to the driving snow as she cradled her deliveries in one hand and closed the car door with the other. The wind was stronger up on this slight rise, and the openness of the farm yard didn't help.

A quick glance around showed no sign of Champ, and Kate hoped he was tucked away in the barn. There were a few lights on in the house, their glow easily visible in the deepening late-afternoon gloom, and an oversized maroon truck was parked next to the garage. Given that building's advanced age and weary slant, Kate imagined its rolling door was no match for ice and snow.

She mounted the kitchen porch steps and juggled her items again to knock at the storm door. The inside door flew open, and a tall, thin man with tired blue eyes and a beard glared at Kate through the glass.

"Post office." Kate raised her voice to be heard over the wind and through the storm door. Despite the smile on her face, a lump of disappointment settled in her stomach. This had to be Wyatt. "I'm Kate. Is Candace home, by chance?"

"No." There was no change to Wyatt's sullen expression. Kate noticed his faded green sweatshirt was badly frayed at the cuffs and collar. "She's running errands. Can I help you?"

His tone implied that was the last thing he wanted to do. A short bark echoed from behind Wyatt, and Champ nosed his way forward with a light of welcome in his eyes.

"I didn't know Champ was an inside dog." Kate struggled to make conversation, as Wyatt had yet to open the storm door or offer any other overture of welcome.

"He is," Wyatt said flatly. "Whenever he wants to be. We don't leave him outside when the weather's poor. We're not that kind of folks, you know."

Kate was taken aback. "Oh, of course. I didn't think ..."

"Look." Wyatt crossed his arms. "I don't care what you thought before, or think now, about my family and what goes on around here."

So tell me, Wyatt, what exactly 'goes on around here'? she thought but didn't say. *You're the one who brought it up.*

"Not my business," she said briskly. "But I did bring you some things from the post office."

"Did you? And here I thought we were on the naughty list this year." Wyatt gave Kate a grin that held no warmth as he finally opened the storm door and relieved her of her burden. "We're not following the rules, last I heard."

"Well, Jack's off today." Kate squared her shoulders. "So I decided, what would be the problem in dropping everything off? There's a package, after all. I know it's aways into town, and everyone is so busy this time of year. And the weather ..."

"I'll ask you to not trouble yourself with us." Wyatt's tone changed from annoyance to one that perhaps carried a hint of warning. "Our business is none of yours."

Candace obviously wasn't home, and Kate now suspected the kids weren't, either. She was alone at this remote farmhouse with a man who clearly wanted her off his land. It hadn't occurred to Kate to alert Roberta when she stopped at the Taylors' farm this afternoon, but Kate now wondered if she'd underestimated the risk of this visit. She glanced down into Champ's friendly eyes, and breathed a bit of thanks that at least the *dog* at this farm was kind.

Her only option was to stand her ground with Wyatt. He'd take any show of fear or awkwardness as a sign he had the upper hand.

"I went against regulations today to bring you your mail." Kate raised her voice, just a little. "And you may not know this, but I went to high school with Candace. There's nothing wrong with being friendly."

Wyatt's brows knit together in anger. "She doesn't need any more friends."

"I think that's her call to make."

He gave a bitter laugh. "Oh, of course you do. You've been gone too long, I'd say. This isn't Chicago. People are expected to mind their own business out here, and we don't like charity." He looked away. "I can provide Christmas gifts for my own kids, you know. Strangers don't have to buy them for me."

So, that's what this was about. Someone at the elementary school must have added ornaments for the Taylor children to the giving tree at the library. The post office crew had gladly accepted the seven requests that had remained on the tree earlier in the week, and Kate now wondered if any of those were meant for these kids.

And she may have moved to Madison, and then Chicago, but Kate was far from being a stranger in Eagle River. "As someone who's lived around here more years than she's been away, I'll remind you that people 'out here' are also willing to lend their neighbors a hand when they need it."

Wyatt's face registered a bit of surprise at Kate's retort before his expression darkened again.

"Charles City is where we shop, as well as work. We don't have much reason to go into Eagle River, anymore," he said derisively.

"You can't even get a drink or two in that town without someone giving you a hard time." Wyatt shook his head in disgust. "A man's got a right to relax, now and then."

"Well, until that post and box are replaced, I guess you'll have to make an exception every once in a while and visit Eagle River." Kate pulled her parka's hood up against the chill before she turned away. "Your mail will continue to be held at the post office."

"Fine." After gently nudging Champ to step back, Wyatt shut the kitchen door with more force than was necessary.

"Merry Christmas," Kate muttered under her breath as she trudged back to where Bertha waited in the gathering dusk. The wind carried her words away, and Kate was filled with frustration and regret as she started down the lane.

* 16 *

The snow flurries finally came to an end overnight, but Friday's skies stubbornly remained overcast. Kate completed her morning kitty chores in a hurry, and admonished the cats not to stir from their insulated shed. Hazel had her freedom, as always, but Kate suspected her dog would spend the day curled up in the house.

Holiday shipping was now in high gear, which meant none of the carriers received their usual weekday off this time around. The best Roberta could promise was a truncated shift on their extra day.

Kate had to be at the post office by seven, and there wasn't anything to look forward to other than a solid six hours of sorting parcels so the on-route carriers could quickly reload as they completed their rounds.

The one bright spot in Kate's gloomy day was that she could remain at the post office, and didn't have to expose her clogged sinuses to continuous blasts of bitterly cold air as she serviced one rural mailbox after another. She only had the sniffles so far, but Kate was physically tired as well as emotionally weary from this rollercoaster of a week.

Yesterday, she'd chalked it up to allergies due to the dusty, filthy conditions inside that shed on Wednesday afternoon. Today, she knew it had to be more than that.

As she scanned boxes' barcodes and organized the parcels by route, Kate had plenty of time to let her exhausted mind wander in a not-so-positive direction.

What if she got really sick? Roberta needed everyone on hand until Christmas, which was still almost two weeks away. And the post office's holiday gathering was Sunday night. If Kate didn't get better, and fast, she couldn't risk having everyone over. What if it was too difficult to reschedule? A Christmas party in January just wouldn't be the same.

Maybe she shouldn't have offered to host in the first place. The sign-up sheet was loaded with promises of good food, but Kate still had to clean her house and finish her party preparations. Along with working her usual Saturday shift. How would she ever get it all done?

The cute area rug she'd ordered to cover a large section of the living room's worn carpet had been backordered, and Kate had given up any hope it would arrive in time for the party. The dining room's wallpaper looked fabulous, but Kate never could have triumphed over the sticky stuff without Gwen's help.

She had managed to hang the lovely new curtains last night, even with Hazel and Charlie's assistance, and fresh throw pillows decked out the living room. But in some ways, the rest of the house looked shabbier than ever by comparison. Maybe she shouldn't have bothered. And it would be a miracle if the Christmas tree survived the weekend.

Hazel was obsessed with it. At least twice a day, she tried to squeeze under the tree so she could bask in the glow of its lights. But that spot had historically been Charlie's domain, and the two now squabbled like cats and dogs over who had first dibs on the most-festive spot in the house. Kate always half-expected to come home after a long day to find her fake tree prostrate on the floor, its light strings in angry tangles and the ornaments flung across the olive-green carpet.

And then, of course, there was the fact that the Panther Junction nativity was nowhere to be found.

How long had it been missing? Kate yawned and rubbed her tired, itchy eyes. Three weeks. From today, if Kate's suspicions were correct.

But she still had no idea who swiped the set. Or where to look next. Or how she and Bev would find the time to follow any new leads before Christmas arrived.

Thank goodness for Chloe! She'd been eager for a brain break from her semester finals, and offered to reach out to several of Gustav Weigmann's direct descendants.

Some of her calls and emails went unanswered, which could partially be blamed on this crazy-busy time of year. A few people were willing to chat, Chloe told Bev last night, but none of them had anything new to share on the nativity's past, much less any idea of where the display might be now.

The situation was frustrating, to say the least. Kate had been thrilled to learn she was related to Gustav, that one branch of her family had proven ties to the artist and his unique creation.

But as the days counted down to Christmas, her hope for new leads dwindled, too. Kate sighed with despair as she contemplated Christmas Eve services at one of the region's oldest churches with its most-prized possession still missing from the altar.

By the time she clocked out, Kate could barely muster the energy needed to brave the pharmacy's bustling aisles to cross a few things off her daunting to-do list.

Chris was often in the back of the store, behind the pharmacy counter, and the bell above the front door was the best way for him to track all the comings and goings. But that afternoon, as everyone tried to squeeze in some shopping before the weekend, the seemingly endless *cling-clang!* only compounded Kate's sinus headache.

The Evertons carried a little of everything on their shop's

shelves, since it was several miles to Prosper Hardware and even further to the stores in Charles City and Swanton, but there wasn't much variety when it came to brand names. Even so, the pharmacy's prices were reasonable compared to the few marked-up goods available at Eagle River's lone convenience store on the south edge of town.

Kate plucked a handbasket from the stack inside the entrance, then skirted around a couple heatedly debating their limited options for paper towels as she aimed for the back of the store.

"Happy holidays!" Chris greeted an elderly woman as he handed her prescription through the pharmacy room's pass-through opening. "Janet is still on late lunch, so let me know if you need anything else. Hey, Kate! Missed you at breakfast yesterday."

"Wish I could have made it. Too busy at the post office these days." Seconds after she spoke, Kate sneezed into the arm of her coat.

"Off to your right." Chris pointed to the display of cough and cold medications. "The stuff is flying off the shelf these days. Holler if something's missing, I might have an extra or two stashed in the back."

Kate nodded her thanks, and was relieved to find what she was looking for. Now, if Chris had miniature marshmallows in stock, her afternoon would really be looking up. She'd decided to make s'mores bars for the party, as the no-bake treats would give her extra time to get her house ready for guests.

The lone grocery aisle was packed with shoppers. Kate spied the marshmallows off to the left, next to the cereal. There were just a few packages remaining, but she only needed one. But only seconds before she could nab the last bag of miniatures, a woman swooped past and tossed them into her basket. Kate's shock, and disappointment, must have been clear on her face.

"Sorry." The woman's shrug indicated she really wasn't. "I need these. Know a better way to make rice krispie treats?"

"How about with the full-size marshmallows?" Kate couldn't help herself. "You're going to melt them, either way. I need those to ..."

"I guess you should be faster next time," the woman called over her shoulder as she scurried away. "I don't have time to leave town."

Kate didn't, either. Maybe she'd have to make something else for a dessert. Or maybe she'd just focus on roasting the turkey Roberta had paid for, and forget about trying to crank out anything else on her own.

And maybe she'd have better luck picking up those last few items she needed for the giving tree. There was a modest selection of clothing just around the corner that included some knit hats, gloves and socks. A few came in bright colors, at least, and Kate felt a little better about how these mundane gifts might cheer up the children on her list.

The store's candy selection was in the next row, and Kate lingered near it for a moment. Surely a little chocolate wasn't a bad thing. Should she throw in a bar for each of the kids? It was Christmas, after all.

"Food allergies," she reminded herself with a sigh. "I'd better stick to the rules. Of course, I could ask Kyle if ..."

Something pointed and hard nipped her side, despite the puffiness of her parka. Then she felt a *smack* on her back. Kate turned just in time to see a teenage girl barge past with one of the full-size shopping carts, which were hard to get your hands on this time of year. Chris only had three.

"She didn't even say 'sorry,'" Kate mumbled as she rubbed her hip. "What is wrong with people these days?"

She sounded old. And cranky. Few people would consider Kate to be the first; although she wondered, some days. But the second? That certainly described her today.

"Hey, can you move over?" A man's voice interrupted

Kate's swarming thoughts. "I really need to get to the soup. The special is only going on until tomorrow."

Kate turned to see Pastor Thorne right behind her with his own handbasket. She wouldn't expect such an impatient comment from a member of the clergy.

But then, Kate decided, maybe she shouldn't be so surprised. After all, she'd been on the wrong side of too many rude people this week.

Travis, for one; and Wyatt, too. Not to mention harried patrons jostling at the post office's counter for another book of holiday stamps, or the scruffy guy who'd cut in front of her at the gas station yesterday in his quest to fill up his rusted-out truck.

Kate was really, really tired of everyone's bad behavior. But mostly, she was just tired. "Sure," she mumbled as she stepped away toward the boxed pasta. "Sorry."

"Oh hello, Miss Duncan." Pastor Thorne's tone was certainly more guarded than friendly. "Didn't recognize you there for a second."

That's convenient, she thought but didn't say. *Because the only other time we've met, I asked you several questions about your church's missing nativity. Questions you couldn't answer.*

"I'm just doing some shopping." But Kate was trapped with Pastor Thorne for at least the next few moments, as the narrow, crowded aisle offered no chance for immediate escape.

Given her sour mood, she couldn't resist. "How are things out at the church? There must be so much going on, with Christmas less than two weeks away."

Oliver Thorne tightened his grip on his plastic basket. "We are busy, to be sure. The church's members are trying their best to focus on the true meaning of the season. But there have been many ... unnecessary distractions, if you will."

He snatched two cans of soup from the shelf, then turned to stare at Kate. "We're determined to keep those to a minimum. I'm sure you can understand."

In other words: *stay out of it.*

"Oh, absolutely." Kate's icy smile made Pastor Thorne flinch, just a bit. "Well, Merry Christmas." She marched away without waiting for his response.

Kate tried to distract herself by choosing a box of cereal, but her simmering outrage was about to boil over. She was pretty certain that the theft of an heirloom artifact, especially one likely worthy of felony-level charges, was a bit more than an "unnecessary distraction." The sheriff would agree.

Out of everyone in Eagle River, Oliver Thorne was the person who should be the most concerned about the nativity's disappearance. He should be the one tirelessly chasing down leads and working closely with the sheriff; two things that, from what Bev had heard, weren't happening.

And what was he doing, instead? Trying to discourage Kate and, apparently, divert his flock's attention from the fact that a crime had been committed at their church. Something wasn't right; Kate could feel it.

Oliver was now at the front counter, where a recently returned Janet rang up his purchases. After a warm smile for Chris' wife and a few holiday greetings, he pulled up his parka's hood and started for the door.

Before Kate even realized what she was doing, she did the same. "God helps those that help themselves," she muttered as she dropped her half-full basket next to the front windows and followed the pastor out onto the sidewalk.

Kate was determined to be a distraction. It was necessary.

"Excuse me." Perhaps her raspy voice wasn't loud enough, as Pastor Thorne didn't break his stride and was soon halfway to his truck, which was parked at the curb.

Kate hurried after him, then stepped into his line of sight. "Hey!"

He blinked and took a quick step back, and nearly collided with an older woman walking her dog.

"Just one thing." Kate pointed at him. "I know you don't want me nosing around, but I really don't care. This is too important."

"Miss Duncan ..."

"Don't call me that! My name is Kate. You want me to stop asking questions? It's not going to happen. I may not attend your church, but it turns out that Gustav Weigmann was my great-great-great grandfather."

Oliver blinked in surprise, but Kate didn't give him a chance to respond. "But more importantly, that nativity is beloved by many in this community. People whose families have been here for generations."

He swallowed hard and glanced around, but didn't try to walk away. Kate had him cornered, and he knew it.

"Just one thing," she said again. "Why didn't you call the sheriff that Saturday afternoon, when Bev and I told you the nativity was missing? Or even Sunday, right after church?" She snorted. "You told me you were going to get on it, right away."

His stare was cold and calculating. "What I said was, I was going to look into it."

"Yeah, right." Kate rolled her eyes. "The sheriff had to find out about it from us on Monday afternoon. *Two whole days* after the set went missing."

"It was the holiday weekend," he said lamely. "I didn't think ..."

"Oh, please! You and I both know that's not a good enough excuse."

Oliver opened the truck's passenger door and dropped his groceries on the seat before he turned back toward Kate. He was buying himself a little time, trying to come up with a suitable response. Kate was tired, she was angry, and she was in a hurry. But she waited.

"That's not for you to decide," he finally said in a quiet voice. "It's not your place to judge my actions." He glanced skyward for only a second, but Kate caught his meaning. "That's someone else's job."

"It was two days," she repeated. "Or more like three, actually, if the nativity was stolen that Friday."

Oliver didn't offer any counter-argument to Kate's assertion the nativity had been stolen. No excuses about it being misplaced, or any hints this was anything other than outright theft. Kate wondered what Pastor Thorne had learned in the past few weeks and what, if anything, he'd shared with the sheriff.

"That's plenty of time for the nativity to be long gone," she told him. "Trucked away to, who knows where? If it had been reported sooner ..."

"The situation would be the same. It would still be gone. Now, I have to stop at the co-op for some dog food, and then I need to get home. Is that OK with you?"

Someone behind them gasped. Kate turned to see a man and woman, shopping bags in hand, watching them closely.

Pastor Thorne sighed and lowered his voice.

"This is a hard time of year for many. There are people in this community dealing with things you can't begin to imagine."

A spark of curiosity flared in Kate's mind, but it was obvious he was not going to elaborate.

"Perhaps it's time to set aside your outrage about an inanimate object that, while it is special in many ways, is just a thing. Instead, perhaps you should contemplate how you can offer support to those who are suffering this holiday season."

Kate didn't know how to react to this sudden swerve in the conversation.

"You're not the only one who's had a difficult year," Pastor Thorne added in a gentle tone. "I hope you are able to find some peace in your heart during this special time of year. Good day."

And with that, he marched around his truck and drove away. The dirty slush along the curb flew out from under the tires and splashed over Kate's boots and across the bottom of her jeans, but she hardly noticed.

Kate barely knew Oliver Thorne, yet he seemed to know a great deal about her.

"Why don't you come back inside?" Chris had his arms crossed against the cold, a fleece pullover his only protection from the wind. "I have just a few more boxes of those bran flakes in stock, and they're popular. Someone might steal yours out of your basket if you don't stay on guard."

"That's true. I know your shipment doesn't come until Monday." Kate stared down Main Street after Pastor Thorne's truck. "Something about him just isn't right. But I'm not sure what it is."

"You're not the first person to tell me that," Chris admitted as they started toward the door. "Sorry, that's all I've got." Then he laughed. "Tell you what. You finish your shopping, and you can have a sucker on the house."

Kate had to smile at Grandpa Wayne's longtime friend. "Really? I haven't gotten a free sucker for, oh, twenty years."

"Well, today's a special day; it's Friday. We have cherry and orange in stock. A little candy always makes things better. And don't tell Janet, but I'll throw in a free bag of cough drops, too."

✳ 17 ✳

Hazel hurried into the kitchen as soon as Kate opened the oven door. "The turkey smells good, huh?" She pulled the lowest rack out aways, then reached for the dish of herbed butter that waited on the counter.

"I'd think this thing is too big to burn in this crazy oven, but who knows?" With another round of basting done, Kate shoved the turkey roaster all the way inside. "We'll just have to *wing* it, I guess."

Hazel gave one of her happy whimpers and a few wags of her tail. "Haha, right? Well, it's too late to do anything but wait and see what happens. I'd better take a shower."

Kate took the long way around to the stairwell to give her farmhouse a final review. Festive floor mats now welcomed guests to the front and back doors. The kitchen had been scrubbed until it shined, and new hand towels were on display. It was the same upstairs in the bathroom.

One pantry shelf was stocked with rolls of festive paper and ribbons so the carriers could wrap their giving-tree offerings. The downstairs curtains looked nice, and the dining room wallpaper looked even better.

She paused mid-stride to adjust the new area rug, which miraculously arrived yesterday evening and was now anchored by the living room's coffee table.

Kate had hoped to hang more holiday decorations, but never found the time. It didn't matter. The Christmas tree glittered in one corner of the dining room, and her thrift-store nativity characters stood watch on the fireplace mantel.

The house looked good. Or at least, good enough. Kate's head cold had departed nearly as fast as it had arrived, and everything was in place for tonight's party. All that was left to do was choose an outfit.

"There's not much to pick from." Hands on hips, Kate studied her closet. Anything that remotely resembled party wear had been donated months ago. As she searched for a solution, she recalled a party last December that had been one of the highlights of her holidays.

It had been hosted by one of Ben's bosses at the federal health and safety administration. The night of the gala, the grand house's foyer had been home to a sixteen-foot-tall artificial Christmas tree studded with hand-blown glass ornaments that shimmered in the light. There had been valet parking, and suited waiters waltzed about with trays of champagne. Ice sculptures glittered on the oyster bar, and an eight-piece orchestra was set up in the receiving room.

Kate had worn an amethyst-hued, matte satin cocktail dress with a deep-vee neckline. Nothing too revealing, of course, just classy. Black jet beading decorated the shoulders and swirled around the hem.

It was a dream dress for a surreal evening. Ben had joked that they'd better leave the party before midnight, because his tuxedo was rented and likely to disappear with the strike of the clock.

Kate remembered how they kissed like teenagers in the ride share's back seat, and how bright their future seemed together. How was she to know that, a few months later ...

A draft of cold air brushed her arm, and she blinked back to the present. "Great. That plastic's come loose again." She checked the west window and, sure enough, it needed more tape and another round with the hair dryer. But that was a chore for tomorrow.

"Well, I have a red sweater." She pulled it from a closet shelf. "And jeans. Practical is the way to go, I guess. And there's no time to waste."

On her way out of the room, Kate paused to peek under the bed. All the afternoon's commotion had told Charlie that something was up. He'd scooted to his safe place as soon as he'd verified that the new throw pillows were perfectly placed on the couch.

"It's not going to be so bad." Kate tried to soothe him with her words, because he'd crawled far-enough back to keep himself out of her reach. "I mean, how could it be that bad? Lots of good food, some laughs, we'll wrap the gifts for the giving tree. I hope you will join us, if nothing else to show off your amazing coat."

Charlie only shifted his paws and turned his head away. "I know, I know, you still have that terrible haircut. Fine. Hazel gets to be the life of the party, then."

As promised, Bev and Clyde were the first to arrive. They brought sage stuffing to go with the turkey, as well as a large folding table and extra chairs. While Bev warmed the stuffing and skimmed off turkey drippings to make the gravy, Kate helped Clyde set up the extra seating in the living room.

Clyde was as quiet as Bev was chatty, but he offered to start a fire in the hearth once the extra table was ready. Then he accepted a cup of coffee, settled in Kate's reading chair, and volunteered to "keep Hazel out of the way."

"Look at the two of them," Bev said while she and Kate spread one of her two green tablecloths over the main table. The linens had been purchased for a family dinner a few years ago, and Bev was happy to use them again. "I think Hazel's made a friend."

"She's very good at reading people. But I don't know how she handles crowds. I guess we're going to find out."

"She knows all the carriers, at least. And she's been nothing but wonderful when she's been at the post office." Bev laughed. "All she has to do is turn on the charm, and she'll have everyone feeding her scraps from their plates."

"I hadn't thought that far ahead. Only turkey, I think. I'd hate for her to get sick. And then, we'd have a mess to clean up."

Any lingering doubts about the evening's potential vanished as more pairs of headlights turned up the lane. The farmhouse soon bustled with people and laughter, and Jared queued up a holiday playlist on his phone. Kate didn't have a speaker to pair with it, but that was just as well. The music played at a high-enough volume to give the gathering a festive air, yet didn't curtail the conversation that flowed through the downstairs.

Jack and his wife, Audrey, brought homemade mashed potatoes to match the stuffing and turkey. The kitchen counters soon filled with an array of appetizers and sides, and an informal dessert buffet.

Most of the carriers were married, and brought their spouses. Marge Koenig was widowed last year, and she caught a ride with Randy and his wife. Allison and Aaron showed up together, furthering Kate's suspicions that two of their youngest team members might be more than coworkers. It wasn't against any policy, as far as Kate knew, and there weren't too many people their age in Eagle River.

Kate, of course, was flying solo tonight. She'd momentarily considered asking Alex if he'd like to come, but decided against it. First of all, he had his bar to look after in the evenings. And then, with so many of the carriers bringing a spouse, the whole thing seemed too much like a date. Besides, she was the hostess and had plenty to occupy her time and attention.

Almost twenty people were packed into Kate's farmhouse, but it didn't seem crowded. And everyone was too busy visiting to pay any attention to the mostly dated decor, other than to "ooh" and "aah" over the wallpaper and laugh about Charlie's fur-raising misfortune.

Because the cat's curiosity finally got the better of him. Or maybe it was the tempting aroma of roasted turkey that brought him downstairs. He made his appearance just before it was time to eat, accepted the adoration of his guests, then sniffed the purses and shoes left in the corner of the kitchen before going back to his under-bed cave.

Just as they started to dig into their plates, there was a knock on the kitchen door. Kate was glad that the oldest guests on the list had decided to come, after all.

"I figured he'd be late," Jack told Audrey, but loud enough the others could hear.

She rolled her eyes at her husband. "Barney was one of the longest-serving carriers in this town. I'd say he can show up whenever he gets around to it."

"Behave yourself," Roberta admonished Jack between bites of Allison's broccoli salad. "You don't want Santa to put a lump of coal in your stocking."

Kate had yet to learn exactly why Jack and Barney butted heads as they did. Bev had been at the Eagle River post office only a few months more than Kate, so she didn't know the details, either. Rumor had it their grudge wasn't over any one thing; they were just two over-opinionated guys who both liked to have the last word. And maybe they sparred more for entertainment than out of spite.

Barney and Evelyn had brought green-bean casserole along with a tray of brownies, and the carriers and their guests were eager to make room on their plates. "You're going to have to roll me out of here," Randy told Kate as he went back for seconds.

Kate was pleased to notice that Hazel made a few polite inquiries but, when no one offered to share, she'd eaten her usual supper in the kitchen and then stretched out by the fire.

Once everyone was stuffed, the tables were cleared and the gift-wrapping party began. Kate had smaller plates and fresh glasses ready so her guests could snack their way through the rest of the evening, and it wasn't long before the rustle of paper nearly drowned out the holiday tunes.

Charlie made two more appearances, and Kate caught on to his game: Every time he showed up downstairs, he was fawned over and admired. When the guests returned to their wrapping, he went upstairs for another nap.

"I really like your nativity," Marge told Kate while she wrapped a set of mittens. "It's humble, you know? I think it's perfect."

Kate explained where she got it, and Randy let out a chuckle. "I'd say that was a few bucks that were well spent. Ours isn't much fancier than that, but it's not Christmas without it. We've had it forever, it seems like."

Discussion soon turned to the Panther Junction nativity. Kate hoped one of her co-workers would offer a bit of gossip that might lead the case in a new direction, but it was soon clear none of them had any leads.

"It's a sad thing," Roberta said as she tied her package with a ribbon. "The closer we get to Christmas, I think people are so distracted by their own plans and preparations that many have forgotten such a rare artifact is still missing."

Kate went into the kitchen to make sure the refrigerator was still stocked with cold beer and pop, and Bev followed close behind.

"What about Myrtle's story?" Bev whispered as they loaded more cans into the fridge. "Should we bring it up? What if it jogs someone's memory?"

Kate considered the idea as she snitched a few chunks of carrot and green pepper off a relish tray. Bev had passed the tale on to Sheriff Preston, and they each had shared it with a few close family members. But otherwise, they'd kept it to themselves.

"Maybe we should. Many of them have lived around here for decades. It's worth a shot."

Once they were settled again, Kate relayed the fascinating tale she'd heard from Myrtle on Monday. Presents and snacks were set aside as everyone listened to every word.

"Well, that's a new one for me." Marge was surprised. "I'd always heard the usual, that the Weigmanns gave it to the church themselves."

Roberta's husband shook his head in disgust.

"I don't want to start a fight, as I'm sure some of you bank there. But I could see old Oswald doing something like that. He was as shady as they come. And my dad had some kind a run-in with Oswald's son, back when he was in charge. We all pulled our accounts and took them to Charles City."

"Well, we do bank here in town." Barney's voice held a note of caution that Kate found interesting. "Haven't had any trouble, ourselves. Just keep an eye on your statements, I guess. They have great interest rates, always have."

"Too good to be true?" Aaron was intrigued.

"Well, who knows what's fact, and what's fiction," Bev said cheerfully as she passed around a plate of Christmas cookies. "Even so, Kate and I talked it over, and I passed Myrtle's tale on to the sheriff. It may not mean a thing, but ..."

"You did what?" Barney nearly spit out a square of fudge.

Kate frowned in confusion. "We told Sheriff Preston. Why wouldn't we?"

"Because it's not the post office's business to get into other people's business." Barney was adamant on that point. "Why, back in the day, we heard and saw all kinds of things. You kept it to yourself. You see people's mail, and you come to their doors with packages; they have to be able to trust you. Discretion has always been a big part of the job."

Kate thought about Candace and her troubles. Where was the ethical line here? What if a carrier suspected someone wasn't treating their animals properly? Or if the wife or children seemed fearful of visitors? Didn't the carriers have a duty to speak up in certain situations?

Years ago, she knew, people didn't talk about their problems like they did now. Welfare organizations didn't exist, or they were shunned by most people as being charity. Those walls of silence had mostly been dismantled, and Kate thought it was for the better. No one should suffer in silence.

"I see what you're saying," Roberta told Barney. "But things have certainly changed. Kate, your grandpa could attest to that. Society's different these days. But anyway, this isn't about someone's personal life. A crime has likely been committed. What if this tip leads to something?"

"People expected us to be discreet, and we were." Barney wouldn't let it drop. "Talking to your mail carrier was like talking to your barber, or your priest or pastor. The conversation stayed where it was; you didn't blab things all over town."

"I don't agree." Jack was working up a head of steam, Kate could sense it. And it didn't help that he, like Barney, had had a few beers.

"We're the eyes and ears of this community. Like when Milton Benniger went missing. You weren't around the post office for that," Jack's voice took on a hint of derision, "but the sheriff specifically asked us to be on the lookout, and that's what we did." Murmurs of agreement echoed around both tables.

Barney leaned forward. "OK, fine. But here's what bothers me the most about this thing with Myrtle. It's not even a question of how many bats she has in her belfry; it's that her belfry is probably empty. She's in her nineties!"

"Going to the sheriff was the right thing to do, for Myrtle's sake." Jack slapped his knee for emphasis, and the sudden movement caught Hazel's attention. Before Kate could reach for her collar, the dog rushed to the cased opening between the two rooms. Her tail low, she watched the men argue.

"Myrtle pointed the finger at some powerful people," Jack reminded Barney. "The Baxters still hold a lot of leverage in this town. Oswald's long dead, thank goodness. But you don't know what the rest of them are capable of."

Barney pushed back his chair and ignored his wife's admonishment to let things go. "We don't interfere in people's business. It's not how things are done!"

Randy chuckled and tried to diffuse the tension. "Guys, drop it! The nativity's going to turn up. And if it doesn't, well, people will get over it, eventually."

"This isn't about some nativity." Jack got out of his seat and stomped around the corner of the dining-room table. "This is about people who've retired and can't move on with their lives. I'm pretty sure about that."

"Oh, come on!" Barney refused to back down. "I'm enjoying retirement, thank you very much. Maybe *you* need to get some hobbies or something."

"Why don't you do the same?"

Jack made a sweeping gesture with his hand as he said this, and his fingers caught the side of Allison's plastic cup.

Several guests jumped out of their chairs and tried to stem the flow of red wine that was ruining Bev's tablecloth and advancing toward the table's edge and the carpet below. Wrapped and unwrapped gifts were swept out of the way, and snack plates flew through the air.

Hazel growled, dashed into the dining room, and barreled past Barney. In a matter of seconds, Jack was down. With her paws on his chest, Hazel barked at a volume Kate hadn't known she possessed.

"Hazel, stop that!" Kate shouted. It was no use.

"Keep it up, I say," Barney chortled. "He's had it coming for some time. Good girl, Hazel!" Barney had landed on the floor next to the Christmas tree, which luckily hadn't toppled over during the chaos, and good-naturedly waved away Jared's offer of assistance.

Jack tried to get up, and that only made Hazel stand her ground.

"Call off your attack dog," he begged Kate. "Hazel, you know me! I'm one of the good guys."

That brought hoots of laughter from Randy and Barney.

"It's her training at the canine facility." Aaron shook his head in awe. "She saw them arguing, and decided Jack was some kind of threat. Oh, Hazel."

"When will she stop?" Marge was blotting the carpet's wine stain with every available paper napkin. "Is there a special command or something?"

"She doesn't listen well." Kate tried to pull the still-barking Hazel away, and realized just how heavy her dog was. Those tense, adrenaline-fueled muscles didn't help. She wasn't about to bite Jack; she just seemed to think it was her job to keep him pinned to the floor so he couldn't get away.

Kate tried several commands. Hazel hesitated for a second, but kept her paws squarely on Jack's chest.

"Let him go!" Kate pleaded. "We're trying to have a nice little party here. You don't have to ..."

"*Nein!*" someone called from across the room. "*Du bist ein schlecht hund. Halt!*"

Hazel stopped barking and immediately stepped away from Jack.

Everyone turned to stare at Bev in amazement.

"I took German in high school, then a little more in college." Bev shrugged. "I remembered reading somewhere that service dogs sometimes learn commands *auf Deutsch*. Thought it was worth a try."

Hazel made a questioning whimper and looked at Kate.

"*Sehr gut!*" That was about all Kate could recall from her second-hand learning at the moment. "Will you go lie down?" She pointed into the living room, and Hazel went. But not before giving Jack one last, wary look.

"Don't worry, Hazel." Randy was laughing so hard, he was

nearly crying. "We've taken the bad guy into custody. Your work is done."

Jack sat up and brushed one hand through his salt-and-pepper hair. "That's quite the attack dog you have there, Duncan."

"You're uninjured," Audrey said coolly. "A little canine justice didn't hurt. Serves you right."

"Both of you," Evelyn added. "Just look at this mess! Thank goodness the gifts didn't get damaged."

Roberta had already retrieved paper towels and trash bags from the kitchen and mobilized her crew to gather up the far-flung snacks and blot up any other spills. Kate gently took Hazel by the collar and guided her upstairs. Charlie waited for them on the landing, a bemused look on his face.

"It's not funny," Kate told him as they passed. Then she started to laugh. "OK, yeah, maybe it is."

Hazel was calm and quiet as Kate guided her into her room and shut the door. It was like Aaron had said: she'd received at least a little intervention instruction, and put her skills to use when a situation came along. Of course, a fully trained service dog would have waited for a handler's command before wading into the fray.

"But that's why you didn't make the cut, huh?" Kate sat next to Hazel's oval bed as the dog dropped into it with a satisfied sigh. "I'm just glad you didn't try to bite Jack or get too aggressive."

Hazel gave her a puzzled look that said, *why would I do that?*

Kate shook her head as she started for the door, which would stay closed until all her guests were gone, just in case.

"It's a good thing I hadn't replaced that carpet yet. And I guess it's good to know you understand German commands. I'd better brush up on mine."

* 18 *

Hazel's presentation of her "obedience" skills didn't ruin the party, after all. The mess was cleaned up, and the carriers and their guests went back to their wrapping duties. Before the evening was over, several staffers declared it was the best holiday gathering the group had enjoyed in many years.

Jack and Barney didn't exactly apologize to each other, but the two men seemed to bury the hatchet, at least for now. Kate suspected Jack's ego had been knocked down a notch or two when Hazel pinned him to the floor. And Barney's annoyance with Jack seemed to be greatly soothed by seeing his co-worker stuck in such a ridiculous predicament in front of the entire crew.

Even so, Kate thought Evelyn was wise to make her husband move into the living room for the rest of the party.

"And I didn't have to renovate the house from top to bottom for us to have a good time," Kate reminded herself Monday morning as she worked her way through a route south of town.

"Maybe we've started a new tradition. Or two, if you count the presents for the giving tree. But I'm not sure I want to host every year; maybe some of the others will step up."

It was a cold morning, and a skim of snow clung to the rural roads. Kate kept an eye on her speed, and was grateful for the gravel under Bertha's tires. These roads didn't get the attention of the paved highways, but their rough surface did offer some traction.

The backseat was piled high with boxes, which made Kate even more cautious with the accelerator and brakes. It was just as well that Hazel seemed to prefer snoozing at home with Charlie on these chilly days; there was no room for a furry co-pilot in this sleigh.

Another crossroads was up ahead. Before Kate made it to the corner, a white SUV appeared over the crest of the hill on her right. Stop signs were rare on these remote gravel roads, and none were posted at this intersection. Kate was closer to the junction but had already decided to yield, given her load of packages. Mere seconds after the other vehicle started down the grade, its driver spotted Kate and flipped on a series of red-and-blue hazard lights.

"It's the sheriff's department!" Kate gasped in surprise while she waited for the SUV to fly past. Once it was through the crossroads, its emergency lights went off again. She glanced at Bertha's dash clock. "It's barely eight in the morning. I wonder what's going on?"

It was a stroke of luck that Kate's route would take her left, as well. She kept far enough behind the SUV that the dust and snow kicked up by its tires didn't obscure her vision. Where was it going? Might it turn in at the next farm?

The county vehicle didn't stop, but Kate had to make a delivery. By the time she dropped her bundle in the mailbox, the sheriff's cruiser had long ago disappeared over the next hill. Maybe it would turn off this road, and maybe it wouldn't. But about fifteen minutes later, Kate spotted it parked just off the driveway of the next farm.

Two more law-enforcement vehicles waited closer to the house, and several members of the sheriff's department huddled near the entrance to a metal machine shed. A woman in a winter chore coat and blaze-orange knit hat was gesturing wildly to the authorities as Kate came up the lane.

"That must be the owner, or one of the owners." Kate checked the name on the box waiting in Bertha's passenger seat. "I bet that's Patricia Redfield."

No one seemed especially in distress, and there was no ambulance at the scene. Once her initial concern that someone was injured had been disproven, Kate decided this was a very, very good day to be a mail carrier. She had an iron-clad reason to be in this farm yard, and find out what was going on.

The woman was obviously frustrated about something, but the officers seemed rather relaxed. Kate offered them a hearty wave and a smile before she parked Bertha next to one of the SUVs. It carried the Eagle River police department's logo, which Kate found interesting. This farm was outside the city limits, and Sheriff Preston already had some of his people here. Why was the city involved?

"I have a package for Patricia Redfield," Kate called out as soon as she opened her door. Two friendly farm dogs dashed through the slush to surround her work boots and demand attention from their latest guest.

"Busy day, huh?" Kate whispered to them as she pulled doggie treats from one parka pocket. "All kinds of excitement, I bet."

The woman in the orange cap followed in the dogs' wake. "That would be me. Is it from Illinois?"

Kate checked the box's label. "Sure is."

The woman's weary face momentarily lit up with joy. "Then it's from Jen, my daughter, and her family. They won't make it home for Christmas this year, so they shipped their presents instead."

When a much-anticipated parcel arrived from a loved one, people's holiday cheer was usually infectious. But the grim-faced middle-aged man coming down the back porch's steps seemed far from merry.

"We got 'em!" He made a fist with one gloved hand, and put his arm around Patricia with the other. "I checked the camera feed, it's all there. The yard light was just bright enough that I think they can zoom in and get a good look at their faces."

Patricia sighed with relief. "Thank goodness!"

"This ends today," her husband said, then gave Kate a triumphant nod. "They aren't going to come back here again. We'll make sure of that."

He started toward the cluster law-enforcement officials, but Kate couldn't bring herself to leave quite yet. She turned toward Patricia. "Can I ask what's going on?"

"Come with me." Patricia sat the box on the porch, then tipped her head toward the shed. "You might want to see this."

As they walked across the yard, Patricia explained how the outbuildings at this farm had been tampered with three times in the past few months. At first, it was just a few items missing from the little shed over by the garden. A hose, a few shovels; the sorts of things Patricia and Jim jokingly blamed on each other and their advancing ages. When the items didn't turn up, Jim put combination locks on the barn doors and shed entrances.

"It seemed excessive, and it was a pain at chore time. But we really started to wonder what had happened to our stuff. And who might be roaming around out here in the middle of the night."

Kate shivered, and not from the cold. "I think that would worry me more than things going missing."

"Exactly."

A few weeks ago, Jim came out one morning to find the padlock on the garage's side door had been cut with some sort of tool. Not much was taken that time, but the overcrowded garage's piles of this-and-that had been ransacked in such a way that both of them were really unnerved. They'd filed another report with the sheriff, of course, but with no proof of anything, there wasn't much anyone could do.

"That's when we got the cameras." Patricia pointed out a small black box strapped up high on the yard light's pole. "That one's pointed at this shed, and we have more near the other buildings' entrances. Nothing happened until last night."

Patricia had found the lock busted off the machine shed's main door that morning. A few power tools were taken this time, items more valuable than what went missing in the past.

"They had the nerve to back their truck right up to the door to make it easier to haul stuff out." She gave a triumphant laugh. "But they didn't know we were getting the whole thing on video."

A young woman in a sheriff's department parka waved to Patricia and Kate, then met them by the side of the shed.

"We got pictures of their boot tracks and the tire marks in the snow, before they can start to melt," she told Patricia. "But those aren't really needed, if Jim has what he says he does. I think we're going to have good news for you folks in a few days."

The female deputy smiled at Kate after Patricia moved on. "Interesting morning for you, huh? I'm sure you are crazy-busy this time of year, and now this." She put out a gloved hand. "I'm Abby Farrell, by the way."

"Kate Duncan, Eagle River post office."

Abby's blue eyes widened slightly in interest. "Oh, yeah! Sheriff Preston just about has you on speed dial, I bet. You and ... what's her name, his childhood sweetheart?"

Kate laughed. "Bev Stewart. We try to help out, when we can." She gestured at the wide skies and empty fields beyond the Redfields' farm. "After all, we're out here on these roads, day after day. Not much gets past us."

"I've only been with the department for two months." A gust of wind raced across the open farm yard, and Abby pulled the hood of her parka up over her knit hat. "A fresh recruit, straight from the state academy."

"I hope the guys don't give you too hard of a time." Kate liked Abby right away. "How long has it been since the department had a female deputy?"

"Never." Abby laughed. "I'm the first one. Everybody's been easy to work with. I wondered if I'd run into any interference but so far, so good. But then, I have Leona in my corner, and she runs that place. She's in charge of way more than the sheriff's calendar, believe me."

Kate nodded in agreement as she studied the group huddled a few feet away. "Maybe you can't tell me this, but ... why is an Eagle River officer here? We're outside of town."

Abby pondered Kate's request, then shrugged. "Well, this is just one of several farms that's been hit lately, as I'm sure you've heard. Whoever is responsible for this job probably isn't acting alone. It's likely some people in Eagle River are mixed up in this burglary ring." She frowned. "And far beyond that. Who knows how far out the tentacles go?"

Kate turned slightly to the left to keep the wind off her face. "I grew up around here. And I can remember when my parents didn't lock the house unless we were going to be gone overnight."

"It was the same when I was a kid, over by Swanton," Abby said. "And now, people have to put up cameras just to feel safe." Then she squared her shoulders. "Well, that's what we're here for!"

The Eagle River officer gestured for Abby to rejoin the group, and she gave Kate a small wave before she moved on. "It was nice to meet you. And Merry Christmas!"

"Merry Christmas!" Kate echoed before she turned back toward Bertha. As she hurried to get behind the wheel and return to her rounds, Kate considered Abby's assessment of the string of thefts in their county.

Who knows how far out the tentacles go?

"All the way to Chicago, I bet." Kate made sure the Redfields' dogs were still on the porch before she turned the key. "Or the Twin Cities, at least. Far enough that the nativity could be long gone. And not likely to ever find its way home."

"I'm not ready to give up hope yet," Bev told Kate the following morning as they prepped for their deliveries. "What if this is the break we've been waiting for? It sounds like the Redfields got what Jeff will need to identify the burglars and press charges."

Kate had vowed to keep what she'd witnessed to herself, at least for a while, but word of the Redfields' discovery was all over town within hours. It was the talk of the post office yesterday afternoon, and continued to be this morning.

"I know." Kate sighed as she sorted parcels. "Even so, the cases might not be related. And if they are, can he get these people to give up their connections?"

"The county attorney certainly could," Jack offered from his side of the metal counter. "Depends on what kind of charges they're facing, and if they already have a record." He set his handheld scanner down for a moment. "I can't remember how it goes, but there's a saying, something about 'honor among thieves' ..."

"They don't have any." Aaron squared one stack of mail and began to sort the next. "And whoever these guys are, they have to be pretty small-time if they are that stupid." He laughed. "The camera was right there, on the light pole! I bet Sheriff Preston can get them to cave, once he figures out who they are."

Marge came by with a container of blueberry muffins. "Take one for the road, if nothing else," she told her co-workers, who were happy to comply.

"And oh, Bev, I have to say I was very impressed with your command of the German language the other night. My grandparents still spoke a few words of it when I was little, but I couldn't come up with any of them if I tried."

Jack muttered something under his breath, and suddenly needed to visit his locker.

"I'm glad I remembered as much as I did," Bev said with a chuckle as they watched him depart. "It was a stretch, for sure."

"You had a whole sentence in there." Kate was impressed. "Better than I could have spit out on a moment's notice."

"I don't care what Barney says," Aaron told Kate and Bev. "If we hear anything of interest out in the field, something important, we need to pass it on." He grinned. "I asked Myrtle yesterday what she knew about the nativity, just to see what she'd say."

Kate's busy hands stopped. "And?"

Myrtle's retelling of the tale was a spot-on match to what she'd revealed to Kate last week. "She's sharp as a tack," Aaron promised. "Didn't falter once."

"Interesting." Bev was intrigued. "Not that I doubted her. But that just adds weight to the idea that the nativity last changed hands in a way everyone else around here seems to have forgotten."

"There's one other thing," Aaron said. "I flat-out asked her who else she's told this story to."

Other than her immediate family, and Kate and Patty, Myrtle said she'd only shared her tale with a young woman who'd called recently, full of questions about the nativity.

"That would have been Abby Farrell," Bev said. "When I passed it on to Jeff, he said he'd have Abby reach out. She's the newest deputy, of course, but he thought Myrtle might feel more comfortable talking to a woman."

The back room of the post office was noisy and bustling that morning, as the carriers chatted and scrambled to prepare for their routes. But even over the din, Roberta's voice was noticeably loud.

"You've got to be kidding me!" the boss shouted into her desk phone. "What are we supposed to tell people? Christmas is still over a week away, not everyone has their cards out yet."

Whatever the other person said in response, it wasn't enough to soothe the postmaster's frustration. "I don't care for his excuses. We're trying to stay relevant in the digital age, as you well know. And this certainly doesn't help!"

Randy looked up from his tasks when Roberta slammed down the receiver. "What's the deal, boss?"

"We're almost out of holiday stamps." Roberta stomped out from behind her desk. "I've been trying for days ... no, *weeks* ... to get more sent to us. But it doesn't matter who I call up the food chain. There are none to be had."

Aaron glowered over his mail case. "You mean, none for us since we're such a tiny shop. I bet Mason City's branch locations are well-stocked."

Marge leaned toward Kate and Bev. "I got some in Charles City yesterday," she whispered. "Aaron's right; we're not a priority."

"Don't let Roberta find out," Bev whispered back.

Too many small towns had lost their post offices due to declining population and revenue. Roberta encouraged her carriers to purchase their personal postal materials from the local shop to help keep its numbers up.

"I was desperate," Mae admitted. "It won't happen again."

Barney came out of the break room with his mug full of coffee. He was still manning the counter, as Roberta was too swamped helping the carriers get everything sorted and delivered. "What should I tell people when they ask?"

Roberta rubbed her face in weary defeat. "You'll have to tell them the truth."

"You may not need to do that." Randy had a solution. "Just tell them the stamps have been backordered, and more are on the way."

Roberta didn't agree. "That'll backfire, I'm afraid. Some of those folks will haunt this shop every day until they get what they want. And there won't be anything to get."

"How about this?" Barney paused for a big gulp of coffee. "I'll tell folks that all the cool people are using standard stamps for their holiday cards this year. After all, those flags will really stand out in a stack of mail compared to the Santas and snowmen."

With his pronouncement made, Barney shuffled through the door into the front of the shop. Roberta threw her arms up in a helpless gesture. "Whatever he thinks might keep people from rioting in the streets is good enough for me."

✳ 19 ✳

Kate smoothed her skirt and marveled at the intricate embroidery around its hem. With a few wiggles of her shoulders, she wedged both of her long-sleeved, thermal tops into their proper place under her outfit's bodice.

"Can you move your arms at all?" Natalie Simpson, a high-school senior, was one of the altos in the community chorus. "Because I don't think I can."

"Here." Kate reached for the back of Natalie's top. "I'll loosen the strings. How's that?"

"Better." Natalie flapped her arms and tried for a twirl. Her layers of petticoats swung into motion, and the countless yards of ruffled fabric nearly pulled her off her feet.

"Watch out!" Kate reached for Natalie's elbow to help her stay steady. "It would be unseemly for an elegant lady such as yourself to end up on the floor, smothered by her skirts, with her insulated fleece pants showing to the world."

"This thing is like an umbrella." Natalie tried to shift her hoops back into position. "But it's below my waist, instead of over my head."

Stacy attempted to glide into the ladies' dressing room, but it took a tug to get her skirts through the door. Even so, Kate noticed her cousin's olive-green ensemble was a flattering match for her blond hair.

"Why, Stacy," Kate gasped with mock drama as she twirled one of her bonnet's strings around her finger. "I do declare, you're pretty as a picture."

"Thank you, milady. Your bonnet is most fetching."

"And yours is, well, quite the fashion statement." Kate waddled over to the nearby table and reached for a tan wool chapeau nearly overcome by sprigs of faux flowers and greenery. Its floppy brim was so wide that Stacy would have to make a deliberate turn to see left or right.

No wonder fashionable ladies of the mid-1800s spent their time sipping tea and watching the world go by from settees and sofas. It was hard enough to walk from A to B, much less take part in anything more active.

Stacy modeled her hat briefly for the others, then dropped it to the floor. "That thing has to weigh five pounds, I swear. I'm not going to tie it on until the very-last minute."

"If there's any wind at all tonight, you might get airborne," Kate warned her cousin. "And I don't know how we are supposed to get into our 'carriage' in these skirts, much less sit in them."

The "carriage" was an Eagle River school bus, which would transport the carolers to the south end of Main Street. They would sing their way north, stroll at a leisurely pace that would allow the throngs of visitors to enjoy the group's seasonal songs. The performers would stop near two intersections, one in the heart of the business district and another just north of the bridge near city hall, to perform a few numbers while standing in place. They would end their journey at the auction barn, where the festival's grand-finale bonfire would be staged in the parking lot.

Stacy reported some of the other singers were already in costume and lingering in the nearby auditorium.

"How does everyone else look?" Natalie wanted to know. "Because I look ridiculous." She tugged at the high neckband on her dress. "It's like a turtleneck that's too tight."

Stacy gave a half-hearted shrug, which was all she could muster in her form-fitting gown. "Historically accurate, I guess. I can report the men have it easy, as they always do. Kevin and Alex are already in costume, and the others are working on it, I hear. I hope they don't make us late."

Kate had yet to run into Alex tonight, and her pulse picked up when Stacy said his name. They'd rehearsed their revamped lines for the final song several times. And it certainly wasn't going to be a tough gig to hold hands with someone that handsome. So why was she so nervous?

"Guys always get ready at the last minute," she reminded the other ladies. "And all they have to deal with tonight is getting their cravats adjusted."

The trio shuffled over to the three-section mirror on the dressing room's far wall.

"Well, we definitely look the part." Stacy adjusted the ruffled cuffs on her long sleeves. "This will certainly help us get into character."

Natalie frowned. "I just hope I remember all the words." While the evening's selections were well-known holiday tunes, the carolers would sing all the verses, not just the familiar ones. "We'll have our songbooks, of course, but I don't know if the streetlights will be bright enough so we can see them clearly."

Stacy reached for her bonnet, but didn't put it on. "It's too bad we can't run inside a few of the stores and see what their specials are. I wish I could say my shopping was done, but it's not."

Kate nodded in sympathetic defeat. "I'm not finished, either. Good thing we have a week to go."

That also meant there was only one week left to find the nativity before Christmas. Kate pushed that depressing thought aside and tried to focus on how much fun tonight could be. *Had* to be. Because no matter how well their voices blended in song, no one wanted to watch a troupe of downhearted singers drag their feet down Main Street.

The ladies collected their capes and headed out into the hallway. Kate forgot all about the missing nativity and her cumbersome costume the moment she spotted Alex standing by the stage. His charcoal greatcoat fit him perfectly, and even the elaborate tangle of his purple-satin cravat couldn't detract from his deep brown eyes and strong jaw.

Don't swoon, Kate reminded herself. *Because if you end up on the floor, you might not be able to get back up again.*

"My goodness," Stacy whispered. "Doesn't Alex look the part!"

Kate gave her cousin a quick jab with an elbow. "You put us up to this. I know you did."

"Oh, so it's 'us' now?" Stacy giggled. "Society ladies are supposed to be discreet, but I want the dirt."

"Nothing is going on." Kate knew the defensiveness in her voice would only make Stacy more suspicious, but she couldn't help it. Natalie had already been absorbed into the cluster of altos and sopranos, and Kate hoped they couldn't overhear this conversation.

"Hmm." Stacy wasn't convinced. "Well, when it does, I hope I'm one of the first to hear about it."

"*When?*" Kate turned swiftly toward her cousin, and nearly lost her balance. "I don't think ..."

"You heard me." Stacy smirked before she moved away.

"Good evening, miss."

Kate took a deep breath before she turned around. More slowly, this time. "Good evening to you, sir. Will you be partaking in the holiday festivities?"

"I believe I will." Alex grandly offered Kate his arm. "Shall we promenade?"

Kate looped her arm through his, and they started up the main aisle at a slow, synchronized pace. They might as well practice this stroll one more time, Kate decided, as the two of them had to lead the rest of the chorus to their marks in front of the bonfire. She just hoped the parking lot wasn't icy. It was a good thing her skirts nearly touched the ground, as she had her work boots on underneath all these layers.

Hanging on the arm of a dashing fellow wasn't so bad. And there were far-worse parts to play in tonight's festivities. Austin's grandfather, George, was playing Santa in the front of Sherwood's Furniture Store, and Austin's sister had been cajoled into dressing up as an elf.

Even so, Kate decided, a few hours in this costume was going to be enough. At least until next year. Because maybe this was going to be fun, after all.

"I think sweatpants and a beer are going to feel pretty good when this is over." Alex's mind was moving in the same direction. "You look lovely, by the way."

Kate smiled as they executed a careful turn at the back of the auditorium. "Thanks. But my hairpins are giving me a headache."

Getting on the bus was a challenge for the ladies, and they each required their own seat once they wrestled their skirts down the narrow aisle. A few snowflakes were drifting about by the time the carolers disembarked at the south end of Main Street. Just enough to add to the ambience, but nothing that would cut short this festive evening in Eagle River's historic downtown district.

And what a magical place it was on this special night! Most of the storefronts were still a mix of red brick and limestone, thanks to a decades-long effort to preserve Main Street's antique architecture. While modern touches had been permitted here and there, mostly to maintain the structures' integrity and meet building codes, there was no vinyl siding or oversized signs. The reproduction lamp posts only added to the nostalgic feel.

Finally, Kate felt at home in her historical getup. She could imagine herself back in time, strolling this street during a holiday season from more than a hundred years ago. It was as if the casually dressed visitors were the odd ones out, in their parkas and fleece and knit caps.

Kate had nearly ditched the chorus after Austin and Alex goaded her into joining it; but now, she was glad she'd seen this through. Why just be part of the crowd when you could stroll along like this, dressed to the nines and singing the songs of the season? It felt really good to participate, not just observe.

"Everyone, huddle up." Lauren clapped her velvet-gloved hands and shooed the singers toward the nearest corner. "We'll start with 'Good King Wenceslas,' just like we planned."

The carolers began their slow stroll up Main Street. While the group's members stayed close together, it was impossible to keep any sort of formation in this jostling crowd. But the ladies' hoop skirts helped clear the way.

Many of the shoppers paused to take in the group's costumes as well as their songs, and the visitors' wide grins and murmurs of admiration encouraged the volunteers to sing with greater enthusiasm. Fred carried a large tin cup in one hand, and there was a steady stream of listeners eager to drop coins and bills into the container.

It was tradition for street musicians to collect cash, and Eagle River's active historical society was certainly a good cause. Kate wondered if, thanks to these costumes, tonight's performance would bring in a bigger haul for the nonprofit organization.

Milton's generosity would allow the society to add costumes to this annual performance for years to come, a new tradition that could pay great dividends. Kate's mind wandered to Milton's lifelong home, which was sitting empty on this winter night, and the three cats that now snuggled, warm and content, in Kate's insulated shed.

"What's wrong?" Stacy asked. "If I had a coat on, instead of this crazy cape, I might have a tissue handy."

"I'm fine." Kate blinked back her unexpected tears. "I think I just got a few snowflakes right in the face."

As the singers wandered along, Kate absorbed the sights and sounds all around her. A vendor dispensed caramel corn from a reproduction-vintage cart at one corner, and restless children endured the wait to sit with Santa in the front window of the furniture store. As they wandered past, Kate caught a glimpse of a costumed George Freitag in a rocking chair at the front of the showroom.

"He's perfect for that role," Kate told Austin, who nodded with pride.

"There's no reason Santa can't come to Eagle River and meet with the kids," he said. "After all, Prosper's holiday fest was a few weeks ago. Maybe their wish lists have changed."

Kate had expected the secular songs to get a rousing response, but she was pleased to notice the religious tunes did as well. The group hadn't planned to pause in front of the Catholic church, which was the only one of the town's three houses of worship that fronted Main Street, but Lauren pulled the group up short.

"Let's do 'Silent Night' right now," she whispered. "No reason we can't change the set list up a bit."

It was a special moment. When the last notes of the third verse drifted away, the large crowd gathered around the church's front steps burst into hearty applause.

"Are you getting nervous?" Alex sidled up to Kate as the chorus made their way through the last block before the auction barn. "It's almost time."

"Sure," she admitted before she flipped her songbook to the next selection. "Aren't you?"

"Well, a little." Alex's relaxed tone put Kate at ease. "But we've run through this how-many times already. We're as prepared as we'll ever be. Besides, I don't think people's expectations are all that high. I mean, they just want to be entertained. That's all."

"I can do that." Kate nodded. "We can do that."

While there were still some shoppers milling about along Main Street, most visitors had begun to move toward the auction barn. Several vendors had set up booths inside that offered housewares and gifts, and decorations and seasonal treats. More food options were available in the parking lot, including hot chocolate, pretzels and popcorn.

Kate was eager to sample whatever she could get her hands on, as supper had been early and rushed and the brisk air and the walking had further whetted her appetite.

But first, she had to get through the grand finale. Hundreds of people were now gathered in the parking lot and, in just minutes, most of them would be focused on the chorus members taking their places in front of the still-unlit bonfire.

Kate just had to sing her solo lines to Alex and the sea of faces, remember the group's rehearsed gestures, and wear a smile the whole time. Easy-peasy, right?

Several members of the fire department milled around the edges of the bonfire's pile, which was banked with wooden pallets and some of the dead tree limbs that had been picked up by city crews over the fall. Once most of the crowd quieted down, Mayor Ward Benson stepped forward. He thanked everyone for attending the night's festivities, then formally announced the choral group's presence to a rousing round of applause.

Alex was right; these people just wanted to be entertained. This wasn't a competition, and the bar was very low. Kate found the crowd's enthusiastic response to the group's first two numbers encouraging, rather than overwhelming.

She saw her parents in the crowd, along with Bryan and Anna. Grandpa Wayne and Grandma Ida were right behind them. *Just sing to your family*, she told herself. *Forget about everyone else.*

"We've got this," Alex whispered to Kate as Ward announced the group's final selection. Alex reached for her hand, and they stepped forward from the rest of the group. A murmur of anticipation ran through the crowd as Kate and Alex took their places. What would happen next? This was something different!

Kate was suddenly glad Lauren and Stacy had forced the two of them to face each other. All she had to do was focus on Alex; she could forget about the crowd.

When Kate sang her first phrase to him, "I wish you a merry Christmas," their listeners fell silent in surprise. But when Alex answered in kind, and the entire chorus chimed in at the end of the verse, the revelers roared with approval.

The beloved song was hundreds of years old, and this fresh take was certainly welcomed by the crowd. Kate's smile was now genuine, as she was filled with relief. Alex grinned back at her, and squeezed both of her hands. The rest of the tune flew by, and when the singers slowed the tempo for the very-last lines, several people in the crowd joined in.

As the chorus held their final notes, church bells began to ring around town. Kate was startled; had that been part of the plan? Lauren must have made some inquiries, but kept her requests secret just in case the added touch didn't come through.

Cheers and applause erupted from the crowd at the end of the performance. Kate was laughing with glee, and she caught Alex's eye.

We did it! she was about to say. And then, before she could absorb what was happening, her handsome singing partner leaned in and kissed her.

Despite the cold, Kate was suddenly warm from head to toe. The cheers around them grew louder and louder, but Kate was lost in the feel of Alex's mouth on hers. It was a simple kiss, the sort that was showcased during a theatrical performance, but Kate certainly hadn't expected it.

They broke apart and stared at each other, and she realized Alex hadn't expected it, either.

Or had he? Was that the start of a smirk at the corner of his mouth?

Well, Kate decided, maybe it was her turn to improvise. She leaned in, grasped the elbows of Alex's waistcoat, and kissed him right back.

The crowd went crazy, and Kate heard more than a few suggestive whistles among the laughter and applause. Or at least, she thought she did. Because it felt like she and Alex were alone on this snow-dusted holiday night.

Finally, she let him go. Kate wished she knew exactly what her friend was thinking.

But, was he just her friend? Or ...

"Let's hear it for our soloists!" Ward stepped forward and motioned for Alex and Kate to face the crowd and take a bow. The audience wanted more than one, and they obliged.

"Come on, man!" a guy in the crowd shouted. "Kiss her again!"

Alex and Kate glanced at each other and burst out laughing. The moment, whatever it was, had passed. There wasn't time for Kate to wonder if there would be another one just like it, because Fire Chief Ben Dvorak stepped forward and announced it was time to ignite the bonfire.

As the singers moved out of the way, Kate's cousin, Corey, gave her a quick high-five. Stacy's brother was a member of the volunteer fire department, and he was decked out in his full gear.

"Nice getup." He gestured at Kate's outfit. "Is that your leading man? He's so handsome!"

"Stop it!" But Kate was laughing. "That was just for show, you know."

But was it?

"And as for this dress," she told her cousin, "it's about as cumbersome as what you're wearing."

✳ 20 ✳

Grandpa Wayne passed Lena the syrup, then nudged Kate with his elbow.

"That was some show last night," he said in a teasing voice. "What a way to get into the holiday spirit, huh?"

Kate was usually quick on her feet when it was time for a snappy retort. But today, she didn't know what to say. Especially because she still had no idea what that kiss at the end of the performance was about.

Both kisses, actually. The one where Alex smooched her in front of hundreds of people, and the one where she kissed him back as the crowd cheered and applauded.

"We were in character." Kate shrugged as she tucked into her scrambled eggs. Henry had been generous with the shredded cheese, just as she'd requested, and they were fabulous. "We were playing a romantic holiday scene. You know, a sprinkle of snowflakes, top hats, hoop skirts and all that."

If Kate hadn't been so tired and distracted, she might have been able to keep the smug smile off her face.

But she'd been awake until after one, pondering last night's twists and turns and wondering how many shopping stops she could squeeze in after work. There was no regular day off again this week, just a promise from Roberta that Kate could come in a little late this morning, sort packages at the post office, and leave by mid-afternoon.

"Well, I'd say you had the plum role in the whole thing." Lena gave Kate a sly wink from across the table. "He's too young for my tastes but, my goodness, Alex Walsh has to be one of the handsomest guys in town."

Max pointed his fork at Lena. "You're also married."

"Oh, there's that, too." Lena laughed as Joan brought a fresh pot of coffee to their table.

"I'd love to hear the details, but I think Kate's going to keep those to herself." Joan shook her head in admiration. "He's a catch, to be sure."

Chris rolled his eyes. "Now, just what is so special about Alex? He's a nice guy and all, but ..."

"Tall, dark and handsome," Lena was quick to say. "Right out of central casting." She put one hand over her heart and gave a dramatic sigh. "And he's a little mysterious, too. I can't put my finger on it, but ..."

"I wouldn't mind putting my hands on him," Joan blurted out, and all three of the ladies burst out laughing. But given the uncomfortable looks on the men's faces, they'd heard enough about last night's dashing hero.

"Hey, here comes Ward." Harvey seemed eager to change the subject. "I'm sure he'd rather discuss something of civic importance or, I don't know, anything but this."

But Harvey was wrong.

"Well hello, Kate!" Ward plucked a stray chair from the next table and settled in. "Are we going to hear church bells again anytime in the future, and for a different reason?"

"We already discussed that." Chris passed Ward the bowl of sweetener packets. "Kate's not saying."

"All teasing aside, that was the best performance that group has put on in years." Ward was pleased. "They usually just stroll along Main Street. You and Alex certainly upped the ante; that last performance at the bonfire was so clever.

And it looked like something out of a Currier and Ives painting!"

"It was the costumes." Kate took a sip of her coffee. "They really helped everyone get into character. And we have Milton to thank for that."

Murmurs of appreciation echoed around the table. "He was one of a kind." Ward nodded. "But his generosity has made our community better, now and in the future."

Talk soon turned to last-minute shopping and how the weather was supposed to shake out in this final week before Christmas. Kate was relieved to have the conversation's spotlight shine somewhere other than on her personal life, and focused on her food. She didn't know what might happen with Alex, or when. Maybe nothing more. But there wasn't much time to think about that right now. Especially when she had to be at the post office in less than thirty minutes.

As the group wrapped up their breakfasts, Ward's cell phone rang. Kate saw a strange look on his face.

"What is it?"

"It's the sheriff." Ward frowned and got out of his chair. "I'll be right back."

"What's going on?" Grandpa Wayne fretted as his friend hustled down the hallway toward the restrooms, away from the din of the dining area.

"Don't know." Max shrugged and sliced up the rest of his plate-size pancake. "Guess he'll tell us, if he can."

The mayor's face was pale when he returned to the table.

"Has there been an accident?" Chris, who volunteered with the town's ambulance crew, checked his phone. "I don't think I got an alert."

"No, nothing like that." Ward dropped into his chair. He glanced around the restaurant for a moment, then leaned his elbows on the table. "Word is going to get out about this, and fast. So I might as well tell all of you, right now."

Three youngsters from the Eagle River area now faced

charges of burglary, trespassing and theft in connection with the break-in at the Redfields' farm Sunday night. The security camera's footage, along with the alleged culprits' confessions, meant the charges against them were likely to hold.

"One of them is eighteen, so he'll be charged as an adult. But the other two? They are just fifteen and sixteen years old," Ward said sadly. "So young to get mixed up in something like this."

"And the nativity?" Kate wanted to know.

"Still gone." Ward was certain about that point. "It hasn't turned up yet."

The teens didn't threaten anyone, Ward said, and were apparently unarmed when they broke into the Redfields' building earlier in the week. It wasn't clear yet if the three boys had been at that farm previously, or if others were responsible for the earlier thefts. Or how their actions might, or might not, fit into the burglary ring that was apparently at work around the region.

"I asked him flat-out if more charges are expected," Ward said. "Because people are going to ask me that, and I want to tell it straight. He hedged a bit, then said he couldn't comment further because the investigation is ongoing."

"I'd say that means more are likely." Grandpa Wayne refilled his coffee cup. "And while the sheriff can't release the names of the juveniles, I bet half the kids over at the high school already know who they are."

"Which brings me to the really shocking part of all this." Ward rubbed the side of his face and sighed. "The pastor at the Panther Junction church was arrested last night, too."

Gasps went up around the table.

"For theft?" Lena's eyes went wide. "I can't believe ..."

"Nope, guess again." Ward shook his head in awe. "Accessory after the fact, the sheriff says."

I think I know where this is going, Kate thought, *and it's very bad for Oliver Thorne.*

"Pastor Thorne was not directly involved in the thefts at the Redfield farm, or elsewhere." Ward was clear on that point.

"And while the sheriff wouldn't confirm this next part for me, I think you can put two and two together."

The charge Oliver Thorne now faced was often applied to situations where someone had knowledge of a criminal act but didn't report it, Ward explained. And it was common for people to seek support from a spiritual advisor during difficult times.

He didn't think the oldest boy's family attended Panther Junction church but, given the twists and turns in this case, it was all-but-certain at least one of the two juveniles was a member.

Harvey was clearly frustrated. "So you're telling us Thorne knew what these boys have been up to, but never went to the sheriff? How does that help them, if they don't face any consequences?"

"He probably thought he could get them started on a better path." Lena was a bit more understanding. "I've never thought about this before, but is there some sort of exemption for clergy members counseling those who are troubled? Especially if they are underage?"

Chris nodded slowly. "Sort of like attorney-client privilege? Well, there must not be."

"Hoo-boy." Max let out a big sigh. "This is going to get everyone talking. You have to wonder, how long has all this been going on? And did Thorne finally pick up the phone and tell the sheriff, or did his role in all this only come out after the boys were arrested?"

Pastor Thorne's odd behavior that afternoon at the church now made a great deal of sense to Kate.

He must have already known what the boys were wrapped up in, and was worried they might have taken the nativity, too.

And then, there was the tense conversation she had with him in front of the drugstore last week.

What had he said?

It's not your place to judge my actions. That's someone else's job.

But now, it seemed God wasn't the only one who would have a say in what happened to Oliver Thorne.

"Folks at the Panther Junction church hadn't completely agreed on hiring Thorne in the first place," Harvey reminded his friends. "I can't imagine this sort of tension is going to make things any better."

Lena crossed her arms. "So that begs the question: Where exactly is the nativity? If the boys don't have it ..."

"So they say." Max didn't seem convinced. "Who knows if they're telling the truth? Or maybe they took it, passed it on to someone else, and honestly don't know where it is now."

Ward let out a low whistle. "For their sakes, I hope they didn't have a hand in its disappearance. Given the nativity's potential value, it's the sort of trouble that would follow them into adulthood. Either way, I wonder if they'll give up the names of some of the others involved in this burglary ring?"

Lena sighed as she refilled her coffee cup. "Whatever is going on, I feel for those boys and their parents. No wonder they turned to their church for help."

"But Thorne should have spoken up sooner." Chris was adamant about that. "Who knows how far-reaching this burglary ring is? How many weeks did he sit on this information?"

Grandpa elbowed Kate as she finished her toast. "Looks like your detective work isn't done yet."

Kate shrugged. "I have to work today; tomorrow, too. Not sure how much time I'll have to snoop around before Christmas."

But a plan was already forming in her mind, one she could set into motion later that afternoon. Bev was walking a town route today, but she might have a few spare minutes in the truck to discuss the situation and help Kate find the right approach.

Kate had no confidence this effort would be tremendously productive. Or anything other than confrontational and stressful. But it was worth a shot.

Eagle River Savings Bank was surprisingly quiet for a Friday afternoon. But then, Kate realized, few people were probably coming in this time of year to apply for mortgages or complete other in-person tasks. And just about everything else could be handled at the drive-up window or online.

"Hello!" A young woman in a royal-blue sweater set greeted Kate from behind the receptionist's desk. "How can I help you today?"

"I'm here to see Leonard Baxter." Kate tipped her head toward the glass-walled office where the bank president was on the phone.

"Oh. Do you have ... is he expecting you?" Given the grimace on her face as she glanced toward her boss, the last thing this woman wanted to do was interrupt his day.

"Not exactly," Kate hedged, then leaned in and lowered her voice. "It's a personal matter."

The other woman blinked, and the practiced smile was back. "We'll let him finish his call, then I'll let him know you're here." She straightened in her chair, as if relieved to have a plan of action. "And you are ..."

"Kate Duncan." She added a confident nod that she didn't quite feel. "Eagle River post office."

For some reason, that relaxed the receptionist a bit.

Kate wondered how often random women arrived at the bank and demanded to see Leonard Baxter about a "personal matter." Just how much did he and his grandfather have in common?

That didn't make Kate feel any better, but her conversation with Bev certainly had. There was only one way into this awkward conversation, and Myrtle Bradford was it.

Leonard looked a bit confused when the receptionist shared her request, but he merely shrugged and turned back to his computer for a moment. The receptionist motioned for Kate to go in as she was on her way out.

"Good afternoon, Miss Duncan." Leonard eyed her with a mix of curiosity and wariness. The first she could understand; the second should have been totally unnecessary unless the bank was somehow shortchanging the federal government on postage.

Kate noticed Leonard's salt-and-pepper hair was suspiciously thick for a man of his age, and the expensive cut of his suit reminded her of how Myrtle's Aunt Amelia always sent away for her fashionable clothes.

"Thank you for seeing me." She closed the door and dropped into the chair across from the bank president's mahogany desk. It looked like an antique; she wondered just how long it had served as the de-facto throne for one of the most powerful families in town. "I promise not to take up too much of your time."

That seemed to be an agreeable offer, and Leonard's shoulders relaxed considerably. "So, what can I do for you today?"

"As you know, our mail carriers are in close contact with everyone in town. And outside of town, as well," she quickly added. "So when we suspect one of our customers might need a little assistance, we like to help when we can."

This earned her a wide smile. "Of course. We all have to look out for one another, don't we? Well, Eagle River Savings Bank certainly has some of the best returns in the area. If you're aware of someone who could use a hand with their finances, that's what we're here for. Referrals are much appreciated."

Kate suspected his next move would be to ask if she was a patron of his fine institution, and she wanted to avoid that conversation if she could.

"This is about Myrtle Bradford." She cut to the chase, and Leonard's smile vanished.

She couldn't be certain, but he might have flinched at the mention of Myrtle's name. Goodness gracious, why would this wealthy, successful man have any reason to worry about his distant relative's take on anything?

"I would guess her finances are in order." Kate was eager to fill the awkward silence. "It's not about that. It's just that she seems a little, well, stuck in the past. I know she has other family in the area, but I don't think I know any of them." Kate smiled. "But she did mention that she is related to you."

Did Leonard just turn pale? This was certainly shaping up to be an interesting conversation.

"You see," Kate leaned in conspiratorially, "she told me this wild story about that missing nativity, the one from the Panther Junction church. Something about your grandfather acquiring it years ago."

Leonard seemed to shrink back in his chair. Kate paused for a moment, let her words sink in, then waved one hand in a dismissive gesture.

"The details don't really matter," she said gently. "Although, it's quite the tale. She's shared it with a few of the other carriers as well. Myrtle is a wonderful lady, quite the pillar of our community, I'm sure you'd agree. But her story is so fantastical, so intriguing, that I'm a little worried she's ... having more than a few 'senior moments,' if you will."

Kate clasped her hands in her lap. "I just wanted to pass on my concerns. She's ninety-two. Perhaps you could put in a kind word with her immediate relatives, let them know about the situation? Then they can decide if they need to make any changes to her medical care."

Leonard crossed his arms. "What exactly did she say?"

Kate and Bev had hoped Leonard would eventually address this topic during the conversation, but they had expected him to feign at least a little interest in his elderly relative's well-being. Obviously, that wasn't a priority.

"About the nativity?" Kate played along. "It's probably not important, it's just that she ..."

"I want to hear it."

Kate took in a breath, let it out. And then, in as casual a tone as she could muster, shared most of Myrtle's story. She carefully skirted the rumors about Oswald Baxter's character, and simply noted he apparently acquired the nativity from the Weigmanns through "some sort of financial exchange."

The fact that Oswald had apparently swindled the Weigmanns out of their land wasn't mentioned. But there was one point Kate and Bev had decided was very important to share.

"She said something else, too, about the nativity." Kate frowned, as if trying to remember. "About there possibly being some sort of curse attached to it. But that has to be nonsense. Elderly folks have too much time on their hands, their imaginations can so easily run away with them."

Leonard's eyes were wider now, from what seemed to be a mix of shock and nervousness ... and maybe, even a little bit of fear? The moment Kate mentioned the curse, most of his bravado had evaporated.

"That's the part that had me the most concerned about Myrtle's memory, to tell you the truth." She smiled at the bank president. "After all, there's no such thing as curses. Right?"

"Of course," he snapped. "Utter nonsense." But the tightness of his jaw said he felt, or even knew, differently.

"Here's the other thing that's so interesting to me," Kate went on.

"I had no idea about this but, well, turns out my family has ties to the Panther Junction church! You can't imagine how surprised I was to find out that Gustav Weigmann was my great-great-great grandfather."

At this news, Leonard rolled his chair back from his desk. And away from Kate. It was only a few inches. But she wondered why this man was, even on a subconscious level, so eager to put more distance between himself and his visitor.

Leonard was apparently very aware of his family's role in the nativity's history. And, given his unsettled reaction to coming face-to-face with one of Gustav's direct descendants, he certainly was cautious about the nativity's alleged powers. If not outright terrified of them.

Kate marveled at the transformation this man had gone through in the past few minutes. From smug and self-assured as he sat behind his forefathers' desk at this bank, to having one hand wrapped around the other as if offering up a prayer.

Here was the chance Bev and Kate had hoped for: An opportunity to pivot this discussion from the veracity of Myrtle's story to the possible whereabouts of the nativity. It wasn't likely Leonard was involved in its disappearance. But if he'd heard anything, anything it all, he just might spill something Kate could use.

"So you see why I'm so concerned." She smiled again. "Not just about Myrtle, but about the nativity. Christmas Eve is just five days away. I think it's imperative the set is found and returned to the church in time for services. Don't you?"

Given his anxious expression, Leonard was imagining all the terrible things that might befall anyone who had a hand in the antique display's disappearance.

"I don't know where it is!" He braced his hands on the armrests of his executive office chair. "I've never seen the thing," he added hastily. "We attend the Catholic church here in town, you see."

Kate couldn't believe how easy this was. Leonard's fear was doing all the heavy lifting for her. "I didn't ask you if you did. I was just saying that ..."

"You may not know about this." His tone quickly turned condescending. "But three young men from this community were charged with theft last night. Word is, two of them attend Panther Junction church."

"I have it on good authority that those boys didn't take the nativity." Kate added just a hint of emphasis to "boys."

Leonard's eyes widened in surprise over Kate's knowledge of this news. "Really." He didn't seem convinced.

Kate decided she wasn't going to get much more out of Leonard Baxter, as he'd clearly shifted blame toward the teenagers. Either in a bid to take the spotlight off his family, or to get Kate out of his office, or both.

"It just would be a shame if the nativity never turns up," she said quietly as she reached for her purse. "It's unique, special. It's nice to have special things." She glanced around the well-appointed office. "And sometimes when they are given away, entitled people wish they could get them back."

A pink stain of anger crept up from the collar of Leonard's perfectly tailored shirt. "Good day, Miss Duncan. I trust you can see yourself out."

It was time to go. Leonard had beckoned to his receptionist, and the visibly nervous woman was heading their way, a smile plastered on her face.

"Happy holidays, Mr. Baxter." Kate stood up. "Let's hope the nativity reappears, and soon."

The fear was back in Leonard's eyes. He stared at Kate as if she were some sort of messenger, that Gustav Weigmann had sent one of his descendants to remind the Baxters that their transgressions hadn't been forgotten.

Good, he's a little scared, Kate thought as she left the bank and zipped her parka against the chill. *Mission accomplished.*

If Leonard Baxter had any idea where the nativity could be, maybe he was now rattled enough to call Sheriff Preston and spill whatever he knew.

✳ 21 ✳

A text from an unknown number flashed across Kate's phone the following afternoon, and she turned off at the next field drive to check it out.

"It's from Candace." Kate frowned, then gasped in delight. "Oh, wow, look at that!"

The attached photo was of a shiny-new mailbox, posing pretty on the side of a snow-dusted gravel road. The weather-treated wooden post was strong and straight. And then, Kate noticed the churned-up dirt and fresh concrete ring around the post's base.

So excited! Candace's text said. *Isn't it great? I'm so grateful we got it fixed before it got too cold. When you see Jack, please tell him thanks again!*

"Jack?" Kate grimaced. "Jack did this? The guy who's always ranting on and on about personal responsibility and following regulations?"

She texted Candace back, told her the mailbox looked wonderful and she was so glad everything had worked out.

As Kate and Bertha resumed their rounds, Kate tried to figure out exactly how Candace's mailbox had been replaced. Money was tight for the Taylors; it was the reason the situation hadn't been rectified weeks ago. And Wyatt had made it clear last week that he wasn't about to accept charity.

Kate assumed his bluster had only been about his children accepting gifts from the giving tree, but had there been more to it than that?

And had Jack really made all this happen? How had he pulled it off, and without anyone else at the post office getting wind of his plan?

Kate still had no idea where the Panther Junction nativity was these days, but this was one mystery she was confident she could solve ... as soon as she got back to the post office.

"He did what?" Roberta gasped when she saw the photo. "No way! Oh, it looks wonderful, but ... Jack playing Santa Claus? I can hardly believe it."

"Maybe he didn't act alone," Jared offered as he looked over Kate's shoulder. They were gathered around one of the metal-topped tables, tidying their work areas after another long week. "Perhaps there's an accomplice involved."

Jared tipped his head toward the closed door into the lobby, where a seasoned department veteran had been in the chair more often than not the past few weeks.

"*Barney?*" This was too much for Kate to absorb. "You're telling me *Jack and Barney* cooked this up? I can't believe it."

"Well, I overheard some things." Jared was grinning. "Jack started it. But then, he usually does around here. It sounded like after the skirmish at the holiday party, they decided to put their stubborn heads together and do some good, for a change."

Hazel's hard-line stance only bruised Jack's ego, but apparently the incident had been just embarrassing enough for him to rethink his ways, at least a little.

And despite Barney's insistence that mail carriers should stay out of their customers' personal lives, he may have started to feel sorry for Candace. Because due to his hours at the counter during the holiday rush, Barney had often been the one to watch over the Taylors' mail and retrieve Candace's bundle when she managed to make it to town.

"Jack should be done with his route any time now." Roberta glanced at the clock. "I don't know about you, but I really want to hear the rest of this story."

Word about Candace's turn of good luck quickly spread among the rest of the crew, who were all on the lookout for Jack when he came in from his rounds.

"Whew! It's windy out there today." He shook off his parka and removed his knit cap. "What?" He frowned. "Why are you all smiling? Or smirking, more like it? What's going on now?"

"This." Kate stepped forward, phone in hand. "We're dying to know what happened."

Jack's eyes sparkled with mischief. "Maybe some elves got word of the trouble out there, and decided to make an early stop at the Taylors' farm."

"It was two elves, from what I hear," Roberta said. "And the last two I'd suspect would have a hand in something like this."

Jack shrugged. "There's nothing wrong with helping out, once in a while. Besides, we all know that if that box didn't get replaced soon, the drama would drag on until spring. I hated the thought of them having to come into town and pick up their mail for that long."

"What about regulations?" Bev teased.

"That's just it! Our only other option was to bend the rules and take their mail to the house." Jack gave Kate a knowing look. "I didn't want to spend the next how-many months having to fishtail it up that driveway in the snow. It'd put me way behind schedule. And that dog! He's as mean as can be; I'd fear for my life every time I had to stop."

"Oh, sure." Kate nodded. "Champ might try to lick you to death."

"Something had to be done. I decided it was up to me to solve the problem, since there didn't seem to be another, easier way out."

Kate wasn't surprised to hear that Jack was the hero of his own story, but she was pleased at how her community had come together to help Candace and her family.

Jack was good friends with Richard Everton, who owned a local construction company, and Richard had been eager to donate the time and some of the materials needed to get the job done. Jack confirmed that Barney had indeed offered to chip in on the cost.

It was Jack who'd approached Candace with their plan. She'd been grateful, of course, but worried Wyatt would refuse anything that seemed like pity. So Jack called Wyatt's dad, and got him in on the project. A serious father-son chat had been the result, and Wyatt had grudgingly agreed to go with the flow. Even so, he intended to pay Richard back over time for the labor and materials.

"I don't know if he will. Or if he can," Jack told the rest of the carriers. "But it gives him a way to keep his pride."

"What about the problem that caused this mess in the first place?" Allison wanted to know. "Do you think his dad can get through to him about that, too?"

Jack shrugged. "He's trying, I guess. Has been for some time. But at least, the mailbox has been taken care of."

The door from the lobby opened, and Barney shuffled through. "Well, it's five bells. I'm calling it; our work is done for the week."

Kate wasn't sure what she expected to happen. Would the two men high-five and have a good laugh? Share smug smiles about the success of their little project?

Barney stopped to chat with Allison and Roberta, who were closest to the lobby door.

"Look at him, sucking up to the boss," Jack muttered to Kate and Bev. "Like we've all been waiting around for him to give us permission to go home."

"Hello, Jack." Barney barely offered him a nod. He pointed at Jack's boots, then toward the rubber mat inside the back door, which was full of melting snow.

"We have one of those in the vestibule, too," Barney told his co-worker. "If you wipe your feet on the first one, it saves trouble on this end. Wet floors are slippery, they're a safety hazard."

"I'll keep that in mind." Jack stared at Barney. "Good of you to show up today. I didn't see you this morning before I headed out; I think you were the last one in the door."

Barney chuckled. "Well, when you get in as many years of service as I have, I guess you can clock in whenever you feel like it."

And with that, Barney turned his back on Jack and busied himself at his locker. Jack muttered something under his breath, then went into the break room to rinse out his coffee thermos.

Roberta paused on her way past Bev and Kate. "I'm so glad the Taylors got a new mailbox. If that situation got those two to work together, then maybe it was worth it."

"We may not have peace on Earth," Bev told the boss. "But at this post office? I'd say this is as close as we're going to get."

* * *

Melinda plopped down in Kate's reading chair and gave the living room an approving nod. "Just look at this place! I know you haven't had the time or money for any serious renovations yet, but it doesn't matter. It's homey and cozy; just what you needed."

"The Christmas decorations really make a difference." Karen came in from the kitchen with a large bowl of snack mix, Hazel at her heels. The dog stretched out at Melinda's feet on the new rug, and Karen joined Kate on the couch.

"You know, I'm thinking of leaving mine up until the end of January, at least. The house always feels so bare when they first come down."

"I've thought the same," Kate admitted. "The tree might have to go back in the box right after Christmas, though." She cut her eyes at Charlie, who presided over this low-key celebration from his stuffed throne by the fireplace. "Someone's having a hard time keeping his furry little paws off anything that's shiny."

This last-minute gathering on Sunday afternoon was as laid-back as it was small. Kate had just two guests. Sweatpants had been required. Along with a bottle of wine, the menu consisted of a smorgasbord of the snacks that had found their way into Kate's house in the past few weeks.

For someone who'd braced herself for a blue Christmas, the past month had overflowed with unexpected blessings and good memories. As she kicked her sock-covered feet up on the coffee table, Kate realized this afternoon's gathering was the third time she'd hosted friends at her farmhouse this season. Those events were in addition to last night's Burberry family party in Prosper, and the Duncan celebration set for next weekend.

She might be the only person living at this farmhouse, but she had Hazel and Charlie, and the Three Mouseketeers. And a crowd of friends and family that would ensure she'd never be lonely back here in Eagle River.

As they snacked and chatted, Kate filled her friends in on the surprise effort to replace the Taylors' mailbox.

"Glenn was talking about it yesterday," Melinda said of Prosper's postmaster. "He heard about it on Friday, I guess. He said it's been a long holiday season, but that gesture of goodwill gave him the boost he needed to get through this last, final push."

The friends' conversation turned to their Christmas plans. Melinda's sister and brother were coming home to Swanton on Wednesday, which made it easy for her. Karen and Doc Ogden always traded holiday on-call shifts for their practice, and Karen had Christmas duties this year.

"Remind Josh to forward some calls to me, if he needs to." Karen's veterinary clinic had a sharing agreement with the practice owned by Melinda's boyfriend. "I'll be around later this week. I'm not going to visit my parents until New Year's Eve."

Melinda nodded her thanks. "He'll be with Aiden part of the time." Josh's son lived with his mother about two hours away, but spent some weekends and holidays with his father. "I'm sure he'll appreciate that."

She turned to Kate. "By the way, we're having a low-key hangout on New Year's Eve at my place. You're welcome to stop by, if you like."

"I might, thanks. I'm having dinner with my parents, and Bryan and Anna." Kate couldn't help but smile. "And I may have another stop to make, depending on how things work out."

"Oh, really?" Karen was all ears. "Does this have anything to do with the handsome gentleman who kissed you in front of hundreds of people at the holiday festival?"

"It just might," Kate teased. "I'm going to take this slow; I would guess Alex feels the same."

Alex was busy on New Year's Eve, of course, but he'd asked Kate to swing by the bar for a little while if she was free. She was looking forward to it, and had asked another new friend to join her. Gwen's boys would be with their father on New Year's Eve, and she'd laughed and said, "why not?" when Kate suggested they head to Paul's Place, if only for one round.

"This New Year's thing isn't a date," she explained to her friends, who didn't seem entirely convinced. "I mean, he owns the bar, it's probably one of his busiest nights of the year. I may barely get a chance to talk to him."

Melinda toasted Kate with her wine glass. "Somehow, I think he'd shut the whole place down for an hour if he could spend it alone with you."

"I see good things in your future." Karen pretended to consult the golden depths of her Moscato. "An intelligent, handsome man. Another bathroom for this house. Oh, and some critters to fill up that pasture ..."

"Don't get ahead of yourself," Kate half-heartedly protested.

"About which part?" Melinda giggled. "It all sounds pretty good to me."

Kate's phone began to chime on the coffee table. Charlie continued to doze by the crackling fire, but Hazel lifted her head in interest.

"Oh, it's Bev. Interesting timing, I'd say. Perhaps she has some predictions for the new year, too." Kate picked up the phone with a smile. "Hey, how's the big bash?"

Bev's extended family potluck was that afternoon at Chloe's parents' house. It was an event Bev and Clyde had been looking forward to for weeks.

"We need to talk." Bev's voice vibrated with emotion, and was perhaps accompanied by a few tears. "I can't believe this! I never would have thought that ... oh, Kate, this is terrible!"

"What happened? What's going on?" Kate returned Melinda and Karen's looks of concern, then hurried into the kitchen.

What Bev said next made Kate put a hand on the counter to steady herself. She'd hardly touched her glass of wine, but her head suddenly swirled with shock and confusion, and questions that had no answers. She wanted to give her friend some words of comfort, anything that might ease Bev's fears, but couldn't think of one positive thought to share.

"What can I do?" she finally said. "Tell me what I can do to help."

"Meet me at the church in fifteen minutes," Bev told Kate in a wavering voice. "I know where the key is. I'll be inside."

* 22 *

Kate marked the miles to Eagle River in stunned silence, then turned south on Main Street at the stoplight. The town's few stores were closed on Sunday afternoon, even the drugstore, but the shops' festive decorations were a bittersweet reminder that Christmas was just days away.

"Even if all of this is true, there's not much time," Kate muttered as she turned west off the highway and drove past the secondary-school complex. This street, which would soon turn to gravel, was the shortest route to Panther Junction. "And it has to be! Given what Bev found, I don't think there's any other explanation."

If Bev was right, Chloe had the nativity. Because Bev had made not one, but two, shocking discoveries at Chloe's childhood home in Elm Springs.

The more Kate reviewed the little she'd just learned, the more angry and frustrated she felt.

She'd been fooled, so had Bev. And not by some shady character with a criminal history. Nope. Just bookish little Chloe, with her retro-trendy glasses, bright-pink laptop and friendly smile.

Too friendly. Too helpful. Kate could see that now.

"She already knew *everything!*" Kate slapped the steering wheel with one hand as she left the outskirts of Eagle River behind. "She knew all the names, all the dates, who fit in where. And here we thought she just wanted to help!"

Kate had only told Melinda and Karen that there was a break in the nativity case, and that she needed to leave. Her friends had rushed to help clean up and then cleared out as quickly as they could, and Kate was grateful they hadn't pressed her for details.

She wanted to trust them, but Bev's discoveries were too shocking, and too important to this case, to risk anyone finding out about them anytime soon.

Other than Sheriff Preston, of course. Which was going to make this very difficult for poor Bev. No wonder she'd asked Kate to meet her at the church.

Bev's truck was the only vehicle parked out front, and just a few lights were on inside the vestibule. But when Kate walked into the sanctuary, she was met with the glorious glow of the sun's late-day rays filtered through the south wall's stained-glass windows. The Christmas tree still glowed in its corner, and the poinsettias radiated their rich colors, but the sight of her friend slouched in a pew near the front of the church made Kate's heart ache.

"Hey," Kate said softly as she edged into the row. "I came as quickly as I could."

Bev only nodded at first, tears streaming down her face. "That's OK. I'm just glad you're here."

She shook her head sadly. "I don't know what to do! Or actually, I know what I must do. How do I find the courage to do it?"

"Well, I think you have a good idea there." Kate gestured at her friend's hands, which were still clasped in prayer. "How about you start from the beginning? Tell me everything that happened."

Bev and Clyde had set out for the party earlier than usual, as Bev had promised to help Anne with any last-minute preparations. Only a handful of folks had arrived so far, so

Bev and her husband were able to hang their coats in the hall closet rather than toss them on a spare room's bed. As she fished out two hangers, something inside the closet caught Bev's eye.

A tweed peacoat was already on the rail, and its wool fabric's blend of charcoal and maroon hues was as pretty as it was unusual. As the jacket's oversized, shiny buttons caught the reflection of the hall's ceiling light, Bev wondered if she'd seen this coat before.

No, she'd decided. But the buttons were certainly familiar.

"They were so distinct," she told Kate. "I noticed them right away. And I instantly remembered the one Hazel found under the railing, right over there."

Bev didn't mention any of this to her husband, as she didn't want anyone to overhear such a conversation. After Clyde ambled into the kitchen for a cup of cider, Bev gave the peacoat a closer look.

All of its front buttons were in place, as were those on the cuffs. But on one inside lining seam, Bev found the loose threads that marked where quality garment makers always tacked a spare button. She managed to snap a quick photo of the coat while she had the flash disabled on her phone.

"I checked it against the photo of the button we gave to Jeff." Bev shook her head in disbelief. "They were a perfect match."

Chloe had mentioned several times that she'd last visited the church months ago. But the sanctuary was vacuumed every Wednesday, and Bev found it hard to believe that button had been forgotten on the floor for so many weeks.

"I started to think she'd been here more recently, then I wondered what else she was hiding from us. And I checked the coat; it has a thick fleece layer inside the usual lining. Something that was too warm for the weather we had this fall."

Bev had certainly felt uneasy, but she went through the motions of greeting her relatives and helping Anne set up the buffet line. Chloe was there, of course.

"Right in front of her mom, she asked me flat-out how the investigation was going." Bev's brow furrowed in frustration. "'It's such an important piece of our family's history,' she said, sweet as pecan pie. 'Let's hope it's not too late for it to be found.'"

"She said that?" Kate's words were clipped with anger. "Seriously? But then, if she's been putting up a false front all this time, she's going to look for opportunities to keep that in place."

Everyone filled their plates and sat down to eat, but Bev managed only a few bites while her relatives feasted and shared memories of Christmases past. She couldn't confront Chloe, not with the house full of guests, and suspected the younger woman would have evasive answers ready for any possible interrogation.

As Bev pondered her less-than-ideal options, she knew the button Hazel had found might turn out to be very important to the case. It was likely Chloe didn't know the extra fastener was missing from the lining of her coat, much less have any idea where she'd lost it. What else might Bev uncover at this house, if she only had a chance to snoop around?

The line for the powder room off the kitchen began to grow, and Bev saw an opportunity to head upstairs. There was a full bath at the end of the hall, and it offered her the perfect excuse to visit the second floor alone.

"My heart was pounding. I didn't know exactly where to look, only that I had just a few minutes to spare. I couldn't imagine Chloe would be stupid enough to attempt to hide anything at her dorm, I know she has a roommate."

Bev found Chloe's childhood room, which was strewn with textbooks and clothes. A peek in the closet netted nothing of interest. There was only time to look in one more location: under the bed.

"That's an obvious hiding place, I know. But it wasn't just that. I can't explain it, but I felt like I was drawn to that spot. So I crouched down, lifted the bedskirt, and peeked underneath."

And there, bookended by old shoe boxes and a plastic storage bag stuffed with extra blankets, Bev saw what appeared to be a long, low box wrapped in holiday paper. After she made sure no one had followed her upstairs, she reached under the bed to touch the mysterious package.

The shape was heavy and solid under its bright wrappings, as if it were made of wood, not cardboard. Bev estimated its dimensions, and decided it was a close match to the nativity's custom oak storage box.

Kate was livid. "She disguised it as a present?"

But it was a clever idea, and a strong indicator of Chloe's shrewdness. The suspense of unwrapping gifts was one of the things that made the holidays so memorable. No one, not even her parents, would touch something like that at this time of year.

Kate was stunned by Bev's revelations. Yet at the same time, they brought her a strange sense of peace. Perhaps the nativity had been located at last after weeks of searching, leads that were still a tangled mix of fact and folklore, and too-many unanswered questions.

No wonder Chloe had volunteered to research the Weigmann family line, then offered to reach out to those descendants on her own.

She'd already made those discoveries, likely months ago, and wanted to prevent Kate and Bev from coming into contact with people who could expose her secrets. It would have been easy for Chloe to drop a few well-placed crumbs here and there, convince Bev and Kate her findings were new.

"I have to wonder, though, when she found out I'm

related to Gustav, too," Kate said as her anger flared again. "Was that months ago? Or did she only make an effort to track me down through the generations once she heard I was helping you search for the nativity?"

She pulled her phone from her purse. "We may never know, but I'll say this: Chloe is going to be very, very sorry she ever crossed paths with me."

Bev motioned for Kate to put her phone away. "Oh, honey, I'll call Jeff."

"There's someone I want to talk to before you do that." Kate tapped her way to an online directory. "Something just occurred to me; if I'm right, it could help this case."

The line rang and rang, but Kate refused to hang up. Myrtle Bradford was likely resting at this hour on a Sunday afternoon, and it might take her some time to answer.

"Hey, Myrtle!" Kate wondered if the relief she felt was noticeable in her voice. "Yes, Merry Christmas to you, too! Yep, only a few days now. Do you have a minute? I need to ask you something; it's very important."

Kate prompted Myrtle to recall the time a sheriff's deputy called and inquired about the nativity and Uncle Oswald. Myrtle was quick to share that the young woman's name was Abby, and she was just the sweetest girl. They'd talked a week ago Thursday, Myrtle was sure about that.

Now, had there been anyone else? Not recently, this might have been months ago, take your time ...

Myrtle's voice faltered as she considered Kate's request. Well, maybe there was another young lady a while back, Myrtle wasn't quite sure. Or maybe, did Abby call twice? Because when the deputy rang her up recently, Myrtle thought the name seemed familiar.

Kate took a deep breath, and closed her eyes. "That other time, was the young woman's name similar to Abby? Chloe, perhaps?"

"Oh, yes!" Myrtle was certain. "Yes, that's right!"

Myrtle then recalled the details with the sudden clarity that sometimes comes to the elderly concerning past events.

It had been a windy day, and the falling leaves swirling and dancing outside the picture window meant Percival barked through most of the call. That young woman was working on her family's history, and its ties to the Panther Junction church, and she wanted to verify something she'd heard from someone ...

"Is there a problem, dear?" Myrtle was concerned. "I can't believe I forgot about the other girl. But their names were so similar."

"Oh, no, everything's fine," Kate lied. "I was just wondering, that's all. Aaron's off Tuesday, so I'll see you then."

Bev crossed her arms. "So Chloe knew about that, too! About Oswald Baxter, and what he'd done. She's a pathological liar. And a thief." Then she put one hand over her face. "And my closest cousin's daughter, too."

Before they called the sheriff, Kate decided, they needed to nail down exactly what they thought happened, and why. Jeff would need every bit of information they could provide to improve his chances of getting a search warrant for the Petersons' home. Of course, the Elm Springs police chief would have to be the one to show up at the family's door.

"Do you think we have enough?" Bev was thinking the same thing.

"I mean, what if they can't get a warrant? Will this be like how it was at the estate company, where Jeff thought it might backfire if he sent a deputy out there?"

"I don't know. Without a warrant, the Elm Springs police will just have to go to the house, ask a bunch of pointed questions from the porch, and hope Chloe confesses."

"And if that doesn't work?" Bev shook her head. "She'll know they know something. Who knows what she'd do then, where she'd hide it next?"

"I don't know who else could help the sheriff, at this point. It has to be us. Especially when this congregation is currently without an official leader."

Pastor Thorne had yet to be removed from his post at Panther Junction, but the charges he faced meant the church's state board was looking into the situation as well as the local authorities. In the meantime, he was officially on a leave of absence. The congregation's retired pastor had agreed to lead services on Christmas Eve and Christmas Day, and until the end of the year. After that? No one was sure what might happen.

"Well, let's start with this," Kate said. "I do believe Chloe when she says she's done research here at the church several times. Because in the end, that's exactly what allowed her to pull this off."

Chloe likely got to know a few of the members during her visits, and gained their trust. Flattered by a young person's interest in the congregation's history, and full of pride for their historic church, they probably talked about where the nativity was stored in the off season. As for the spare door key, Chloe might have overheard people discussing where it was hidden or even stumbled across its location.

"She had all the information she needed." Bev picked up Kate's theory. "She was home on Thanksgiving break and, for whatever reason, decided this was her chance to take the nativity. She must have slipped over here Friday night to steal it. I bet her nerves got the better of her in the end. Between stashing the nativity's box in her car and getting the key back to its rightful place, she probably forgot to double check the side door was securely shut behind her."

Kate thought about the marks in the snow Hazel found the following afternoon. Were those Chloe's distorted tracks, or had they been made by someone else? She could imagine Chloe being in such a hurry, and so nervous, that she didn't bother to go around on the cleared sidewalk.

"I'm sure you're right. Despite how smart she is, she's not a career criminal." Kate studied the painfully bare space on the altar. "So, I think we've figured out how she pulled it off. But why would she feel the need to steal the nativity? You know, I've heard that genealogy can become rather addictive, that people feel compelled to track down one more ancestor, find one more piece of the puzzle."

Bev managed a small smile. "Oh, you mean like us when something unexpected happens in this community?"

"Yeah, I guess you're right. But stealing is stealing. It doesn't matter if you're related to the person who created the item. Or how emotionally attached you are to the thing. If it doesn't belong to you ... well, it just doesn't."

Bev sat up straighter in the pew. "Wait a second. What if the curse is real? I don't think it is," she hurried to explain. "But what if Chloe does? Did she somehow think that if she 'takes back' the nativity from the church, it'll do the opposite of what the Baxters apparently believe? Bring her good luck, not bad?"

Kate hadn't considered that idea before, but it did make sense in a twisted way. Legends could be powerful things, just like memories. And as Vicki Colton had said, an item's sentimental value could be far-more important than any monetary price someone might be willing to pay.

"I wouldn't be surprised if that's why she did this. Who knows what she's thinking? Or what she plans to do with it after the holidays? I mean, she can only leave it under that bed for a few more days. What then?"

Bev swallowed hard. "As difficult as this is going to be for me, for my family, I'm not going to give her a chance to find out." Her lower lip trembled, and Kate wrapped an arm around her friend's shoulder.

"I'm not going to let you do this alone." Then she smiled. "After all, what are cousins for? Even if they're four times removed, or whatever?"

Bev barked out a laugh. "I can call Jeff. I mean, I *will* call Jeff. I have no choice."

Then she sighed. "It's Anne and Ted I'm worried about. She and I were so close growing up, almost like sisters. This will be hard on them, on all of us, no matter what turns out to be the truth."

She turned to Kate with tears in her eyes. "That's what I'm worried about the most. I was snooping, even though it was for a good reason. But what if I point the finger at Chloe, and it turns out I'm wrong?"

"Then we'll be wrong together."

But as Kate stared at the altar, something told her they were right. She gazed up at the lofty ceiling of this historic church, and wondered again if Gustav himself was guiding them onward.

We'll get it back, she promised in her heart. *Get it back to where it's supposed to be.*

The day's light had dimmed in the past half hour, and the sun was about to set behind a bank of gathering clouds. Kate suddenly remembered that this was the winter solstice, the longest night of the year. Bev was facing a dark night of the soul, one that would require her to set her family allegiances aside and do what was right. And Kate was determined to be there with her, every step of the way.

But they needed to hurry. What if Chloe had any suspicions that Bev stumbled across something in that house? Bev and Clyde had left early, claiming Bev didn't feel well, which was the truth. If Chloe got the jitters, there was no telling what she might do out of desperation.

"We have to tell Jeff what we know as soon as possible," Kate said as she folded her hands in prayer. "But I think we can take a minute or two to seek some guidance before we make that call."

With Sheriff Preston on speakerphone, Bev shared what transpired at the Petersons' house and Kate relayed the conversation Myrtle Bradford had with Chloe. Jeff asked a few questions at first, then lapsed into stunned silence as the ladies detailed the intricate web of lies Chloe had apparently constructed over the past several weeks.

"The photos you snapped this afternoon should greatly improve our chances of getting that search warrant," he told Bev. "Well done! You two make all of us proud."

The sheriff promised to start reaching out to the appropriate people as soon as he ended the call. A Sunday evening during the holidays wasn't the ideal time to hit up any of the local judges for a search warrant, but he agreed with Kate and Bev that there was no time to waste.

If he could get the paperwork approved yet tonight, Jeff said, someone would be on the Petersons' doorstep first thing tomorrow morning.

"I went to the academy with the chief in Elm Springs, he'll get right on board. And I'm definitely going along. Let's see if we can make a Christmas miracle happen."

* 23 *

From what Kate heard later, Anne Peterson was understandably shocked when three members of local law enforcement rang the front porch's bell just after seven on Monday morning. After they explained their errand and showed her the search warrant, she set her mouth in a firm line, pointed toward the coat closet, then went upstairs to rouse her adult daughter from sleep.

Sheriff Preston's interrogation at the kitchen table got off to a slow start, as Chloe offered evasive answers and claimed complete ignorance about the nativity's history and its current whereabouts. But when the Elm Springs chief brought the still-wrapped box downstairs and peeled away its festive paper, the young woman burst into tears.

The only explanation Chloe offered was that her ancestral ties to Gustav Weigmann, along with her self-appointed role as the family's historian, gave her the right to retrieve the set from the church.

Bev heard through the family grapevine that Chloe had struggled emotionally since a nasty breakup with her boyfriend in the spring. Her grades had suffered as well, which in turn put her scholarship in jeopardy. Perhaps the mounting pressures in her personal life caused her to go all-in on genealogy as a distraction from her troubles.

Sheriff Preston had the final say on which charges Chloe faced, since the theft occurred within his jurisdiction. Upon consultation with the county attorney, he started with misdemeanor theft and trespassing.

Chloe's theft charge could still be upgraded to a felony if the nativity's current financial value reached that fifteen-hundred-dollar threshold. The sheriff was searching for an experienced appraiser of sculptures and folk art who could shed light on the nativity's current financial value, perhaps someone from the Twin Cities or Chicago.

Along with the potential revisions to her charges, Chloe's punishment was also up in the air. As a first-time offender, it was possible her fines might be reduced, or that hours of community service could be applied to whatever sentence was ultimately handed down. She'd already pleaded guilty, which was the first step in easing her legal woes.

And the congregation's official position on the situation could also influence Chloe's future. Bev told Kate that its members were debating which charges should be pursued.

The church got its beloved nativity back, that was what mattered; should its elders take a position of forgiveness and leniency? At the same time, the rule of law demanded respect; perhaps a firm example needed to be made.

But first, there was a homecoming of sorts set for Tuesday afternoon. Roberta gave Bev and Kate permission to take a long, late lunch break, and they were among the dozen or so ladies that waited expectantly in the vestibule at Panther Junction Christian Church for the sight of a sheriff's department SUV arriving at the snow-dusted crossroads.

The group erupted into cheers and hearty applause as Sheriff Preston and Deputy Collins lifted the wooden crate out of the back of the cruiser.

"They've been photographed and processed," the sheriff said. "We didn't try for any fingerprints, of course."

There were tears of joy when the carton was carefully

lowered to the carpet in front of the altar, and its lid removed to reveal the characters nestled safely in their custom crate.

After everyone donned white cotton gloves, the carvings and their backdrop were carefully dusted and arranged in their traditional configuration in the center of the altar: the wisemen and camel to the right; the shepherd, his flock and the other animals on the left; the angel above; and the Holy Family in the middle.

"You do the honors." One of the circle's members handed Bev the carving of Baby Jesus in the manger. "They're back where they belong, and just in time."

Bev settled the final statue in place, and then took a small step back. They all just stared at the nativity for a moment. The one photo Kate had seen of the set hadn't begun to do it justice. She was enthralled by the wondrous expressions on the characters' faces.

Mary gazed lovingly upon her baby, and Joseph's faint smile was filled with pride. Even the animal sculptures conveyed feeling. The cow lowered its head in a show of reverence, and the lamb's eyes were wide with curiosity as it studied the newest visitor to this humble stable.

Gustav had left no detail unnoticed. The folds in the humans' robes were clearly visible, as well as the wooly coats of the sheep. Hundreds of tiny notches marked the fringed hems of the wise men's robes, and even the camel's blanket carried an elaborate pattern of vines and leaves.

"Look at His little hand," Bev whispered to Kate as she pointed at the Baby Jesus. "See how He has that one out from under the blanket? Like He's reaching toward the sky? It's incredible."

"The whole feeling in the church has changed," one of the women said. "What was missing has now come home."

※　※　※

The church's gravel parking area was already full by the time Kate's family arrived Wednesday night for the congregation's lone Christmas Eve service. Curtis turned west at the crossroads, and inched past the line of vehicles already parked along the road.

"Look at this crowd." He eased the car onto the snow-packed shoulder. "I'm glad we bundled up and wore boots, since we'll have to hike it. No church shoes tonight."

"We won't be the only ones." Kate was squished in the back seat with Bryan and Anna. "Everyone else had the same idea, looks like. I just hope there's room inside that little church for all the folks who want to be here."

"There wasn't any room at the inn, on the first Christmas Eve," her dad reminded them as they got out of the car. "And I bet it'll be standing-room only here before the service starts."

Christmas Eve in Panther Junction was a special time even for those who weren't current members of the congregation. With a history that dated back over a hundred and fifty years, countless families had attended the church at one time or another. And many of those with sentimental ties to the congregation made it a priority to visit on Christmas Eve.

The little church always held its service at five, due to the aging of its congregation and its location in a rural area. That also allowed the service's attendees to have the rest of the evening free to spend with family or go to a later service at their regular church, as the Duncans would that evening.

As her family trudged up the gravel road toward the church, Kate eyed the other clusters of visitors making their own pilgrimages to the crossroads. She wondered how many of them weren't even past members or neighborhood residents, but people who just wanted to witness the return of Gustav Weigmann's masterpiece to this charming, historic landmark.

"Just look at it!" Charlotte marveled as they reached the corner. All the lights were on inside the church, and its stained-glass windows sparkled and glowed in the twilight. "It's so serene, so beautiful."

The entryway's coat hangers were already filled, and ushers stood by to collect armloads of jackets and take them to tables that waited downstairs. Kate handed her parka to a member of the youth group, then sought out Bev on the other side of the packed vestibule.

"How are you holding up? Any word from Anne?"

Bev sadly shook her head. "She hasn't called. Clyde says to give it time, and I know he's right. She and Ted must be devastated, and embarrassed. But I did what I had to do."

"That's right. Maybe once the charges are settled and some of the shock wears off, Anne will reach out."

"I hope so." Then Bev smiled. "Why don't all of you sit with us? You and I can grab some seats before the line to view the nativity dwindles down."

Kate's parents, and Bryan and Anna, joined the queue of visitors moving toward the front of the church, where a velvet rope stretched between two posts allowed people to get an up-close glimpse of nativity while keeping too-curious hands at bay.

Ushers beckoned people forward, then guided them to the left and right as they made their way to the back and into the pews. By the time the service neared, folding chairs had been brought up from the basement to pack more visitors into the side aisles and out in the vestibule.

With a cane aiding his steps, the church's retired pastor soon made his way up the main aisle while the organist played an opening selection that contained bits of treasured Christmas hymns.

"My dear friends," Pastor Fiske began after taking his place behind the pulpit. "We gather on this special night to celebrate the birth of our Savior. And something else, which

I'm sure all of you are very-much aware of: the return of our beloved nativity and its reminder of the real reason for the season."

Murmurs of agreement rippled through the crowd, accompanied by a smattering of applause.

"Some of you may find this hard to believe," Pastor Fiske's blue eyes twinkled with mirth, "but that nativity set is even older than I am. It was created by one of our founding members, a man of great faith. We are filled with gratitude, and rejoice over its return."

Then suddenly, he gave a big grin.

"As you all know, the Holy Family had a rough go of it on their way to Bethlehem. I don't know which would have been worse, traveling all those miles on foot or bouncing along on the back of a donkey while pregnant. But somehow, with God's help, Mary and Joseph made it to their destination."

He turned to gesture at the characters on the altar.

"I'd say that despite their recent troubles, our little friends had it easy in the end. As many of you have likely heard, they hitched a ride in the back of a Hartland County sheriff's cruiser yesterday, which got them home in record time."

Many in the church burst into laughter at the pastor's witty observation. Kate thought of Auggie's "missing persons" poster at his co-op, and was surprised she hadn't picked him out in this crowd. He and Jane must have had family commitments that night, as this was the sort of hot-topic event Auggie wouldn't want to miss.

As she glanced around the sanctuary, Kate spotted one visitor that gave her a jolt of surprise.

Leonard Baxter stood in the back of the church, near the entrance to the vestibule. He still wore his wool overcoat, as if he didn't plan to stay. Kate suspected he'd come to see for himself that the Weigmann family's most-prized possession was indeed unharmed and back where it belonged.

Leonard noticed Kate staring at him, and gave her an

unreadable look and a quick nod before he left the sanctuary.

Bev would get the reward that had been offered for the nativity's safe return, and she'd already decided to give all the money to the church. And while the reward's donor would remain anonymous, it wasn't too tough for Kate to figure out who had put up the cash.

As the laughter in the church ebbed away, Pastor Fiske held up a hand. "I've always said I believe that God has a sense of humor, even if we often don't understand the 'why' of His ways." Then he turned more serious.

"But along with celebrating our precious nativity's return, let's also remember those in our community who are struggling, for whatever reason, and anxiously seeking their own paths forward."

He didn't need to say more. Kate thought of Oliver Thorne and Chloe, and the three teenagers charged with burglary and theft.

"And now, let's begin our service." Pastor Fiske reached for his hymnal. "We'll start with 'Angels We Have Heard on High, number 285."

The program continued with scriptures and a sermon, as well as more hymns and a special message for the children. But it was the end of the service that Kate was most looking forward to, even though she would repeat it later at her family's home church in Prosper.

Many of the region's congregations had been founded by German settlers, and it was tradition to close Christmas Eve services by singing at least one verse of "Silent Night" in the song's native language.

The original words were printed on the back of the bulletins, and the attendees acquainted themselves with the German lyrics as the sanctuary's lights were dimmed and ushers carrying lit candles stepped to the end of every pew. Small tapers with plastic drip trays were already in place in the communion-cup holders, and the light was passed from person to person as the opening strains of the beloved hymn filled the sanctuary.

"Good thing Hazel isn't here," Bev murmured to Kate. "Who knows what 'commands' she might pick out of these lyrics?"

Kate smothered her laughter as she thought of her beloved dog, who was probably curled up on the couch with Charlie. And of Scout, Maggie, and Jerry, safe and snug in their shed. Of her family, who shared this pew, and all the new friends she'd made in this past year.

Her own journey had been long and hard at times, but Kate had arrived at her destination by putting one foot in front of the other. She'd circled back to where she started, but Kate had no doubt she was exactly where she was supposed to be.

This was certainly a "holy night," but Panther Junction Christian Church was far from silent. The well-known tune carried everyone through the less-familiar words as they lifted their joyful voices in song.

And up on the altar, bathed in soft candlelight, Gustav Weigmann's likeness of the Baby Jesus reached one tiny hand toward heaven.

Kate nudged Bev with an elbow. "Merry Christmas," she whispered.

Bev bumped her back. "You, too ... *cousin.*"

WHAT'S NEXT

So much more to come! Look for the next book in the "Mailbox Mysteries" series in 2024.

If you aren't already on the email list, go to the "connect" tab at fremontcreekpress.com and sign up. As soon as I have the new book ready for preorder, I'll let everyone know.

Want more holiday cheer? Check out "A Tin Train Christmas," a short story set during the Great Depression at what later became Melinda Foster's farm. While it highlights a few of the characters from the "Growing Season" series, you don't need to have read those books to enjoy this heartwarming holiday tale.

Tasty recipes: Dive into the dishes posted under the "extras" tab on the website. There are several sweets from the "Growing Season" books, as well as appetizers and much more, to share with your family and friends this holiday season.

Thanks for reading!
Melanie

ABOUT THE BOOKS

Don't miss any of the titles
in these heartwarming rural fiction series

THE GROWING SEASON SERIES

Melinda is at a crossroads when the "for rent" sign beckons her down a dusty gravel lane. Facing forty, single and downsized from her stellar career at a big-city ad agency, she's struggling to start over when a phone call brings her home to Iowa.

She moves to the country, takes on a rundown farm and its headstrong animals, and lands behind the counter of her family's hardware store in the community of Prosper, whose motto is "The Great Little Town That Didn't." And just like the sprawling garden she tends under the summer sun, Melinda begins to thrive. But when storm clouds arrive on her horizon, can she hold on to the new life she's worked so hard to create?

Filled with memorable characters, from a big-hearted farm dog to the weather-obsessed owner of the local co-op, "Growing Season" celebrates the twists and turns of small-town life. Discover the heartwarming series that's filled with new friends, fresh starts and second chances.

FOR DETAILS ON ALL THE TITLES
VISIT FREMONTCREEKPRESS.COM

THE MAILBOX MYSTERIES SERIES

It's been a rough year for Kate Duncan, both on and off the job. Being a mail carrier puts her in close proximity to her customers, with consequences that can't always be foreseen. So when a position opens at her hometown post office, she decides to leave Chicago in her rearview mirror.

Kate and her cat settle into a charming apartment above Eagle River's historic Main Street, but she dreams of a different home to call her own. And as she drives the back roads around Eagle River, Kate begins to take a personal interest in the people on her route.

So when an elderly resident goes missing, she feels compelled to help track him down. It's a quest marked not by miles of gravel, but matters of the heart: friendship, family, and the small connections that add up to a well-lived life.

------------------------ ✳✳✳ ------------------------

A TIN TRAIN CHRISTMAS

The toy train was everything two boys could want: colorful, shiny, and the perfect vehicle for their imaginations. But was it meant to be theirs? Revisit Horace's childhood for this special holiday short story inspired by the "Growing Season" series!

Printed in the USA
CPSIA information can be obtained
at www.ICGtesting.com
LVHW051951131223
766217LV00031B/1075/J

9 781952 066368